The Norwich Victms

Also in the Crime Classics series:

MY FRIEND MR CAMPION AND OTHER MYSTERIES
Margery Allingham

BLUEPRINT FOR MURDER
Roger Bax

DEATH WALKS IN EASTREPPS
Francis Beeding

TRIAL AND ERROR
Anthony Berkeley

THE PYTHON PROJECT
THE WHIP HAND
Victor Canning

MY BROTHER'S KILLER
THE SLEEPING TIGER
Dominic Devine

BAT OUT OF HELL
THE TYLER MYSTERY
THE WORLD OF TIM FRAZER
TIM FRAZER AGAIN
Francis Durbridge

ALL THE LONELY PEOPLE
YESTERDAY'S PAPERS
Martin Edwards

THE CASE OF THE CROOKED CANDLE
Eric Stanley Gardner

NO TEARS FOR HILDA
Andrew Garve

BEFORE THE FACT
Francis Ilesy

THROUGH A GLASS, DARKLY
Helen McCloy

JOHNNY UNDER GROUND
WHO SAW HER DIE?
Patricia Moyes

CLOSE UP ON DEATH
Maureen O'Brien

LONELY MAGDALEN
Henry Wade

SOME MUST WATCH
Ethel Lina White

CRIME CLASSICS

The Norwich Victims

AN INSPECTOR MARTIN MYSTERY

FRANCIS BEEDING

ABOUT THE AUTHOR

'Francis Beeding comes into the front rank of those who succeed in making their readers sit up until the book is finished.' *The Times*

Francis Beeding is the pseudonym for the writers Hilary St George Saunders (1898–51) and John Palmer (1885–44), who collaboratively wrote crime and thriller fiction novels throughout the 1920s and 30s, and into the 1940s. Of the thirty-plus novels that they penned together, five have been adapted into feature films.

This edition published in the UK by Arcturus Publishing Limited
26/27 Bickels Yard, 151–153 Bermondsey Street, London SE1 3HA

Design and layout copyright © 2013 Arcturus Publishing Limited
Text copyright © The Estate of Hilary St George Saunders 1931

Cover artwork by Steve Beaumont
Typesetting by Couper Street Type Co.

AD003689EN

Printed in the UK

HERMIONE TAYLOR
Prepared to commit murder, but
not to make a habit of it.

JOHN THROGMORTON
Whose crimes are obvious, but not
easily detected.

ELIZABETH ORME
Who held a final clue to the mystery
without being aware of it.

ROBERT HEDLAM
Who, at a critical moment, brought information
to Scotland Yard with a view to the arrest of
Throgmorton.

INSPECTOR GEORGE MARTIN
The officer in charge of the case.

CHAPTER I

1   *Saturday, November 21st*

'Why not the Tivoli? They say it's a good picture – George Arliss in *The House of Rothschild*. Might pick up a few hints on high finance.'

Hermione Taylor looked without enthusiasm at the man in front of her. He was standing with his back to the wireless set, smiling at her vaguely. He smiled like that, as she knew, when he was ill at ease – uncertain of himself, wondering what she might say or do. The smile exasperated her and yet filled her with an odd compunction.

She looked away from him impatiently and her eye fell on the calendar clock on the mantel-piece: eight o'clock and the day was Saturday, November 21st. Her attention, evading the man, was caught irrelevantly by objects here and there. Those printed cotton curtains at two and elevenpence a yard from Heathcote's were really not unsatisfactory – an old Tudor pattern of stiff, conventional flowers. Not a bad makeshift, but all was makeshift in this poky little flat. There were days when she had dreamed of Dover Street or of Whitehall Court, but Warwick Avenue, Maida Vale, was as far as she had got or was likely to get.

A ring of tobacco smoke came spinning towards her from lips foolishly rounded. Why did John insist on smoking those cheap cigars? Perhaps they gave him a feeling of success. John Throgmorton, financier. Successful financiers usually smoked cigars. But not the kind that John smoked – a bit of good tobacco twisted up anyhow, as stated on the round drum in which they were packed.

What had induced her to throw in her life with this nondescript? She looked at him with the question in her eyes as he stood before her in his short black coat, striped trousers and spotted, blue tie. There was no glamour in the man. The round, clean-shaven face with its broad expanse of forehead and double chin carried no sort of force or persuasion. Its normal expression was one of simple kindness. It suggested a benevolent interest in men and things – a useful face, she thought bitterly, for the work he had to do. People trusted him and that was how he earned his money.

For the moment, however, the face had ceased to be kind. Even propitiation was extinguished. It had become amorphous – inert and therefore mysterious; and behind the horn-rimmed spectacles, whose lenses were completely circular, were concealed a pair of blue eyes shaded with a pair of light eyebrows and flanking a considerable nose. Everything about him was strangely colourless, including the hair, of palest yellow, streaked here and there with grey. His most decisive feature was a set of remarkably white and even teeth which gave to his mouth a sensual prominence in striking contrast to the impression of faded vitality conveyed by the rest of the face. He seemed entirely empty, drained of life, waiting to be moved. She was prompted to remember the man delivered of a devil, whose mind, all swept and garnished, had waited to receive seven other devils worse than the first.

There was ash on the lapels of his coat. Hermione crossed the room and flicked it off, wrinkling her nose as she did so.

John's hand, smooth and rather plump, closed on her fingers.

'You shouldn't wrinkle your nose,' he admonished, the uneasy smile coming back to his face. 'It's bad for you – bad for your looks, you know.'

He put a forefinger under her chin and gazed at her. She knew that it stirred him to look at her like that. But the face remained almost without expression.

He kissed her slowly. Not for the first time it astonished her to find his full, smooth lips so shockingly alive in that featureless mask.

She found herself struggling in his grasp.

'Well,' he said, releasing her suddenly, 'what about it? Shall we go to the movies?'

Hermione was staring into the looking-glass where she had been assessing the damage.

Her thoughts in that brief interval had returned to the question: Why had she given herself to this nondescript? True, he had been kind, passionately kind – at a time when she had needed kindness and had been ready to pay any price for a little security and attention. She had even, for an instant, imagined herself to be in love with him – only to discover that she still belonged to the feckless young fool who had ruined himself for her sake. Where was Richard now? Somewhere in France – where he must remain till his uncle allowed him to return.

There were times when her thoughts were so full of Richard that she feared to utter his name in her sleep. Once even she had awakened, after a vivid dream, to find Throgmorton looking at her queerly, and she had half-expected him to say: *So that is how we stand. You are in love with Richard Feiling.* And she had felt a sudden terror of the placid face with the pale blue eyes and the living mouth.

She turned from the looking-glass.

'I wish you would take things more seriously, John,' she said.

'Here am I out of a "shop", and you heading straight for the official receiver. Yet you can quite calmly talk about going to the movies.'

Throgmorton shrugged his shoulders.

'Isn't that what the movies are for – to make us forget our troubles?'

Hermione turned on him impatiently. She felt that she must try to get him to realise the position.

'John,' she said sharply, 'it's time we began to face things. I've worked like a slave at this business of yours, but it's no good. We haven't made a penny for the last two months. The rent is due again, and God knows what else is to pay.'

He stared at her a moment.

'Leave all this, my dear. I've only just come up. Missing you badly. I don't see you often enough these days.'

His face was blank and the round lenses of his spectacles gleamed like the windows of an empty room.

'Then why don't you come up more often? Give the business a chance. Put your mind into it. I don't know what you do with yourself. Half the time you are out of London, and when you *are* here you want to spend most of the time playing about with me.'

He stared at her unwinking.

'My God,' he said, with sudden violence, 'and isn't it worth it?'

He stepped forward and put a hand on her shoulder, but impatiently she shook him off.

'We have no time for that now,' she snapped.

'All right – all right,' he muttered.

'You've said yourself that things are getting desperate, and, if things are desperate, we must face up to them. You leave me to do most of the facing, and I'm sick of it. You have not been near the office for a week.'

'Nothing to do at the office,' he murmured.

'Business doesn't come to you. You must go to meet it. We don't do so badly with the clients you bring in, but we want bigger and better ones, and more of them. You can't run a high-class bucket-shop on a twelve-hour week – which is about the time you give to it.'

The pale eyes blinked rapidly behind the round lenses. She knew what he was thinking. He disliked having his business referred to as a bucket-shop. He liked to feel respectable. There was nothing disreputable in being an unlicensed stockbroker, who was also ready to play the part, when opportunity offered, of an accommodating banker to customers in need. Bucket-shop was a term which had originated in the professional jealousy of the big houses.

He would try to change the subject, of course.

'Tell me', he said, 'about yourself. You were hoping to get a part in that new piece at the Royalty.'

He looked at her critically, and again she knew what he was thinking.

She was still slim, and, if her face was a little lined, she was still, for professional purposes, a young woman. But you could not reach thirty-five and lead the life she had been leading without showing something of the past.

'I was at Drew's only yesterday,' she answered steadily. 'The part has eight lines. I was the thirty-seventh applicant, and it went to a girl of twenty who had never trod the stage before.'

The pale eyes of the man glared.

'And the fool managers wonder why we no longer come to their god-forsaken theatres,' he said.

She looked at him more kindly. He was easily angry when she was disappointed or undervalued. That was one of his better features. She went up to him and fingered the lapel of his black coat.

'John,' she said, 'what do you do with yourself half the time?'

She passed her hand over his forehead and lightly touched the grey-yellow hair. He drew back quickly. He could never bear to have his hair touched.

'Don't do that,' he said nervously. 'And please remember anything I do out of London is my own affair.'

'Just as you like,' she responded quickly. 'I grant that it is no concern of mine. On the other hand, I'm your secretary and partner in this business, and I have a right to insist that you give to it the attention it so badly needs.'

She certainly had no desire to call him to account – except for strictly business purposes. She rarely inquired into his private arrangements. Live and let live was a principle that suited her well. She had no desire to be saddled with him continuously, and she had her own reasons for wishing to be free to move.

Richard was in Paris, and it was not often possible to see him, but she must be ready to slip away when he suggested it. She had not seen him for months. When would he write again?

She looked up to find Throgmorton placid and smiling.

'Perhaps the share business is not so good,' he admitted. 'Nobody is buying anything these days.'

'The loans bring in very little and things are not likely to improve till you put the fear of God into your clients. I saw Charlie Bingham the other day. He can't even pay the interest. You ought to prosecute.'

'Think of the scandal,' he protested.

'It's the scandal we need. It would bring the others to heel.'

Smiling still, he patted her shoulder.

'Hermione,' he protested mildly, 'you worry too much. Things aren't so bad as they seem. I have other irons. That is why I am away from the office so much.'

She had a gleam of hope.

'You mean that you are getting money in the provinces?'

He stood, however, blank and unresponsive, smiling no longer, and, in her mind, she could hear his next words before he spoke them.

'Things are tight everywhere,' he said.

She looked at him in something like despair. There seemed no way of nailing him down.

In the short silence that followed there came a double knock on the door. The post had come.

'I will go,' said Throgmorton.

He turned and moved quietly on the balls of his feet as he walked towards the little hall to get the letters.

'Just like him,' she thought. 'He will never face the issue.'

Throgmorton padded lightly back into the room.

'Only one letter,' he said. 'It's from Paris.'

Hermione's heart gave a jump.

'For me?'

He held it out to her and, at sight of the handwriting, her face changed.

She tore open the envelope and read eagerly, becoming aware, however, as she read of Throgmorton waiting and watching.

'It's from Richard Feiling,' she said, holding the letter.

There was a pause. Throgmorton was still waiting.

'He wants five thousand pounds,' she added seriously.

'Not the sort of client you would recommend, Hermione,' said Throgmorton dryly. 'Why does he want the money?'

She unfolded the letter and looked at it again.

'"Give me five thousand pounds," he says, "and I'll make it fifty. No risk at all and money back if the deal miscarries."'

She looked over the edge of the letter. Throgmorton had lit another of his cigars and was moodily regarding the window-curtains.

'Well, John, you know Richard. He usually speaks to the point.'

'You believe in Richard?'

'I do.'

'He proposes to multiply his capital by ten – not for the first time.'

With difficulty she restrained herself. She could have struck him for saying that. Her thoughts went back to the miserable interview with Richard, when he had confessed his folly and she had urged him to go quickly to France lest Sir Oswald, who had decided not to prosecute, might change his mind. Come to think of it, the old man had behaved rather well, though Richard refused to admit it . . . Richard . . . She could still see his angry face: *I asked him for fifty; he could have spared twenty times as much. But I only added a nought to the cheque.* And now here was John Throgmorton, financier, reminding her that her Richard was, in effect, a forger and a thief.

'Richard has put you on to one or two good things in his time,' she said steadily. 'He has brains and he never lets you down.'

Throgmorton turned away to the mantelpiece, smoothing his yellow-grey hair.

'What's the use of this discussion anyway?' he said. 'We haven't got five thousand pounds, or any chance of raising it.'

For a while there was silence between them. Then came the crackle of a newspaper unfolded.

Throgmorton had picked up the *Evening Standard* and was looking at the list of entertainments.

'Won't you put on your hat?' he said.

She walked wearily to the tiny bedroom.

'Very well,' she replied. 'What shall it be?'

'*The House of Rothschild,*' he suggested.

He was smiling again.

2   *Monday, November 23rd*

Elizabeth Orme placed a sheet of paper in the typewriter, glancing aside at the young man who sprawled on the window-sill swinging his legs. He was so obviously unnecessary. He straggled. A high forehead drifted down by way of a long nose and a weak mouth towards an indeterminate chin. He was formless and large. The small room in which she worked was full enough without him.

Papers lay rather untidily piled on open shelves. There was a roll-top desk in one corner and opposite it a filing cabinet. Two chairs filled most of the space that remained.

'Joseph,' she said, 'what is the day of the month?'

Mr Joseph Greening removed a battered pipe from his mouth.

'This,' he said, 'is the twenty-third of November.'

Elizabeth typed rapidly for a moment and pulled away the sheet.

Mr Greening again removed his pipe.

'Well,' he said, 'what's the latest effort? What says Daniel, the decree. . . . Uriah, the ukase. . . . Percival, the proclamation?'

Elizabeth read the notice to herself.

She could not stop Mr Greening trying to be funny, but she could limit the field of play.

ST. JULIAN'S PREPARATORY SCHOOL

NOVEMBER 24TH, 193–

MORNING MILK

ALL BOYS TAKING MORNING MILK WILL LEAVE

HALL AT II A.M. PROMPTLY. THE BREAK IS

INTENDED FOR EXERCISE AND NOT FOR

EATING.   (SIGNED) ROBERT HEDLAM

The swing-door, covered with green baize, which led to the main portion of the school, swung back suddenly and a small boy appeared on the threshold. The open door let in a high clamour:

> By the Nine Gods he swore
> That the great house of Tarquin
> Should suffer wrong no more;
> By the Nine Gods he swore it,
> And named a trysting day. . . .

The shrill treble of some twenty voices was cut off abruptly as the door closed and the small boy breathlessly delivered himself.

'If-you-please-Miss-Orme-will-you-please-come-to-Mr-Hedlam's-study-at-once,' he said.

'Williams Minor,' said Mr Greening severely, 'that's no way to deliver a message. Speak the speech, I pray you, trippingly on the tongue; for in the very torrent, tempest, and, as I may say, the whirlwind of passion, you must acquire and beget a temperance that may give it smoothness.'

Williams Minor stared at Mr Greening, and, seeing that humour was intended, he smiled dutifully. Mr Greening was pulling his leg. Mr Greening must be indulged.

'Yes, Mr Greening.'

The small boy disappeared.

Elizabeth rose and moved towards the green-baize door.

'One moment, Lizzy,' said Greening.

She turned and looked at him. As usual, his hair was tousled and the B.A. gown, worn over a tweed coat and baggy grey trousers, was threadbare.

'What is it, Joseph?' she asked.

'Why this indecent haste?' he complained. 'The Old Man won't run away. I would have speech with you.'

Elizabeth inspected him closely. Greening was in one of his facetious moods, and yet he looked uneasy. She knew the signs. Greening had been drinking.

'You will be late for your History Form,' she said.

'Poor little beggars. All yearning to know what happened in ten sixty-six. But don't be so harsh with me, Lizzie. A word of comfort to an aching heart, please. And, talking of hearts, how is Bertram the Bobby this morning?'

Elizabeth looked at him steadily.

'Inspector Martin is very well, I thank you,' she said with dignity.

'He was in Norwich this week-end, I believe,' said Greening in a voice especially refined.

'He was,' said Elizabeth shortly.

'Norwich in November! Try our bracing breezes. Straight from the Pole!'

Elizabeth moved to the door.

'Oh, I say, for God's sake don't go,' Greening ended suddenly.

'Broke, I suppose?' she said.

Greening was usually in that condition towards the end of the month.

'Well,' he said, falsely casual, 'half a guinea would come in devilish useful. Pay you back on the first. Honour bright. So help me St Michael and all angels.'

He made a rapid gesture in the direction of his heart.

Elizabeth sighed.

'I suppose it fell at the first fence,' she said.

'Third,' he corrected her promptly.

'Very well, Joseph. After lunch. But you must pay me back for certain on the first.'

'Peace, peace, perturbèd spirit.'

He made a sweeping gesture and a box file fell to the ground.

'Pick it up and be sensible,' said Elizabeth, and left the room.

She walked quickly down the corridor. From a distance came the penetrating sing-song. They had reached Arretium now:

> This year, young boys in Umbro
> Shall plunge the struggling sheep,
> And in the vats of Luna
> This year the must shall foam
> Round the white feet of laughing girls
> Whose sires have marched to Rome.

She knocked at a white-painted door at the far end and a soft voice bade her enter.

She found herself in the familiar study with the green-baize curtains. A familiar bald head winked and glittered in the pale sunshine and a pair of pale blue eyes looked at her from under a pair of eyebrows startlingly black.

That was Uncle Robert Hedlam, proprietor of St Julian's. He was seated as usual at his desk in his neat, grey suit with the little black tie. Underneath the desk, as she knew, was a pair of surprisingly small feet in creased shoes. His clothes were always shabby and never varied except in texture. He always wore grey.

She wondered, as often before, why Aunt Dorothy had ever married him. Presumably because he was safe, and certainly he had never given Aunt Dorothy a moment's trouble from the day when he had led her to the altar at St Peter Mancroft's to the day when he had laid her to rest in the cemetery in Bowthorpe Road.

'Come in, child,' repeated Hedlam softly.

Elizabeth groaned inwardly. Uncle Robert was going to be kind to her, and she never quite knew how to respond. His little orphan girl, he was wont to call her on such occasions. What does one say to a person like that?

He had nevertheless earned the right to be sentimental if it pleased him. After all, he had provided her with a home, the only real home which, as an Anglo-Indian child, she had ever known. He was kind and he had pushed her into a job. Not the sort of job she would have chosen for herself, but it was, as he said, a stepping-stone to higher things. She had never quite determined whether Uncle Robert, when he produced that sort of phrase, meant it in all good faith or whether he was pulling her leg. Uncle Robert was like that. You never did know.

Strange that he should have decided to sink their small capital in a school. He had no notion of teaching and no intention of taking it up. For him the school was simply an investment. Part of the money came from Aunt Dorothy, and always very scrupulously he referred to it as 'their little fortune'.

And now it was all embarked in St Julian's, and on the whole Uncle Robert had been singularly successful. The school was not of the highest class, perhaps, for the county was shy of it, but it had for the last twenty years established itself as a fit and proper place for the sons of the more successful tradesmen of Norwich. Uncle Robert had secured the result largely by charging higher fees than anyone else in the county and creating the impression that he never had more than a few vacancies and a long waiting list, so that most of the boys were there as a special favour to their parents. He saw to it that the masters he engaged to run the school were efficient, if somewhat colourless, and, though he was often absent, he gave it his personal attention down to the smallest detail.

'Sit down, Elizabeth,' said Uncle Robert.

Elizabeth did as he bade her, noticing, as she did so, that there was another occupant of the room standing upright near the bust of Socrates on the rosewood pedestal in the far corner.

'Good morning, Miss Haslett,' said Elizabeth.

'Good morning, Miss Orme.'

Elizabeth glanced curiously at the woman with whom she had exchanged these greetings.

Miss Veronica Haslett seemed hardly her usual self. Her eyes were bright with excitement and her face, flushed and shiny, contrasted forcibly with the neat grey hair strained almost to breaking point to form a hard bun at the back of the head.

Had the boys been ragging her again? It looked like it. Poor old Hazelnut – a silly nickname. She bore not the slightest resemblance to a nut of any kind, but she was exactly the sort of person to be ragged, quite pointlessly, by the young – a matron of the old type, a relic of the days before Uncle Robert had bought St Julian's and turned it into a paying concern.

What had happened to excite her so obviously? Her face was bright red – almost as red as the disfiguring port-wine mark which marred the lower part of her left cheek.

Elizabeth, unconsciously looking at the mark, realised that Uncle Robert was speaking.

'Elizabeth,' he was saying, 'I want you to do Miss Haslett a service.'

'Of course,' said Elizabeth.

'Miss Haslett will shortly be leaving us.'

The voice of Miss Haslett, its unchanging refinement but slightly ruffled by her manifest excitement, intervened.

'Only for a few days, Miss Orme. I shall not be away for very long.'

Elizabeth looked at Miss Haslett in surprise. Miss Haslett had never been known to leave the school during term-time even for an hour.

'No bad news, I hope,' said Elizabeth.

'On the contrary, Miss Haslett has had a wonderful stroke of luck.'

Elizabeth turned to Uncle Robert. He was leaning slightly forward across his desk and the light winked and flickered on his bald head.

'I shouldn't be surprised,' he continued, 'if she should decide to leave St Julian's for good.'

'I'm sure, Doctor—' began Miss Haslett, but Uncle Robert stayed her protest with a plump hand.

Miss Haslett always referred to Uncle Robert as 'Doctor', though he had no right to the title.

'I'm afraid, Miss Haslett,' he said with a slight smile, 'that you don't yet realise the extent of your good fortune. You have served St Julian's faithfully and well for many years, and, now that Providence has seen fit to bless you, I should be the last to complain if you should wish to spend your remaining years in more restful surroundings.'

'I have no wish for the moment to leave St Julian's, Doctor. On the other hand, I should be grateful if Miss Orme would kindly consent to act as matron during my absence in Paris.'

'Paris!' exclaimed Elizabeth.

Miss Haslett nodded violently as though someone had jerked her head with a string.

'Paris,' she repeated.

'On business,' added Uncle Robert.

He turned to Elizabeth.

'Miss Haslett has won a considerable sum of money,' he explained. 'Seven hundred and fifty thousand francs in the French lottery.'

Elizabeth sat back in her chair.

'I did not buy the ticket,' put in Miss Haslett quickly. 'It was sent to me.'

'Miss Haslett's cousin sent it to her,' said Uncle Robert.

'Nephew,' corrected Miss Haslett.

Uncle Robert accepted the correction with a smile.

'Nephew,' he said. 'And the ticket was a winner and Miss Haslett is now a lady of means.'

He smiled genially.

'I am sure we shall wish to congratulate her,' he prompted gently.

'Seven hundred and fifty thousand francs,' gasped Elizabeth.

Again Miss Haslett nodded.

'The Doctor tells me,' she announced, 'that at the present rate of exchange, seven hundred and fifty thousand francs is equal to about ten thousand pounds.'

Elizabeth leaned forward.

'What a wonderful bit of luck. I do congratulate you, Miss Haslett.'

Elizabeth tried to feel sincere. She *was* sincere, but could not help feeling also a little envious. What was that faded spinster going to do with seven hundred and fifty thousand francs?

'Miss Haslett must go to Paris *quam celerrime*, as they say, to draw the money.'

'When do you propose to go?' inquired Elizabeth.

'In two or three days' time,' put in Uncle Robert. 'There is the question of Miss Haslett's passport. Miss Haslett has never been abroad before, so we must send in an application. She will probably be able to leave on Friday.'

'I see,' said Elizabeth slowly. 'That means that you will want me here for long leave?'

She tried to keep the disappointment out of her voice.

'Long leave', borrowed like the boys' Sunday jackets from Eton, fell next week-end, when a holiday on Monday would be accorded in commemoration of the occasion when Mr Hedlam had taken over the school. Elizabeth saw her small but precious plans crashing to the ground.

She had meant to spend the holiday with Inspector George Martin from Scotland Yard. They had been engaged only two months and he was to take her to Cromer, where he lived, to be viewed by the family. That ceremony would now have to be postponed – indefinitely, she supposed, for George's holidays were as infrequent as her own. She had meant to enjoy herself with

George – one of Lord Trenchard's bright young men, and no one brighter to her way of thinking.

She was recalled to herself by the voice of Miss Haslett.

'I hope it will not greatly inconvenience you, Miss Orme,' she was saying.

Elizabeth hesitated a moment and found Uncle Robert's rather prominent blue eyes fixed firmly upon her.

'Not at all,' she said weakly.

Uncle Robert was very gentle but very firm, and Elizabeth was by nature obedient.

'Very well then,' said Uncle Robert, 'we will consider it settled.'

He smiled, disclosing a row of imperfect teeth with manifest omissions, opened a cigarette-box and pushed it across the table towards Elizabeth. At the same time he stooped and pulled open the bottom drawer of his desk.

Elizabeth passed the cigarette-box to Miss Haslett, who shook her head. Meanwhile Uncle Robert's head had reappeared above his desk and in his hand was a bottle.

Elizabeth's eyes, as she lit her cigarette, grew round.

'This,' said Uncle Robert, 'is an occasion. You are going to drink a glass of sherry with me, Miss Haslett.'

'I have been accustomed to drinking sherry only at funerals, Doctor,' said Miss Haslett.

Uncle Robert looked at her gravely.

'What could be more appropriate, Miss Haslett? We will bury the past – all the years of hard work and, I am afraid, not too much pleasure.'

'You are very kind, Doctor, I am sure.'

Miss Haslett's eyes, fixed on the sherry, were suspiciously moist, and Elizabeth felt suddenly ashamed of her failure to rejoice. Poor old Hazelnut – she had earned every right to a few warm years in the sun.

'Elizabeth,' said Uncle Robert, 'there are some glasses in the pantry.'

Elizabeth turned and left the room. She discovered, after rummaging, three wine-glasses and returned to find Uncle Robert talking finance.

'Four hundred a year at four per cent,' he was saying as she opened the door of the study.

Old Hazelnut was still standing stiff as a grenadier under the bust of Socrates.

'That is,' he continued, 'if you can still find a Government four per cent stock at par. Otherwise you will have to be content with three and a half.'

'Quite,' said Miss Haslett, but it was obvious that she did not understand, or even wish to understand. She had won seven hundred and fifty thousand francs. That was enough for one day.

Elizabeth bent forward and placed the glasses on the desk. Uncle Robert pulled the cork.

'Fine old Amontillado,' he said. 'From my father's cellar. Here's to your good health, Miss Haslett. I wish you every happiness.'

All three raised their glasses. Elizabeth supposed it was good stuff. Terribly dry. Not really very nice, she decided.

'And now, my dear Miss Haslett,' continued Uncle Robert, 'let me give you a word of advice. I expect your good fortune will get into the papers and you will be simply flooded with circulars and – er – propositions.'

He paused a moment, drained his glass and looked at her gravely.

'Touts,' he added.

There was a short silence.

'Touts,' repeated Uncle Robert. 'Persons who want to invest your money for you. There are a lot of them about, I assure you. I get quite a number of enticing circulars myself and I put them all into the waste-paper basket. I should advise you to do the same. When it comes to investments, there is only one really safe and proper course. Consult your banker or a good solicitor, and, if you buy anything yourself, employ a registered stockbroker. But beware of touts.'

He broke off as a deafening clamour smote their ears.

'The bell, I think,' concluded Uncle Robert gently.

Elizabeth emptied her glass and, rising from her chair, left the room to attend to her duties.

3   *Friday, November 27th*

On the morning of Friday, November 27th, 193-, Mr Joseph Greening, Assistant-Master of St Julian's Preparatory School, Norwich, an impressive modern residence standing in its own grounds of over ten acres bordering the Aylsham Road, clad in overalls and smoking an after-breakfast pipe, set forth from his lodgings in St Saviour's Lane on his way to the small garage in Magdalen Street where he kept his motor-cycle. Mr Greening was in spirits. Normally he would at that hour have been on his way to St Julian's, but his colleague, Rutherford, had decided not to go away during long leave and had consented to 'hold the fort', releasing Joseph for a really satisfactory weekend.

Joseph was going to London, and he was starting a day earlier than he had anticipated. This meant, of course, what he was pleased to call some preliminary staff work. First he must send a telegram to his friend Barton at Worthing. Barton was to be his boon companion for the week-end and he had arranged to meet Barton on Saturday at Victoria. Would Barton be able to meet him instead that very evening? They would then have two whole days together. Barton was one of the best – the only one of his Oxford friends with whom he had kept in touch. They had shared with each other the amenities of Wadham and kept together in fair and foul weather.

Poor old Barton, scraping along like himself at a dingy school on two-fifty a year and all found.

Greening wheeled his motor-bicycle from the garage and made for the post office, chugging slowly through the traffic in the narrow street. He stared about him indulgently. Norwich was good to look upon that fine morning. The pale November sun was already dispersing the veils of mist that hung over the city. To his left was a wide, open space where a man could breathe. Beyond him bulked a medieval gateway and beyond it the Close and the great Cathedral.

He passed into the post office and dispatched his telegram to Barton. Then he paused a moment. More staff work. He must telephone to Billy Blossop at Brancaster.

He stepped into a call-box.

'That you Blossop? Listen, old boy. I'll be coming to the King's Head on Sunday week, but this week I'm going up to Town and I want you to send the usual post card. Let Mrs Cardew have it first thing to-morrow morning. That all right? Thank you, Blossop.'

Greening left the post office and, mounting his motor-bicycle, set off down the Ipswich Road for London, smiling thoughtfully to himself. Useful chap, Blossop. Blossop understood. Blossop, as Blossop was accustomed to say rather too often, had been young himself once and made no bones about the small deceptions required of him. It would never do for Hedlam to know that his assistant-master was in the habit of slipping off to London on pleasure bent. Officially Mr Greening spent all his spare time in Brancaster – not to play golf – he could not afford it – but to watch the birds in the sanctuary.

Greening on British Birds. Would he ever find time to write the book of his dreams?

Whenever he went to Brancaster he put up at the King's Head and now and then, when he didn't go to Brancaster, but was supposed to be there, he arranged for Blossop to send a post card to his landlady, Mrs Cardew – photographs of the sanctuary, the golf-course, the church and the village street. Blossop had a small supply of them, each with a little message, signed 'Joseph Greening,' affirming that he was having a good time and would be back for supper on Monday. It had all worked like a charm for over a year now.

Greening smiled happily as he pulled out to avoid a dray, but presently he frowned. Things were devilish tight at the moment – tight in a financial sense.

He hoped to be *tight* in another sense later on. Joke. He laughed a little and, humming the waltz tune out of Conversation Piece, 'I'll follow my secret heart,' accelerated to forty.

Things were certainly tight and Barton was not likely to be flush of cash. Strictly, he could not afford three days in Town, but it was two months since he had really enjoyed himself, and the prospect of spending long leave anywhere within twenty miles of Norwich was too appalling.

Greening swerved uneasily. There was a special reason why he disliked the idea of spending long leave in Norwich. He did not like to admit it, but there it was. If he had stayed in Norwich or gone to Brancaster he would have had to see Phyllis. He did not want to see Phyllis. She had written to him twice in the last week and he had left her letters unanswered. Phyllis was all right, but she was taking too much for granted. He had an uneasy feeling that she wanted to have it out with him.

As if that would do any good. What was the use of discussing marriage on two hundred and fifty and all found?

He decided not to think of Phyllis. He would think instead of the treat in store. There was a place in Maddox Street. . . . His eyes brightened and again he accelerated.

But the place in Maddox Street was expensive, and that show at the Hippodrome, which he must certainly see, would cost a bit. Moreover, there would have to be supper afterwards, and, though Harry would pay his share, money didn't go very far these days in spite of all this talk about the fall in prices.

This brought him to the great idea. Any sum up to five thousand pounds on note of hand alone. Moneylenders, of course, were in principle to be avoided, but, approached with sense and moderation, they had their use. He would have to be careful, but he was not the sort of man to be cheated. He knew his way about.

He removed a hand from the bar and felt his coat pocket. The circular was there safe enough – Mr John Throgmorton of 153 Shaftesbury Avenue.

Not only a moneylender, it seemed. He also sold shares and probably had lots of customers in Norwich. There had been a regular hail of his prospectuses on the town just recently. Everyone at the school and some of his friends had received one. Sierra Grande Preferred were booming apparently. Mr Throgmorton had a packet of them and seemed anxious to dispose of them. Perhaps old Hazelnut would have a shot. She, too, had received a circular and would soon have a whole packet of boodle to invest. Lucky old trout.

He had found her looking at the circular after prayers, and he had begun to tell her what she ought to do. Then old Hedlam had descended on them and Hedlam had firmly advised her to tear the thing up.

But the old girl had tucked it away in her bag.

It was a little past midday when Joseph Greening dismounted from his bicycle outside the Lowestoft Family Hotel in Bloomsbury Square. He usually stayed at the Lowestoft when in London. It was cheap but clean and he preferred it to one of the popular hotels in the Strand or Piccadilly. He booked his room, however, for one night only. Heaven only knew where he would be staying the next night, if old Barton turned up.

Unpacking, he placed his evening-trousers carefully beneath the mattress. It was rather a feat to carry on his motor-bicycle a suit-case containing evening-clothes, but he had reduced packing to a fine art.

He was on the point of leaving his room when a telegram from Barton was brought to him. Barton could not get away in time to meet him that night. Would he therefore meet the train at Victoria on the following day?

Greening, resigning himself to independent measures, set out at once for Shaftesbury Avenue. It was already one o'clock and he assumed that Mr Throgmorton would be at lunch. He therefore turned into a sandwich-bar and consumed a frugal meal at leisure. From outside came the sweet murmur of traffic and the shifting of many feet on the flagstones. It was good to be in London, and even better to think of the pleasant evening that lay before him – a

very pleasant evening if only Mr Throgmorton proved to be suffi-
ciently accommodating.

Shortly after two o'clock Joseph found himself climbing four
flights of dusty stairs in a business block at the top of Shaftesbury
Avenue.

In the outer room of Mr Throgmorton's establishment he found
to his surprise, not the scrubby office-boy of his imagination, but
an attractive young woman – well, not young perhaps, but with a
face which was beautiful in its haggard way. She asked him to sit
down and returned to her papers.

She was brisk and businesslike. Mr Throgmorton would see
him in five minutes.

True enough, some five minutes later he was shown into Mr
Throgmorton's presence, to emerge, ten minutes later still, a happier
man. In his pocket-book were seven five-pound notes. It had all
been absurdly easy – terms one per cent per month with an obligation to repay at a month's notice. Pretty stiff but not outrageous
considering that he had no security to offer. Mr Throgmorton had
seemed a decent sort of chap, but not very easy to read. Face like
a blank wall. No expression at all. But very civil and businesslike.

And he had delivered the goods.

Joseph Greening fingered his pocket-book and whistled a merry
tune. He would have no cause to stint himself that day.

4   *Friday, November 27th*

Miss Veronica Haslett, a little flustered, re-adjusted her veil and
sat down in the corner of the third-class compartment. She had
meant to take the early train which reached Liverpool Street at

11.20, but, what with packing and making what she called her arrangements, this had proved impossible.

She would now have to incur the expense of lunching on the train, having forgotten to provide herself with sandwiches – a nasty, dear meal and everything joggled so. But she was not going to meet a man of business on an empty stomach.

She sat back in her carriage gazing at the trim Norfolk landscape as it wheeled and slipped past the window. At last she was on her way. The incredible dream had come true. Underneath her best silk petticoat, for nothing else, she felt, would suit the occasion, was the little bag which she had made with her own hands, tied securely with tape and fastened to her stays with two large safety-pins, one on each side. In it were bestowed the lottery ticket and three one-pound notes as a reserve against emergencies.

Was it possible? That small slip of paper was worth some ten thousand pounds of English money. It would, so she understood, be handed to her in notes quite casually across the counter by a clerk. Her bank-manager had explained it all to her most carefully, urging her to take special care of the notes, for they would not even be numbered – or rather, of course, they would be numbered, but no record of the numbers was kept, so that, if they were stolen, it would be very difficult to trace the thief. The French were very careless in these matters.

These things were managed better in England. But then, there were no lotteries in England.

Miss Haslett paused in her train of thought. Her conscience pricked. She would owe her fortune to a lottery, and a lottery was just wicked gambling. But then, of course, she had not bought the ticket. She had merely received it from her disreputable nephew and godson, Timothy Bell. Timothy was always going to Paris, and he had sent her the ticket as a joke – pulling her leg, as he would call it. Timothy was like that.

Miss Haslett pressed her lips gravely together. She would write Timothy a nice letter to thank him for his gift, and she would inform him of its consequences. That would teach him to make game of his aunt. Nice and mad he would feel about it all. Inscrutable were the ways of Providence!

Everyone had been extraordinarily nice to her. Young Mr Joseph Greening had seemed genuinely pleased, while Mr Hedlam had been kindness itself, and they had both given her all sorts of advice.

Mr Hedlam had urged her to do nothing rash. Something safe at four per cent was what he favoured, while the bank-manager had talked about British credit going on a three per cent basis, whatever that might mean. Her income from the lottery would at that rate not exceed three hundred a year. A nice little sum, of course, but hardly enough on which to retire – not when you had to pay income tax, on unearned income at that.

Surely one could do better with so large a sum of money? Mr Greening had been quite emphatic about it. He had even shown her a prospectus and she, too, had received one. So, it seemed, had Mr Hedlam and Mr Rutherford, and others that she knew. It had been sent to her by a Mr Throgmorton of Shaftesbury Avenue.

Mr Throgmorton was a most persuasive and apparently a most philanthropic gentleman. He was what Mr Greening described as an outside broker. He did not believe in a safe three or even four per cent. Mr Throgmorton was ready to guarantee his clients at least six per cent without risk or peril, and, certainly, the list of investments which he had submitted was most attractive. There was one company which apparently had not failed to pay six per cent for years, and it could show a lord and two baronets on the board. It was true that the lord, if Mr Hedlam was to be believed, had twice been through the Bankruptcy Court, but that might happen to anybody. In any case, all that had happened before the lord had become a director – before, that was to say, he had learned wisdom. Then there were those gold-mines in Mexico. She knew something about gold. Her sister Jane had money in gold and the shares had risen from twenty-five shillings to four pounds ten.

Miss Haslett nodded her head wisely. She was her own mistress and intended to manage her own affairs. She had been dependent on the counsels and wishes of others long enough. Henceforth she would think and act for herself. Already she had taken the first step towards emancipation. She had written to Mr Throgmorton explaining to him all the circumstances, and she had suggested consulting him on Monday.

This was Friday. She was to sleep that night in London at the Westmoreland Hotel. Mr Hedlam had remembered it was cheap and comfortable. She was to go over to Paris first thing in the morning by Imperial Airways and return by it in the afternoon, having lodged her money with the Paris agents of the Norfolk and Suffolk Bank, Head Office, London Street, Norwich, with which she had kept an account for thirty years.

On Monday, therefore, she would be ready to discuss investments.

Mr Throgmorton had been most kind. Not only had he answered her letter by return, but his secretary – evidently a lady – had rung her up from London. Unfortunately Mr Throgmorton would not be in London on Monday, possibly not for some time, but he would meet Miss Haslett on her arrival at Liverpool Street. She would be reaching London at half-past four, after business hours, but Mr Throgmorton would be most happy to talk things over with his client and to arrange, if Miss Haslett so desired, for a more formal interview later on.

Miss Haslett would have liked to consult Mr Hedlam on the subject. But Mr Hedlam had spent the whole of that week, except for a brief visit to the school on Wednesday, visiting his mother in Kensington. Mr Hedlam was lucky. The school belonged to him, but he did not belong to the school. He merely owned it and paid people to run it for him – a gentleman of leisure.

Miss Haslett smiled at the passing landscape. She, too, might now be a lady of leisure if she pleased.

But here was the lunch all ready and they were not yet at Ipswich. Miss Haslett, outwardly serene but inwardly a little tremulous, passed to the dining-car.

Two hours later she was refusing the services of a porter at Liverpool Street who offered to carry her light dispatch case. It was all the luggage she had, for, when one travels by air, one must travel light. She walked steadily down the platform.

Where was Mr Throgmorton? Her attention was drawn to a man of middle height who was obviously looking for a passenger. He had a featureless face, with rather full lips and a prominent right eye that gleamed benevolently from behind spectacles of light-coloured horn. He wore a moustache and a neatly trimmed beard. The left eye was covered by a small black patch. He wore a well-cut overcoat and silk hat.

Miss Haslett felt her heart beat a little faster as the silk-hatted stranger, after speaking to one other lady, alone like herself, came towards her.

'Excuse me,' he said, removing the hat, 'but have I the honour to address Miss Haslett?'

Miss Haslett bowed.

'I am Mr John Throgmorton, at your service,' continued the stranger. 'I hope you have had a pleasant journey.'

'Thank you, yes. It was quite pleasant. It is very kind of you to meet the train, Mr Throgmorton.'

Miss Haslett flushed as he gallantly relieved her of the dispatch case.

'Not at all, not at all,' he said. 'It is for me to apologise – for being out of Town on Monday. Where are you staying, Miss Haslett?'

'At the Westmoreland Hotel.'

Mr Throgmorton nodded wisely.

'Very comfortable, I believe. Every modern convenience. Let me get you a taxi.'

'A taxi?'

She hesitated.

Mr Throgmorton was smiling.

'You can afford a taxi now, Miss Haslett,' he said, 'if what you tell me is true. Seven hundred and fifty thousand francs, I think was the sum mentioned.'

Miss Haslett nodded. She was a rich woman now, of course, and could take a taxi whenever she so desired. And Mr Throgmorton was really most kind – a most understanding man.

A taxi swept to the pavement and, still holding her dispatch case, he handed her into it. Soon they were in the thick of the city traffic, moving slowly towards the West End.

'Excuse me, Miss Haslett,' Mr Throgmorton was saying, 'but may I ask whether you have engaged a private sitting-room?'

Miss Haslett looked at him in surprise.

'No,' she said. 'I am staying only for one night. I go to Paris to-morrow by air.'

'Of course,' said Mr Throgmorton. 'I was merely wondering where we could best have our little talk. The public rooms in an hotel are so crowded, and I could scarcely ask you to receive me in your bedroom, could I?'

Miss Haslett flushed a deep crimson.

'Could we perhaps take a walk in the park?' she suggested.

Mr Throgmorton smilingly waved a plump hand at the window. 'It is raining,' he pointed out, 'and it will be dark in half an hour.'

He thought a moment.

'In the circumstances perhaps it might be as well if we went to my rooms. I frequently do business there. I can introduce you to my secretary. You have already met her, I believe, on the telephone. She will give you a cup of tea and we can go over things together quietly and in comfort.'

'You are very kind, I am sure,' murmured Miss Haslett.

'Not at all. I shall be only too pleased to make your better acquaintance. Investment is necessarily a matter of confidence, and I want you to know me a little better before you decide to entrust me with your affairs.'

Miss Haslett felt herself beginning to glow faintly.

'You understand, Mr Throgmorton,' she said, 'I have no wish to – er – speculate.'

Mr Throgmorton looked at her reproachfully.

'We are not going to speculate, Miss Haslett. There is all the difference in the world between speculation and the policy of bold but sound investment which I advocate and practise on behalf of my clients. But please do not let us talk till you have had a cup of tea. You must be tired after your long journey?'

They sat back silent for a moment and Miss Haslett found herself looking surreptitiously at her companion.

'Admiring my black patch?' asked Mr Throgmorton. 'That was a golf ball. I got it straight in the eye at Moor Park only yesterday. It was lucky that the fellow hadn't really hit his shot, otherwise I might have had to have my eye removed. My oculist tells me to keep it covered for a day or two.'

He broke off as the taxi, which a moment ago had swung into Edgware Road from the Marble Arch, drew towards the pavement.

'Here is your hotel,' he concluded. 'I suggest that you should leave your luggage here and sign the register. We can then go on to my office.'

He helped her from the taxi and, telling the driver to wait, walked with her to the reception counter. Miss Haslett signed the register and Throgmorton noted the number of her room.

'Thirty-six,' he said, and smilingly advised her not to forget it.

They left the hotel and Throgmorton gave the driver an address in Cadbury Road, Maida Vale.

'It is a kind of office-flat,' he explained. 'I have many clients in this district and it is not always convenient for them to come to my place in Shaftesbury Avenue.'

It was now five o'clock and the winter day was closing. The taxi swung into a dark road and pulled up beside a row of houses which left it at right angles.

'Bit of a nuisance for taxi-drivers,' said Mr Throgmorton as he jumped out and helped Miss Haslett to alight. 'I live in a cul-de-sac.'

With a gesture he prevented Miss Haslett from settling the taxi fare, and, paying the man himself, led her into the blind road. They climbed a flight of steps belonging to a three-storied house. He unlocked the door, and presently she was seated in a comfortable chair in a sitting-room full of Edwardian furniture.

A roll-top desk suggested that the sitting-room was also an office.

Mr Throgmorton walked to the door.

'If you will excuse me,' he said, 'I will look for Miss Taylor and ask her to make us some tea.'

Miss Haslett, left alone, walked to the window. The curtains were drawn, but parting them she looked down, over a small back garden, upon a large railway siding. It was nearly dark and the lines were picked out with gleaming signal lights. Long rows of trucks stretched away into the shadows. Here and there men were waving lamps and a small engine was busy.

'Admiring the view, Miss Haslett?'

Mr Throgmorton was back again.

'Miss Taylor is out for the moment,' he continued; 'but I fully intend that you shall have that cup of tea. I will get it myself.'

Miss Haslett came from the window.

'Can I help?' she asked.

Mr Throgmorton raised a plump hand.

'I could not dream of it, my dear lady. I am an old bachelor and accustomed to looking after myself. I suggest that you come over here and look at these investment lists while the kettle is boiling.'

Miss Haslett approached the roll-top desk and sat down in the swivel chair. Mr Throgmorton bent over and the top of the desk rolled back. There were papers on the ledge and his hand went across her shoulder to get them.

Suddenly it stopped.

At the same instant Miss Haslett felt a firm and agonising pressure beneath her ears. Merciful God, what was happening? The pressure was increased. The whole world was shot with stars.

She felt she was screaming with agony, but not a sound passed her lips.

Then a dark curtain shot with vivid light fell like a heavy blanket and she felt no more.

Mr Throgmorton drew himself up – breathing heavily.

'It's all over, Hermione,' he said. 'You must help me now with the clothes.'

CHAPTER II

1 *Friday, November 27th*

Mr Joseph Greening, feeling that life was good to him, followed his companion down the narrow passage. All was quiet and uncommonly dark. No one would have thought that Tottenham Court Road, with its heavy traffic, was only a few yards away. Mr Greening thoroughly approved of his companion. Ruby was cheerful and matey. She was going to cost him a pretty penny, and, of Mr Throgmorton's notes, only three of the original six remained.

It seemed no time at all since he had seen Mr Throgmorton and borrowed the cash. Nevertheless it was now nearly midnight. But time flies when life is pleasant. Hats off to Ruby! She knew her way about. It was a stroke of luck picking up a girl like that – not only good to look upon but sympathetic. He had even been moved to confess that he was not greatly in funds and, doing her best to be helpful, she had suggested a visit to her 'club'. It was known as the 'Emerald' and one could do most things at the Emerald, including what she called a little flutter on the baize.

They came to a flight of steps and Ruby said something to a man at a half-open door. Joseph could not see the man very clearly. Soon, however, the door opened a little wider and threw a shaft of light on to the paving-stones of the alley. Instinctively Joseph glanced down at his shirt front. It was a little crumpled and there was a faint smudge near one of the stud-holes, but the breastplate was intact.

He climbed some stairs. They were covered with thick carpet and at the top stood a footman in livery so that Joseph wished suddenly that he had been wearing a white tie. Another door was thrust open.

'Just going to powder my nose, dear. See you soon.'

Ruby vanished behind a velvet curtain and Joseph handed his hat, coat and scarf to the footman. It was not, he felt, the sort of coat to hand to a gentleman in livery – an elderly and somewhat greasy trench-coat. The footman, however, took it as though it had been lined with sable and collared with astrakhan.

A stoutish man approached him as he stood in the doorway.

'And now,' thought Joseph, 'I know what they mean by immaculate evening-dress.'

For the stranger was glossy all over, from his brilliant hair down to his twinkling shoes.

'Come right in,' he said. 'Friend of Rube, I guess. Have a drink?'

'You're very kind,' murmured Joseph and felt suddenly that a drink would do him good.

The room into which he had come was small, handsomely carpeted and discreetly lit. A cabinet gramophone was playing softly in a corner. Two proud youths, also immaculate, were sitting on a sofa along the far wall, and there were three or four girls sunken in armchairs before an electric fire.

Joseph began to wonder what he should do next. His host solved the problem for him by dividing a curtain and inviting him to come forward. Joseph obediently advanced into another room.

It was a large room, the distant end of which was filled by a long table at which a number of people were seated. A blue dome of cigar smoke hung between the table and the ceiling.

'Stake 'em up, lads, and chance it. Stake 'em up. Roll, bowl or pitch. Every time a blood orange or a good cigar,' were the first words he heard.

They came from a little man sitting in front of the long table. The table was covered with green baize and in the centre of it was a roulette wheel. There were perhaps twenty people in the room, grouped round the table, some standing behind chairs and some sitting, the baize being covered with various coloured counters of different shapes and sizes.

The immaculate gentleman laid a hand on Joseph's arm.

'You'll be wanting to have a little flutter, I reckon, but first you'll come along with me.'

Joseph was led to a buffet covered with a shining white cloth which cut off one corner of the room. A rather splendid butler stood to attention.

'A glass of the old and bold before we start,' suggested his conductor genially, and signed to the butler, who began pouring out champagne.

Joseph had a qualm.

'I say,' he protested.

His host stopped him with an impressive gesture.

'The drinks', he said solemnly, 'are on the house.'

The eyes of Joseph gleamed wild and wide.

'On the house?' he murmured.

This was something like a club.

He felt a hand on his arm.

'Finding your way about, dear?'

Ruby was beside him.

'Here's how,' said Joseph, draining his glass.

'What about a fiver for chips?' suggested his host.

Half an hour later Joseph found himself sitting in the outer room. He was not quite clear as to the sequence of events which had brought him there, but the room, he noticed, was empty except for the immaculate gentleman. Ruby, of course, must have gone to get her cloak.

Joseph was sitting at a small desk.

'Really bad luck,' his host was saying; 'and you were shaping for a winner at the start. Such is life. Ups and downs. Make it payable to "Bearer," please.'

Joseph tried to realise what he was doing. What had become of his fifteen pounds? Where were the snows of yester-year? At one time he had been forty pounds up. Yet here he was writing a cheque for thirty-five.

He had a last spasm of caution.

'Do I really owe all this?' he asked.

'You counted your chips, didn't you?' answered his host shortly.

Joseph nodded. He had counted his chips and the little white ones were worth five pounds each. He had bought seven of them and the last one had fallen under the rake five minutes ago.

He signed the cheque with an effort.

'I've post-dated it a week,' he said. 'Is that all right?'

'Quite all right,' said his host and folded the cheque with fat fingers.

Joseph moved towards the door. Mechanically he took his hat and coat and scarf.

Where was Ruby? Of course. She had promised to wait outside. He descended the steps and looked about him.

There was no sign of Ruby.

He walked down the dark passage towards Tottenham Court Road. It was past one o'clock and there was not much traffic in the streets. Still there was no sign of Ruby.

For a moment he stood silent under a lamp.

'Had for a mug,' he muttered and walked back moodily to his hotel.

2   Saturday, November 28th

Hermione Taylor, descending the stairs, walked quietly into the lounge of the Westmoreland Hotel. She was carrying a light dispatch case. It was early morning, not yet seven o'clock, and no one was on duty at the reception counter.

She laid upon it a key bearing the number thirty-six and passed out into the street.

She had seen no one that morning but the chambermaid, who, according to her orders overnight, had delivered the bill with her breakfast at six.

It was a grey morning with a hint of rain in the sky. She did not notice the weather, however, but turned to the right and walked rapidly away from the hotel. She tried not to feel conscious of her clothes. But that was easier said than done. It would have been difficult at any time to feel at ease wearing such garments as these, and it did not add to her comfort that only a few hours previously the late owner had been stripped and huddled away in a sack – a stiff, disfigured creature; all that was left of the late Veronica Haslett from the city of Norwich.

John had been amazingly kind and thoughtful. He had spared her as much as possible. But she had been obliged to help him with the clothes and to take a last look at the features of the dead woman whom she would have to impersonate.

She had not attempted to make up her face. It was not really necessary for her to look exactly like Miss Haslett. One distinctive feature was enough – provided the clothes were right and the general appearance as to age and calling. That port-wine mark on the left cheek was providential. Nobody could fail to notice that, and it had been the work of a few minutes to paint it on to her face. She was unlikely to meet anyone who *knew* Miss Haslett and the photograph on the passport was the usual nondescript affair.

The risk was small and could not, in any case, be avoided.

She glanced at her watch – Miss Haslett's watch, an old-fashioned, clumsy thing, pinned inside the lapel of her coat.

She quickened her pace and picked up a taxi in the Edgware Road.

'Imperial Airways, Victoria,' she directed the driver.

Half an hour later she was running smoothly in the charabanc to Croydon and at half-past ten she was at Le Bourget. Her flight had been entirely uneventful, but she had never been in the air before, and for a moment the novelty took her mind off things past, present and to come.

But the journey soon ceased to interest her. The Kentish Weald and the South Downs seen from the air were robbed of all distinction and her mind inevitably returned to the business in hand.

John had been cool and collected throughout. When it had come to the point – all preparations made – he had wanted her to have as little to do as possible. He had not called her into the room till Miss Haslett was dead and, once she had taken the clothes, he had insisted on finishing the job himself without further assistance. She had felt no sort of compunction or remorse for having killed the woman. But Miss Haslett had not been nice to look upon. She had hated having to see and handle the body.

She had even felt a little sick, and John, seeing how it was with her, had given her a glass of brandy to drink.

The waiting, too, had been pretty bad. She had sat, seemingly for hours, by the window, staring into the little scrubby garden which ran down from the dining-room to the fence which bordered the railway.

John, on returning, had claimed to have been at work for not more than forty minutes. All that time hardly a sound had come from the tool-shed, a rough shelter whose fourth wall was the fence itself, where he was cutting a hole through to the siding with its waiting trucks.

She remembered his words at parting.

'Good-bye and good luck.'

He had drawn her close and she had felt his hands pressing her towards him – the hands which only an hour before . . .

She shivered at the memory.

How quickly it had all happened. She had seen Miss Haslett lying dead in the flat at five o'clock and in less than an hour, wearing Miss Haslett's clothes, she had hailed a taxi in the Edgware Road. Within ten minutes she had stood, safe and unsuspected, in Room 36 of the Westmoreland Hotel.

With a beating heart she had walked up to the reception counter and claimed the key. But the clerk had given her only the briefest glance. John had been most emphatic on the subject and John had been right.

'They will notice nothing,' he had said, 'but your clothes and the mark on your face.'

Where would the body be ultimately found? Would it be traced back to the house where the crime had been committed? Well, they had very carefully considered all that – allowed for every possibility – and, if the police should find their way to that ground-floor flat in the blind alley they would still have to find Mrs Beck, the decayed British gentle-woman, who had occupied it for two days only and then effectually disappeared.

Hermione smiled grimly to herself. She had not so far contrived to make much out of her talents – very considerable talents, as she thought – for realistic impersonation. The stage had not offered her much scope for the exercise of her gifts. Life was proving more generous. Two parts – parts which, if the luck held, would pay her extremely well – had come her way within the last forty-eight hours.

Her performance as Mrs Beck in search of a home had been well within her repertory, and fate was starring her now in the role of Miss Haslett, lately of Norwich.

There had not been the slightest hitch in finding, renting or leaving the flat, and there would remain not the slightest trace of their brief tenancy, except for that gap in the fence large enough to serve as a practicable exit for a man of average size and shape.

Mrs Carroll, the owner of the house, had been only too thankful to find a tenant, and had made no attempt to conceal her satisfaction at receiving a month's rent in advance on condition that she vacated within twenty-four hours.

But here at last was the Rue des Italiens. Hermione Taylor dismounted stiffly from the omnibus which had brought her from Le Bourget, as befitted a woman of fifty, and, giving the dispatch case to one of the porters of Imperial Airways, asked him to get her a taxi. Ten minutes later she drew up outside the Government lottery office in the Pavilion de Flore.

It was not the impressive temple of fortune she had expected to find. Two or three shabby clerks were waiting behind a counter. She approached one of them and said in halting French:

'Is this where I present a winning ticket?'

The man nodded.

She fumbled in the handbag hanging from her wrist, Miss Haslett's bag, a depressing receptacle of black pigskin, and produced the ticket. The clerk looked at it carefully, went away and returned about two minutes later. Hermione, strangely cool, noticed that his collar, chafing an ill-shaven neck, was soiled with blood. He bent over the counter and scribbled something on a piece of paper which he pushed towards her.

'First cashier on the left,' he said.

She picked up the paper and walked without a word in the direction indicated. Upon the paper was an order to pay bearer seven hundred and fifty thousand francs. She pushed it beneath the wire. The cashier, an elderly man with greying hair and a mole on his right cheek, looked at the paper.

'How will you have it?' he asked.

Hermione laid Miss Haslett's dispatch case on the counter beside her.

'I will take it in five-thousand franc notes, if I may.'

The man nodded and began to hand her little packages. There were ten notes in each of them. Hermione stowed them in the dispatch case and closed the lid with a snap.

'Don't you keep a record of these notes?' she asked, and waited a little breathlessly for his reply.

The man shook his head.

'No time for that,' he answered. 'This is not a bank. Good morning, madam, and my congratulations.'

Hermione found herself in the street.

'And now,' she said to herself with elation, 'for part number three.'

She hailed a taxi and was driven to the Gare du Nord. There, in the ladies' cloak-room, she rapidly removed Miss Haslett's clothes, took from the dispatch case a frock of her own, put it on and at the same time wiped the port-wine stain from her cheek.

She then left the cloak-room, slipping past the woman attendant when her back was turned.

Outside she glanced at the watch on her wrist. It was already midday.

A quarter of an hour later she was sitting on the terrace at the Café de la Paix drinking a glass of vermuth and looking with the eager eyes of a tourist at the people walking down the Boulevard des Capucines. On her knees was the dispatch case with Miss Haslett's clothes crushed into it beneath the precious notes.

She had not been there five minutes when she felt a hand on her shoulder.

'Hermione,' came a voice from beside her.

She had been waiting to hear it and yet was taken by surprise. It was always like that with Richard.

She looked up at him, noting that he was well and that he seemed in spirits.

'I got your telegram,' he said. 'What on earth does it mean and why must I carry a brief bag?'

He was smiling down at her and his grey eyes were soft and kind. It would be difficult to send him away.

'Dick,' she said, 'how lovely to see you again. Sit down for a moment.'

He looked at her uncertainly.

'Finish your drink,' he urged, 'and let's go where we can be human. I've missed you badly, my dear.'

His eyes were less kind but more possessive.

He looked her over from head to foot.

'You are looking tired,' he said. 'What are you doing in Paris, anyway?'

'Listen, Dick. I can't spend any time with you this visit. But I've got the money.'

Dick stared at her incredulously.

'Not the five thousand?'

She nodded.

'It's in French notes. I want you to take them and carry out the instructions in a letter which I am also going to give you. Call a taxi and drive me to the Gare du Nord. I'll hand over the notes in the cab.'

'You don't mean that you're going back at once?'

She bent her head.

'I must be in London this evening.'

'Hermione.'

'Please, Dick. I shall see you again soon. Read my letter carefully. Change these notes as directed and call at Throgmorton's office in Shaftesbury Avenue as soon as you can.'

'Look here,' he said jealously, 'what does this mean? Has Throgmorton . . .'

'No, Dick. But he is with us in this business. We must discuss the whole thing with him when you come to London.'

He looked at her uneasily.

'How did you get the money?' he asked. 'Is anything wrong?'

'One doesn't pick up five thousand pounds in the street. We are running a certain risk. I collected the money this morning on behalf of Throgmorton. The only way you can help us is to carry out your instructions and come to London as soon as possible.'

'But my dear,' he protested, 'this is more than flesh and blood can stand. I can't see you like this and let you go again without a word.'

'It's not for long, Dick. I'll make up for it in London. I promise. It's just as hard for me.'

Dick looked at his watch – mystified and inclined to resent it.

'Time for lunch, anyhow,' he suggested.

'No, Dick. I mustn't be seen with you to-day in Paris.'

Dick grasped her by the arm.

'All right,' he said gruffly. 'Finish your drink and I'll call a taxi.'

On the way to the Gare du Nord – once the notes had been transferred and the letter thrust into his pocket – she sank back into his arms. For a moment she forgot her errand. She was indifferent to the traffic outside. The movement of the taxi flung them from side to side, but she was conscious only of the grasp and pressure which held her firm.

They drew up all too quickly at the Gare du Nord. A porter opened the door, intruding suddenly from the world she had lost. Dick waved him aside, scrambled to the pavement and waited while she adjusted her hat.

'Keep the taxi,' she said firmly. 'Here we must separate.'

'Hermione!'

'I shall be waiting for you in London. Goodbye, Dick.'

She jumped from the taxi and left him standing by the open door. Only when she had reached the entrance to the station did she venture to turn and, when she did so, she saw the back of the cab disappearing into the stream of traffic on the boulevard.

She walked slowly away, bringing her mind with difficulty back to the business in hand. First she must change again. She walked, as before, into the ladies' cloak-room, to emerge ten minutes later wearing Miss Haslett's clothes and bearing on her face the port-wine disfigurement.

The aeroplane did not leave Le Bourget until three o'clock. She accordingly took a taxi to the Place de la Madeleine and lunched at Bernard's restaurant behind the church. Thence she walked to the office of Imperial Airways and within an hour was looking down on Paris dwindling to a toy city behind her.

The following wind which had blown her so rapidly to Paris was now against the aeroplane, which did not land at Croydon till dusk was falling, so that it was almost dark when she reached Victoria.

She stepped from the omnibus, which had brought her from the aerodrome, and walked in the direction of the station. As she did so, she brushed against a man who was about to cross the road with a male companion. The man turned towards her with a muttered apology.

She stopped a moment, startled by a vague impression that she had seen him before, but looked quickly away again as she perceived that he, too, had come to a standstill and was staring back at her.

Ten minutes later, Hermione Taylor, in her own clothes – after visiting the ladies' cloak-room at Victoria – was driving in a taxi to Warwick Avenue.

3   *Saturday, November 28th*

'Had for a mug,' repeated Mr Joseph Greening for the eleventh time.

His friend, Harry Barton, looked at him.

'You always were a mug,' he responded cheerfully. 'But luckily I have a spare fiver. So what about a quick one?'

'They are not open yet,' said Joseph.

Joseph Greening had met his friend at Victoria according to programme.

They had left the station on foot, making for Wilton Road, where Harry had a room intermittently at his disposal.

Joseph, stepping from the pavement, jostled a lady in black wearing an old-fashioned hat with a small veil. He muttered an apology and stared after her a moment.

'Come on,' urged Harry Barton peevishly.

'Coming,' said Joseph, and suffered himself to be led away.

4   *Saturday, November 28th*

Hermione Taylor shut the door carefully and advanced into the middle of the room. Throgmorton sprang to his feet. He moved round the office desk, his hands outstretched.

'Well?' he said eagerly.

He placed his hands on her shoulders.

She drew back, removed her hat and put it on the desk.

'It's all right,' she said quickly. 'Everything went according to programme – just as we planned.'

He pulled her slowly towards him. The light eyes behind the spectacles opened a fraction wider as he felt her instinctive recoil. Then the head came forward and the full mouth closed upon her own. Automatically she responded. Throgmorton released her, a little breathless. He was trembling slightly.

'The notes?' he inquired.

'I handed them over to Dick – in a taxi on the way to the Gare du Nord. There was not the smallest difficulty.'

Throgmorton wiped from his forehead the small beads of sweat.

'My God, Hermione, it's been pretty awful – waiting here. If anything were to happen to you. . . . The last half-hour was the worst. I was expecting you sooner.'

'It was the head wind,' she explained. 'The plane was late.'

There was a short silence.

'Did you get the Brannocks?' she asked.

'Yes, but Thornton was engaged. So I've invited Butterworth.'

'What are we going to do?'

'Cochran's new review. I've taken a box.'

'A bit extravagant, isn't it?'

'We're going to the theatre to be noticed. Hence the box. Besides, we might as well be hung for a sheep as a lamb.'

Not a fortunate remark, she considered, but it was difficult to bear continually in mind that if things went wrong hanging might become for them more than a figure of speech. Not for a lamb, perhaps. Miss Haslett could hardly pass for a lamb. She shivered slightly and found his eyes fixed anxiously upon her.

'This has been the devil of a time for you, my dear. Your nerves must be all to pieces.'

She thrust out her arm and stared at the slim wrist at the end of it.

'Look,' she said. 'Steady as a rock.'

But Throgmorton was groping beneath the desk. His head came up and he produced a bottle of gin, followed by a cocktail shaker.

'Time for a quick one,' he said.

He manipulated the shaker – an ingenious machine. All you

had to do was to press the lid up and down. He had bought it at Fortnum & Mason's.

He filled two glasses. The cocktail was sticky and not iced, but she felt the glow – felt also that this man, with his obstinate care and consideration, was her friend. She squeezed his arm with a gesture of affection as he turned to open the door.

An hour later, in the vestibule of the Trocadero, they stood awaiting their guests. Butterworth came first, lean, languid and probably hungry. He, at any rate, would enjoy his dinner. Fleet Street was not treating him any too well.

John was cordial – overdoing the carefree host, she considered.

'A snake in the grass, or a pirate's breath, or why not one after the other?' he suggested.

Hermione glanced at him anxiously. He had a strong head and she had never seen him worse for drink, but to-night he must be normal. Her quick fancy already heard prosecuting counsel:

'Did you notice anything at all unusual in the behaviour of Mr Throgmorton on that occasion?'

The black barman was shaking up the drinks as the Brannocks entered. Joyce Brannock was looking more than usually lovely.

Hermione regarded her coolly and without envy. Glowing from her brief encounter with Dick in Paris she feared no rival and could afford to be generous. Joyce had a beautiful back and was not afraid to show it. The new fashions suited her.

They returned to the flat in Warwick Avenue at one in the morning. Throgmorton sighed heavily as he removed his tie.

'A very nice party, my dear,' he said over his shoulder. 'But I hope Dick Feiling will be with us soon. Till then we shall be living on my overdraft.'

5   *Tuesday, December 1st*

Shunter Wilcox stepped out briskly. It was a nasty, raw morning – the first of December. Brighton was at its worst, and there was, as yet, no hint of dawn in the sky. A fine drizzle was streaming before the wind and a day's work stretched before him monotonous and cold.

A quarter of an hour's walk brought him to a spot a little beyond the railway station, where he joined the other members of his shift. They turned into the goods yard by twos and threes, clocking their time as they passed the foreman.

"Ullo, Albert,' said one of them.

"Ullo, Tom,' responded Albert.

Tom looked at the morning, but he was a cheerful soul.

'Come to the sunny South. Be bright in breezy Brighton, what?'

There came a scurry of rain as, dressed in the railway company's voluminous tarpaulin coats, the two men walked along the glistening track. They made their way between two lines of trucks towards a distant siding which ran under a beetling cliff of dirty chalk. From the round house, a hundred yards away, came sounds of escaping steam, a clang of metal and occasional sharp cries from a driver.

'Got to uncouple the first three,' said Tom.

Albert nodded and moved down the line. His hands were cold and stiff. He approached the first of the three trucks.

'Empties,' said Tom.

Albert said nothing but fell to work on the coupling. As he did so, his eye, through a crack in the wall of the truck, fell upon a sack in one corner of it.

'Someone's left summat,' he said.

'These trucks is supposed to be empties,' repeated Tom, as he approached his mate.

'Have a look,' said Albert.

Tom applied his eye to the crack.

'There's somethin' there all right,' he said, wrinkling his broad nose.

'Funny it should be a sack,' said Albert. 'This is a coal truck.'

He pointed to letters painted on the side of the truck, indicating that it belonged to a colliery in Merthyr Tydfil.

Albert swung himself up and dropped heavily into the grimy interior. The floor was thick with coal-dust but in one corner lay a discoloured sack. He began to pick at the cord confining its neck.

'Gotcher knife, Tom?' he called back.

'Leave it alone,' came the reply.

'Gotcher knife?' he repeated obstinately.

There was a crunching of footsteps beneath.

''Ere you are, old curiosity shop.'

A large jack-knife, tossed into the air, fell with a thud beside Albert Wilcox.

He picked it up, cut the cord round the neck of the sack and pulled it wide.

The next moment he staggered back.

For in the sack, very naked and very dead, was crammed the body of a woman.

6   *Tuesday, December 1st*

Inspector Martin pushed his chair back from the big desk and filled his pipe. He then crossed the room and shut the window. Fresh air

was all very well, but this morning it brought with it cold flaws of
rain. The prospect from the window was uninviting. Scotland Yard
– unless you had a high room overlooking the river – was a gloomy
place at the best of times, and on a day when the English climate
was at its worst only a naturally happy disposition and a store of
pleasant thoughts could live it down.

'Grin and bear it,' said Inspector Martin to himself, and duly
grinned into the mirror above the mantelpiece.

Inspector Martin was of a cheerful countenance. His blue eyes
twinkled back at him from a freckled face and the firm jaw, which
at times had a formidable, are-you-coming-quickly thrust about
it, relaxed easily into a smile which few were able to resist.

He soothed the tuft of dark hair which had a tendency to stand
up like a chicken's feathers on the crown of his head and went back
to his table in a better frame of mind.

It was true that his week-end – one of the rare long week-ends
he was able to take – had been spoiled. He had hoped to have
Elizabeth very much to himself, but all their heavenly plans had
been upset by the inconsiderate behaviour of Miss Haslett. Elizabeth had been obliged to remain on duty at the school and he had
seen her only in snatches. Elizabeth was like that – a girl of infinite
spirit but allowing herself too readily to be exploited. A sense of
duty was an excellent thing in a woman and would be invaluable
in a policeman's wife. But there were limits, and she had no reason
to be so confoundedly grateful to her employer.

Hedlam was not a bad old thing in his way, but he certainly
contrived to get a great deal of work for very little pay out of his
'poor little orphan child.'

Still, she had been free for a couple of hours on Sunday afternoon and the memory was sweet.

Inspector Martin smiled happily as he began to turn over the pile of routine reports which lay on his table, for Inspector Martin was very much in love.

He worked steadily for an hour, looking through the reports and making an occasional note. He was still thus engaged when the door opened.

James Crosby, his good friend and colleague, stood on the threshold. He came into the room and removed a dripping Burberry.

'Well, George,' was his greeting, 'how is the great brain this morning?'

Crosby, born within sound of Bow Bells, had worked himself up from a beat in Whitechapel to the rank of inspector attached to the Yard. There was naturally a certain amount of jealousy between the older type of Yard official and those who, like Martin, had entered under the new scheme. But Martin and Crosby were firm friends, presenting in all their dealings a perfect example of the attraction of opposites.

Martin was the son of a country doctor at Cromer with a good practice; Crosby owned to no origin but the institution which had gleaned him from a tenement in which he had all but ended his days at the age of three. Martin was a Conservative and a member of the Joint Universities' Club; Crosby was a Labour man, verging on Communist, and a prominent member of the Socialist group in Bethnal Green. They entertained each other at respective head-quarters and worked together or in rivalry on the best of terms.

Crosby, as the mood took him, affected, in his reference to Martin's intellectual achievements as a university graduate, to be alternatively contemptuous or overawed.

'What's the great idea?' he continued, taking his seat at a desk on the opposite side of the room. 'Still working on the Babcock forgeries?'

'Finished, thank God,' answered Inspector Martin. 'The papers went off to the P.P.'s Department on Friday.'

'Heard the news?'

'Anything particular?'

'That's as may be. Brighton is on the map again.'

'Another trunk crime?'

'Truck, this time, not trunk. Woman's body discovered in a sack. Found this morning. The news came in half an hour ago.'

'Not for either of us, I'm afraid,' went on Crosby. 'Sandison will get it.'

As he spoke the buzzer on Martin's desk sounded sharply.

Martin rose, picked up a file and obediently went to his master.

He found Chief Inspector McPherson standing in front of the fire in his office.

'So Babcock is finished,' he said, as Martin laid the file upon his desk. 'Good work. I shall read your report with interest.'

Martin, flushing to the ears, waited.

'Good work,' repeated McPherson.

'Thank you, sir. Anything special for me to-day?'

McPherson shook his head.

'No, Martin. I'll leave you to get on with the Milbank case.'

'Very good, sir,' said Martin without enthusiasm.

The Milbank case was what the papers called 'an unsolved mystery,' and such it was likely to remain – a peculiarly skilful burglary. Everyone in the Yard knew it to be the work of Teddy Bishop, but no one had as yet collected enough evidence to bring him into Court for it, and it seemed doubtful if anybody ever would.

Inspector Martin turned about and passed his chief's desk on the way to the door. He glanced idly at it and suddenly stopped. Lying on the blotting pad was a hastily developed photograph.

'Not for you, I'm afraid, Martin,' came the voice of his chief. 'That's the Brighton truck victim. It came in half an hour ago. Quick work, for they only discovered the body this morning.'

Martin had picked up the photograph. It was not a pretty picture, but he examined it with unflinching care.

'But, look here, sir,' he stammered. 'This is really rather extraordinary. Has the victim yet been identified?'

Chief Inspector McPherson moved away from the fire and sat down at his desk.

'Not yet,' he said. 'Why do you ask?'

'Only that I happen to know who it is.'

'Indeed!'

McPherson twisted round in the swivel-chair and looked at him. Then he picked up the photograph.

'Are you sure?'

'Quite sure. It is a woman by the name of Haslett. She was housekeeper at St Julian's Preparatory School, Aylsham Road, Norwich.'

There was a short silence.

'This is a bit of luck,' said McPherson. 'It short-circuits things – though I suppose we should have traced her pretty soon by that mark on the left cheek.'

Again he paused and looked doubtfully at Martin.

'Well,' he said at last, 'I suppose I shall have to give you the job. Normally I should put on a senior man, for it's a case that is going to thrust us right into the public eye.'

He looked again at the photograph.

'Friend of yours?'

'Not exactly, but I know a good deal about her and can soon discover the rest.'

'Then you'd better not lose any time. Get off to Brighton at once and identify the body. Write me a report in the train of all you know concerning Miss Haslett. Drop it here on your return and go straight on to Norwich. I'll have the local people warned, but I'll leave you to deal with them personally when you arrive.'

Martin turned to leave the room but paused.

'I think I can guess the motive of the crime, sir,' he said.

'Indeed! You seem to know a great deal about it.'

'Miss Haslett won seven hundred and fifty thousand francs in a French lottery last week. She went over to Paris on Saturday or Sunday last to claim it. I suggest, sir, that we at once follow up two lines of inquiry.'

McPherson nodded.

'The truck, of course. We are already on to that. I expect to receive a time-table of its movements any minute. What else do you suggest?'

'The lottery office in Paris. When did Miss Haslett cash the ticket? It should be easy to find out when she made the crossing and where she stayed both in Paris and London.'

McPherson looked at him approvingly.

'Anybody you fancy for the job?'

'Might I have Crosby to work with me on the case?'

'Crosby will do. See him before you go and send him to me.'

He paused.

'One other thing,' he added. 'The Press will be on to this with headlines in the lunch editions. I shall say nothing on the subject of identity till you start your inquiries in Norwich.'

'Very good, sir.'

Inspector Martin returned to his room and briefly acquainted Crosby with the facts. His colleague made no effort to conceal his satisfaction. Martin, though he could not help feeling elated professionally, was personally in a different position. The case came too nearly home. Above all he did not relish the task of breaking the news to Elizabeth.

He had little time, however, to brood on this aspect of the matter. Half an hour later he was on his way to Brighton.

He formally identified the body lying on the cold slabs of the mortuary off King's Road, and within twenty minutes he was on his way back to London and busy writing as full a report as he could of all that he knew of Miss Haslett and of her friends and circumstances. This he dropped at the Yard and was just in time to catch the 5.15 for Norwich from Liverpool Street Station.

He put up at the 'Maid's Head' and half an hour later was shown into the presence of Mr Robert Hedlam, proprietor of St Julian's Preparatory School.

He found Hedlam sitting in his study, with his right foot resting upon a chair. He had, as he explained, slightly twisted his ankle that morning on the stairs. A rubber-shod stick was propped on the desk beside him.

Inspector Martin looked at him uneasily. It was not the first time he had been called upon to bring bad news to persons quite unprepared to receive it.

Hedlam was smiling and the lamplight shone cosily upon his bald head.

'Sure you want to see *me?*' he inquired pleasantly. 'Wouldn't it be more to the point if I were to send for Elizabeth?'

'Nice old boy, Hedlam,' thought Martin.

'No, Mr Hedlam,' he said gravely. 'I'm here on business, and it's you I want to see.'

Mr Hedlam raised his eyebrows.

'Really? Well, of course I'm entirely at your disposal. What's it all about?'

'I want you to tell me what you know about the movements of Miss Haslett during the last week-end. When, for example, did you expect her to return from Paris?'

Mr Hedlam opened his pale blue eyes.

'She intended, so she said, to return to us yesterday. But I never really expected her back so soon. She will feel that she is her own mistress now, you know.'

Inspector Martin reflected a moment.

'Mr Hedlam,' he said at last, 'I've bad news for you. Miss Haslett will never return to St Julian's.'

Hedlam raised his eyebrows.

'Never return?'

'Miss Haslett has been murdered.'

Hedlam sat back in his chair. His face had gone white. His mild eyes were staring hard at the Inspector.

'I'm afraid this is a terrible shock to you, Mr Hedlam,' Martin continued, 'but it's essential you should know the facts. I'm relying on your help. Miss Haslett's body was discovered in a railway truck at Brighton this morning.'

'Impossible!' said Mr Hedlam.

Inspector Martin nodded slowly.

'I myself identified the body.'

'But Miss Haslett has been here for thirty years,' stammered Hedlam. 'She has not an enemy in the world. And why should she go to Brighton?'

'The motive for the crime is obvious enough,' answered Martin. 'She had just received a large sum of money.'

Mr Hedlam produced a silk handkerchief and wiped the sweat from his forehead.

'This is terrible,' he said. 'Terrible.'

'For the moment,' continued Martin, 'we have nothing to go upon, and I can only hope you will be able to throw some light on the case.'

Mr Hedlam was groping. Rather shakily he produced a bottle and stood it on the desk.

'If you don't mind,' he said, 'perhaps you will join me?'

Inspector Martin shook his head.

'Sherry,' said Mr Hedlam. 'I never drink anything else, as you know.'

He dived again beneath the desk, produced a glass and poured out the wine with a trembling hand. Martin waited till he had finished drinking.

'Now,' he said briskly, 'I'm sure you want to help me all you can, Mr Hedlam.'

Hedlam set the glass firmly down and looked straight across the desk.

'No stone shall be left unturned,' he said emphatically.

He was about to continue when the door opened abruptly and Elizabeth entered. On seeing Martin she stopped short and her face lit up.

'Why, George,' she said, 'I never expected to see you here this evening.' Martin was on his feet.

'Inspector Martin is here on official business, Elizabeth,' put in Hedlam.

Martin nodded.

'Yes,' he said. 'Bad business, I'm afraid.'

Elizabeth looked from one to the other.

'If it's private—' she began.

'You will have to hear about it sooner or later, Lizzie,' said Martin.

He was thinking how lovely she looked sitting on the worn arm of the leather chair, slim and straight. And there was determination too, in the face. No one could call that chin anything but firm.

Martin pulled himself together with a jerk.

'George is here to-night in his professional capacity, my dear,' said Hedlam. 'It's about Miss Haslett. The news is rather shocking. It seems that Miss Haslett has been murdered.'

Martin looked anxiously at Elizabeth as she took the blow. Her eyes opened wide and her hand went reaching for the other arm of the chair.

'George,' she protested, 'you don't mean that? There must be some mistake.'

'No mistake, Lizzie. Miss Haslett's body was discovered in a truck at Brighton early this morning. I am here to make inquiries.'

Elizabeth slid softly from the arm of the chair into the seat.

'Killed for her money, I suppose,' she said.

Martin sat down. That was like Elizabeth, jumping to the point at once.

He nodded.

'Not a doubt of it, I'm afraid,' he said.

'But what on earth was she doing in Brighton?' pursued Elizabeth.

'I had hoped one of you would be able to tell me that,' answered Inspector Martin. 'Has she any relatives?'

Mr Hedlam leaned across his desk.

'She has a sister Jane – Mrs Bell – who lives at Exeter, I believe, and is married to a solicitor. They have one son and it was the son who sent Miss Haslett the lottery ticket from Paris.'

Martin instinctively felt for his note-book.

'You didn't hear from Miss Haslett, I suppose, whilst she was away?'

'Not a word. There has scarcely been time. She left only last Friday.'

'I suppose everyone here knew of her good fortune?'

'It was all over the school. The boys were ragging her about it.'

'What precisely were her plans?'

'I can tell you that,' said Mr Hedlam. 'She was to take the aeroplane from Imperial Airways on Saturday morning to Paris. She intended to collect the money and lodge it, I believe, with the Paris agents of the Norfolk and Suffolk Bank, with whom she has dealt for many years. She told me that she would return either that same day or, if she felt like it, on the Sunday or Monday. I insisted, however, that there was no need for her to hurry back if she wanted to see something of Paris. It was her first visit abroad.'

'Can you give any further particulars, Elizabeth?'

Martin turned to Elizabeth as he spoke. She tilted her head, wrinkling her forehead as she did so.

'I don't know any more than Uncle Robert,' she answered, 'except that Miss Haslett was in good spirits. But that was not unnatural. She even gave me a present before leaving.'

'Really?'

'Or, rather, she promised me one – a cheque for ten pounds. Towards my trousseau, poor old dear.'

Elizabeth turned away and her shoulders were trembling. Martin crossed over to her. He might be there on official business but he was only human after all.

'Lizzie, darling.'

'Sorry, George. I am all right now.'

Martin turned to Hedlam.

'Do you know where Miss Haslett stayed in London?'

'I recommended her to go to the Westmoreland Hotel, that big new place near the Marble Arch.'

'Was she to see anyone in London?'

'Not to my knowledge,' said Elizabeth.

'Wait a moment,' she added quickly. 'I wonder if she did anything about that circular?'

Hedlam leaned forward eagerly.

'The bucket-shop fellow, you mean,' he said.

'Sorry,' said George, 'but I am out of my depth.'

'There may be nothing in it,' said Elizabeth; 'but a day or two before she left Miss Haslett received a circular from somebody who offered to buy shares for her – a broker, I suppose.'

'Was this circular addressed only to her?'

'We all had one,' put in Hedlam. 'I warned Miss Haslett strongly against the man.'

'Have you got a copy?'

Hedlam shook his head. 'I threw mine into the waste-paper basket.'

'I think I can find one,' said Elizabeth. 'There are plenty of them about. Mr Greening had one and Mr Rutherford.'

She got up and left the room. Martin occupied the brief moments of her absence in looking through his notes.

'I must see Greening and the rest of them,' he said.

'Of course,' agreed Mr Hedlam.

'Here you are,' said Elizabeth, returning.

Inspector Martin glanced at the sheet – a typical production, rather expensively multigraphed. He read:

'CRANFORD MANSIONS,
'153, SHAFTESBURY AVENUE,
'LONDON, W.C.2.

'Are you content with a safe 3% on your money? Very probably – because in these difficult times you feel it would be tempting Providence to ask for more.

'That, if you will allow me to say so, is where you make a mistake. Why be content with 3% when, by consulting an expert, you can obtain 6% or even 6¼%?

'If you will write to me and put yourself in my hands, I guarantee to double your income.

'As proof of my good faith in the matter, I refuse to accept any commission on our first transaction.

'(Signed) JOHN THROGMORTON.'

There was a postscript in which John Throgmorton announced that he was also prepared to advance money with or without security to those in need of it.

Martin folded the circular and put it in his pocket.

'Has Miss Haslett been receiving any other letters lately?' he asked, looking at Hedlam.

'That question I am afraid I cannot answer,' replied Mr Hedlam.

'Do you know, Elizabeth?'

Elizabeth shook her head.

'I don't know anything about her correspondence, but on the day before she left she had a trunk-call from London on the telephone.'

'Do you know from whom it was?'

Elizabeth shook her head.

'I must look into that,' said Martin, rising as he spoke. 'Meanwhile I should like, if I may, to see the rest of the staff.'

At that moment the telephone bell rang. Hedlam picked up the instrument and, after a word or two, handed it to Inspector Martin.

The call was from the local police with whom Scotland Yard had communicated earlier in the day. Sergeant Sharpen of the Norwich Constabulary declared himself to be at Inspector Martin's disposal.

Martin felt a little guilty. He ought to have called on the local police before coming to interview Hedlam. It had been discourteous on his part, and he hoped they were not offended. The provincial police were sometimes a little touchy. He excused himself somewhat effusively on the telephone and asked Sergeant Sharpen whether he would be good enough to come at once to St Julian's.

A little later, in the masters' common room, Inspector Martin took a number of statements from members of the school staff. Mr Joseph Greening, with whom he had a slight acquaintance, was voluble but not of much assistance, being over-ready to impart a great deal of information which was irrelevant. Among other things he announced that, during the fatal week-end, he had been away from Norwich.

Mr Hedlam, present at the interview, smiled and nodded.

'Mr Greening is frequently away for weekends,' he said. 'He has a passion for bird-life.'

'The Brancaster sanctuary, you know,' put in Greening.

George Martin looked at Greening curiously. He did not look the sort of man for country pleasures.

'So you were at Brancaster?' he said, closing his note-book.

Mr Greening blinked and looked at the ceiling.

'At Brancaster,' he confirmed. 'Among the birds.'

7   *Wednesday, December 2nd*

'Another drink,' suggested Mr Throgmorton.

Hermione moved away as he began to manipulate the patent cocktail-shaker over the office table.

On the chair beside her lay an early edition of the *Evening Standard*. It had been left there from the previous day and on the front page in thick black letters stood the headlines:

WOMAN'S BODY FOUND IN A TRUCK
ANOTHER BRIGHTON MYSTERY

Hermione suddenly swept it up and crushed it into the waste-paper basket beside the desk.

'Not for me,' she said shortly, as Throgmorton began to open a fresh bottle of gin.

'No news from Richard?' he inquired.

'The last Continental post came in half an hour ago,' answered Hermione wearily.

'Damn the fellow,' said Throgmorton peevishly. 'He's taking his time.'

'Why shouldn't he take his time?'

Throgmorton looked at her, startled by the warmth and quickness of her defence.

'Have you considered, my dear, that we are taking a bit of a risk with that young man? What's to prevent him fading away?'

Hermione stiffened. She was trying hard not to lose control.

'I have absolute trust in Dick,' she said quietly.

There was a short silence.

'Come on, old girl,' said Throgmorton suddenly. 'Another drink will put heart into you.' He put a hand on her shoulder. 'No call to worry,' he assured her.

'They will have traced the truck by now,' said Hermione.

Throgmorton nodded.

'They will also,' he said, 'have made their inquiries in Paris. The Yard doesn't lose time.'

Throgmorton drained his glass. His face was flushed – a rosy pink. The prominent eyes glittered behind his spectacles.

Hermione stared at him resentfully. This was how he kept his courage up – drinking cocktails and going over the ground. He was always going over the ground. Recapitulation, he called it.

'The truck,' he said, 'will lead them to the flat in Cadbury Road. Here they will in due course ascertain that it was let furnished to a middle-aged spinster lady. Her name was Mrs Beck. She paid the rent in advance and a deposit on the gas. The neighbours may have noticed that she received a visit from a gentleman with a black patch over one eye, who brought with him a lady friend. But Mrs Beck vacated the flat next day and she has never been seen again. Nor has the gentleman with the black patch. Nor has—'

Hermione put down her glass with so abrupt a movement that the stem snapped between her fingers.

'For God's sake shut up!' she exclaimed.

Throgmorton smiled.

'That was blank No. 1,' he continued. 'Paris will be blank No. 2. We shall probably read all about that in the papers.'

He began to walk about the room, declaiming excitedly.

'It has now been ascertained that Miss Haslett, identified by the port-wine mark on her left cheek, called at the lottery office in Paris on Saturday morning and received notes to the value of seven hundred and fifty thousand francs. It has been further ascertained that Miss Haslett returned immediately by air to London, where she was last seen in the neighbourhood of Victoria Station. We understand from the authorities in charge of the case that further developments may be expected at any moment.'

He broke off and came back to where Hermione was still standing beside the table.

'But there won't be any further developments,' he concluded.

He reached out for the cocktail-shaker. As he did so the telephone bell on his desk rang sharply.

Hermione removed the receiver.

'Is that the office of Mr John Throgmorton?' came a quiet voice.

'Yes,' she said. 'This is Mr Throgmorton's secretary speaking. Mr Throgmorton will be leaving shortly.'

'Will you kindly ask him to remain?' continued the voice.

There was a touch of authority in the request and she looked uneasily across at Throgmorton, who was pouring himself out another drink from the shaker.

'Who is it speaking, please?'

'This is Inspector Martin of Scotland Yard,' came the answer. 'Would you please tell Mr Throgmorton that I am coming round to see him at once?'

CHAPTER III

1   *Wednesday, December 2nd*

Inspector Martin left the police car and approached the entrance to Shaftesbury Avenue.

A tall man in plain clothes was standing by the open door.

'Nobody passed out, sir,' said Sergeant Babbington, touching his hat.

Inspector Martin nodded.

'Keep an eye on the door, Sergeant. I'll whistle if I want you to come up.'

Inspector Martin passed up the stairs. He had planted Babbington to watch the building before telephoning to Throgmorton merely as a matter of routine. He had nothing definite against the man and must approach him with an open mind. Throgmorton had sent a circular to Miss Haslett a day or two before her departure for Paris. Miss Haslett, moreover, had received a trunk-call from London, put through, as Martin had ascertained, from Throgmorton's office on the morning before she had started on her journey. There was nothing more to go upon than that.

He stood for a moment outside a brown-painted door with the words 'Maitland Investment Trust' painted on it in peeling white letters. He passed through the door and entered a small office, hearing, as he did so, a murmur of voices on the farther side of a partition the upper part of which was of frosted glass. An inner door was thrust open and a woman came through.

George Martin looked at her – a neat and businesslike figure in a plain black dress, with white collar and cuffs.

'Inspector Martin of Scotland Yard,' he said with a slight bow.

'I am Mr Throgmorton's secretary. Will you please come this way?'

He stepped past her into the inner room.

So this was Mr John Throgmorton. The room was badly lit and the man was in shadow – a heavy man, with a remarkably expressionless face, prominent eyes distorted by a pair of horn-rimmed spectacles, and a thatch of grey-yellow hair.

He rose from the desk as Martin entered and extended a well-kept hand across the top of it.

The room was reeking with Vapex. The man, it seemed, was suffering from a severe cold in the head.

Correctly dressed for the city, George Martin noted. Short black coat, striped trousers and the rest of it. In that case why were his offices in Shaftesbury Avenue? Presumably he was not very prosperous. Rents in the city were notoriously high.

'What can I do for you, Inspector?'

The voice was hoarse and the enunciation that of a man with a stuffed nose. Martin, who had a horror of colds, hoped that he would escape infection.

Mr Throgmorton was in no way nervous. The man was entirely at his ease.

'I am in charge of the investigation into the murder of the woman whose body was found in a truck at Brighton early yesterday,' Martin announced.

Throgmorton nodded and waited, expressing neither alarm nor surprise. 'Yes, Inspector?'

'We have discovered that the woman in question was a Miss

Haslett of St Julian's Preparatory School, Norwich. May I ask whether you knew her?'

'I can hardly say that I knew her, Inspector, but I had a small business acquaintance with her.'

'I am trying to trace her movements during the week-end from November 27th to November 30th. Can you help me at all in the matter?'

'I doubt whether I can be of very much assistance,' he answered smoothly. 'Miss Haslett wrote to me asking for an appointment. Her letter was unusually long and confidential. She held a winning ticket in a lottery and wished to consult me about investments!'

'You have her letter?'

The well-kept hand pressed a bell on the desk and the door opened.

'Bring me our correspondence with Miss Haslett, please, Miss Taylor,' said Throgmorton.

A moment later Inspector Martin was examining two letters neatly enclosed in a cardboard folder. The first letter was dated Tuesday, November 24th. It was signed 'Veronica Haslett' and in brackets after the signature she had written 'Miss'.

Miss Haslett stated that she had seen one of Mr Throgmorton's circulars. She related her good fortune with the lottery ticket, gave particulars as to her plans for obtaining the money in Paris and ended by asking whether it would be convenient for her to call at his office on Monday, November 30th. The second letter, dated Wednesday, November 25th, was a formal acknowledgment signed by Throgmorton stating that Monday was unfortunately impossible, but that he would suggest another day.

Throgmorton waited quietly as the letters were being read.

Inspector Martin put down the file and produced a note-book.

'Was there any sequel to this correspondence?' he asked.

Throgmorton nodded.

'Yes, Inspector. There was a sequel. You will understand, I am sure, that the prospect of securing a client with a considerable sum of money to invest was not one to be lightly dismissed. I therefore told my secretary to ring up Miss Haslett and to discover whether we might not arrange a meeting on the Friday or Saturday. As a consequence of that conversation Miss Haslett, shortly after her arrival in London on Friday, came to see me here. I think I can tell you the exact time.'

He turned over the pages of a memorandum calendar on the desk in front of him.

'Miss Haslett called at this office shortly after six o'clock, and was here for nearly an hour.'

'May I inquire as to the subject of your interview?'

'Investments, Inspector.'

'Did she mention any particular sum?'

'Eight or ten thousand pounds, I think she said. We had a long and friendly conversation and she professed herself anxious to obtain my advice.'

'Did you, in fact, advise her?'

'I gave her a list of certain securities which I thought might suit her,' answered Throgmorton smoothly. 'But we only discussed the matter in general terms. We were to have met again on Monday last. She even made an appointment for the purpose, but of course she never came.'

'What did you conclude from that?'

'I was disappointed, especially as I had rearranged my programme for Monday because of her visit. But I was not altogether surprised. I have said that she professed herself anxious to obtain my advice.

But I felt somehow that she had other irons in the fire and that I was not entirely in her confidence.'

'Had you any definite grounds for that impression?'

'She referred more than once to other plans. I even suspected that she had already seen someone else.'

Martin looked keenly at the man in front of him.

'That is an important point, Mr Throgmorton. Can you remember anything which she said or did to justify such a suspicion?'

Throgmorton smiled sadly upon the Inspector.

'Nothing definite,' he said. 'But I have a long experience of such interviews, and one gets to know by a sort of instinct whether one's client is really in earnest or likely to go elsewhere. Miss Haslett was attracted by certain suggestions which I made to her, but I felt that she was comparing them with other and possibly more attractive proposals which she had already received.'

There was a short pause.

'If it is not an indiscreet question,' ventured Throgmorton at last, 'have the police any idea as to when the crime was committed?'

'Miss Haslett was last seen alive on the evening of Saturday, November 28th,' Inspector Martin found himself replying.

'On her return from Paris, no doubt,' suggested Throgmorton. He paused and added: 'The police, I presume, have already ascertained whether she cashed the ticket?' Martin nodded.

'She did not call upon you again – after her return to London on Saturday, I mean?'

'Subsequent to our interview on Friday, November 27th,' he said, 'I never saw Miss Haslett alive again.'

Martin wrote busily a moment in his note-book.

'I must apologise for these inquiries,' he said, 'and you will forgive me if I go a little further yet.' He hesitated a moment and added:

'It is my duty,' he said, 'as a matter of routine, to ask any persons who saw Miss Haslett over the week-end to give me an account of their movements on Saturday, November 28th. You will appreciate the importance of such information. It helps us to eliminate certain . . . possibilities.'

Throgmorton nodded.

'I quite understand,' he said. 'You naturally want to narrow the field of inquiry.'

Inspector Martin waited.

'Let me see,' Throgmorton continued. 'On Saturday I stayed late at the office. I then went to my flat in Warwick Avenue and changed for dinner. That would be about half-past six. At seven I met a party of friends at the Trocadero and we went on afterwards to the new revue at the Pavilion. My secretary, Miss Taylor, was of the party. There was also Mr Butterworth of the *Morning Herald* and Mr and Mrs Brannock of 21 Arizona Avenue, Hampstead.'

Throgmorton paused.

'Is that all right for an alibi, Inspector?' he asked.

Martin closed his note-book.

'Thank you, Mr Throgmorton,' he said. 'That will be more than sufficient.'

2   *Thursday, December 3rd*

'Truck No. GC 143769.'

The head of the Goods Department of the London and North Eastern Railway looked up briskly from the small pile of papers in front of him.

'Here's your report, Inspector.'

'Thank you,' said Inspector Martin.'It was very good of you to be so quick about it. If you don't mind I will read it here.'

A few moments later Inspector Martin was installed in a dusty office full of clacking typewriters. He glanced rapidly through the report. It traced the movements of the truck, in which the body of Veronica Haslett had been discovered, from the evening of Friday, November 27th to the morning of Tuesday, December 1st. The truck, it appeared, belonged to the Morgan Jones Colliery of Merthyr Tydfil. It had left the private sidings of the colliery on Monday, November 23rd, arriving at the main goods yard of the London and North Eastern Railway two days later, where it had been unloaded and shifted to a siding. It had stayed on the siding from the 25th to the 28th November and had then been used to make up a goods train, part of which had been detached at Red Hill Junction. The remainder, including truck No. GC 143769, had been sent to Brighton. The Morgan Jones Colliery had purchased certain machine parts manufactured at Brighton which were to have been loaded on the truck the day on which the body had been found.

Inspector Martin made his way back to the Yard, where Sergeant Babbington awaited him.

'Inspector Crosby back yet?'

'No, sir. He is expected on the afternoon plane.'

'No further messages from Paris?'

'No, sir.'

Martin wondered how Crosby was faring. He had reported by telephone the results of his first inquiries into the movements of Miss Haslett and was now trying to discover what had become of the notes. The customs officers at Croydon remembered a woman, wearing clothes corresponding to the police description, with a port-wine mark on the left cheek. They had examined the small case which she carried and refused to believe that she had smuggled notes to the value of seven hundred and fifty thousand francs. What had become of the money? The Paris agents of the Norfolk and Suffolk Bank, with whom she had intended to lodge the notes, had been expecting her visit, but she had not kept the appointment.

Was the money still in Paris? Had she disposed of it herself? Had she been robbed of it or had she entrusted it to someone else?

If she had been robbed of the money in Paris, why should she have been murdered in London?

Inspector Martin, followed by Sergeant Babbington, made his way thoughtfully to the goods depot of the London and North Eastern Railway. A thin rain was falling.

The superintendent, who had been warned to expect them, was bright and helpful.

'I've got a man to show you the place. He has been waiting this half-hour,' he announced.

'Wilson!'

A shunter in overalls stepped forward and touched his cap.

'Show these gentlemen where the truck was parked.'

'Yes, sir. Step this way, sir, please.'

Inspector Martin and Sergeant Babbington climbed over long lines of wet rails. The air was loud with the whistling of engines and the ring of buffers. Martin produced the report of the head of the Goods Traffic Department and glanced at it once more in the driving rain. The truck, he confirmed, had reached the depot on the morning of November 27th. There was no need to go further back than that.

'Holy Moses!' said the sergeant, as he tripped over a rail.

Martin watched the bubbles of mist which glistened on his moustache.

'This is the place,' said the little shunter suddenly. 'I handled them trucks myself. That's how I know.'

Martin looked about him. The goods yard was bounded here by a fence beyond which ran dingy gardens lying at the back of a row of Victorian houses.

'One of fourteen,' continued the little man, 'and I little thought I was shunting that poor old girl to Kingdom Come – with all her clothes took orf, so it said in the paper.'

Inspector Martin, turning up his coat collar, looked at the fence and at the row of houses beyond it. Did one of them hold the secret of the murder?

There were very few windows looking towards the railway.

'Folks wouldn't want to look out of the window more than they could help,' the Sergeant pointed out. 'And they wouldn't want to open them neither – what with all the noise and smoke.'

'Better have a look at the fence,' said Inspector Martin.

He walked down the line to the fence, leaving the shunter standing where the truck had rested. The fence was tarred and about the height of a man. There were chinks in the boards through which he could get glimpses of the gardens behind. Their flora consisted mostly of empty tins, with here and there a valiant evergreen.

How would the body have been brought to the siding? Over or through the barrier? Martin, as he walked beneath the fence, struck the board smartly at regular intervals with the heel of his boot. He repeated this operation for perhaps half a dozen times when one of them moved. He bent down and examined it. The board which he had kicked, with the three boards adjoining it, had been cut through about half-way up their length by a saw. They had afterwards been pushed back into place and the crevices daubed with soot. He gave another kick to the boards and all three of them caved in, revealing the interior of a small tool-shed.

Martin whistled to Babbington, who came up with the shunter. At the same time he bent down and thrust his head through the gap.

Sergeant Babbington, behind him, struck a match and thrust a thick arm over his shoulder.

'Sacks,' said Martin, 'and there is sawdust on the floor. The dirt of ages has been trodden into the ground and brushed from the walls. There are shreds of sacking on the edges of the sawn wood. Stay here, Babbington, and keep an eye on the place. I am going to have a word with the people in that house.'

He turned to the shunter.

'Where is the nearest telephone?' he asked.

'Signal-box, sir,' said the shunter.

A moment later Martin climbed the iron ladder into the signal-box. There, amid the polished signal levers, he telephoned to Scotland Yard and informed Chief Inspector McPherson of his discovery.

'Good,' said the Chief Inspector. 'Go at once to the house and keep it under view. I will have a search-warrant sent along immediately.'

Inspector Martin left the signal-box and, crossing the shiny rails once more, presently entered the street which led to the goods depot.

Miss Haslett had been decoyed to the house in Cadbury Road and there murdered. The body had been stripped, put into a sack, hidden in the tool-shed, taken through the gap in the fence and placed in the truck.

But how had Miss Haslett come to be visiting this shabby house? She must somehow have been decoyed to the place, and, if that were so, the murder had been carefully planned. Inspector Martin shook his head thoughtfully. It was unlikely that so many obvious clues should have been left broadcast if they were leading him straight to a solution.

Not for the first time his thoughts went back to the interview with Throgmorton – a plausible fellow, quite unruffled and prompt, a little too prompt perhaps, with his evidence – suspiciously ready to account for every moment of his time on the night of Saturday, November 28th, the night on which Miss Haslett had returned from Paris.

But the Yard had checked his alibi and found it proof.

Had Miss Haslett, during that week-end, met someone else?

Martin made a mental note that an effort must be made to trace her movements in greater detail from the moment of her arrival at Liverpool Street. He must cast back to the station and go over the trail more carefully. It had seemed sufficient to know that she had registered at the Westmoreland Hotel towards five o'clock, and that a little more than an hour later she had called upon Throgmorton in Shaftesbury Avenue. But, according to Throgmorton, she had seemed to have other plans. Throgmorton had at any rate received that impression. Whom else had she seen between her arrival in London and her departure for Paris on the following day?

Inspector Martin was by this time in Cadbury Road. He walked on the side of it opposite to the suspected house. It stood fifth from the end and differed in no way in shape from that of its neighbours. The windows on the ground floor, he noted, were dirty and partly obscured by Nottingham lace curtains. The steps leading to the front door had not been cleaned for some days. The place had a neglected air.

Martin walked back to the end of the road and waited for the search-warrant. Some twenty minutes later a car pulled up beside him. Sergeant Hitchcock of the Yard, and two constables, all in plain clothes, alighted and walked with him to the house.

Martin pressed the bell, but there was no response. Sergeant Hitchcock thereupon lifted the knocker and beat a tattoo on the door.

A window above their heads was thrust open and a woman looked down resentfully upon these proceedings.

'The door ain't locked,' she said in the manner of one addressing persons of no intelligence; 'but if you want the people on the ground floor they've gorn away.'

Inspector Martin, blushing under the eyes of his assistants, turned the handle of the door. It gave upon a dingy hall of which the floor was covered with worn linoleum. Immediately to the right hand was another stout door. On a tarnished brass plate screwed to its panels was the inscription: 'Flat No. 1.'

'It's what they call maisonettes, sir,' said Sergeant Hitchcock helpfully.

'See if you can get into Flat No. 1,' said Inspector Martin. 'I'm going to talk to the woman up above.'

He began to climb the stairs as he spoke and had just reached the door of Flat No. 2 when the door opened to display a loose, untidy female wearing an apron of sacking and a cloth bound round her head.

'If you're looking for Mrs Carroll, she ain't there, cause she's let the flat,' the woman said abruptly.

'Indeed! May I have a word with you, Mrs—?'

'Webster, my name is. Step this way.'

Martin stepped into a small corridor littered with brooms and a large pail.

'Is it the p'lice?' asked the woman hopefully.

'From Scotland Yard,' said Martin.

'You don't say so? But as I said to Jim only the other day – Jim's my 'usband – Mrs Carroll won't be with us long. Owes money all over the place – four pounds ten to Tomlinson's down the road and Salter's, the fish people, will never see a penny if you ask me.'

'The flat below you say is let.'

'That's right. Mrs Carroll let it for a month and got the rent in advance.'

'Do you know the tenant?'

'Not to say know. Elderly lady. Didn't get more'n a glimpse of her.'

'When did she move in?'

'About a week ago, if you can call it movin' in. Just come and went and never been seen since. There was a gentleman, too. He had a black patch over his eye and a brown beard. But he always came after dark and was uncommon quiet. I never set eyes on either of them properly – not to notice. Jim and me lives mostly in the back room.'

'The room with a window looking on to the garden?'

'Some might call it a winder, but we ain't tempted to treat it as such – what with the smuts and the noise they make on the sidin'. I ain't seen nothin', if that's what you mean.'

'Can you tell me, Mrs Webster, whether Mrs Carroll's tenant was here on Saturday night of last week?'

Mrs Webster reflected a minute.

'That was the day after Jim won two pound ten for the *Daily 'Erald* cross-word.'

'Helps to fix it,' said Martin encouragingly. 'Did you see or hear anything on Saturday, and, in particular, were there any visitors?'

'We wasn't at home on Saturday. Jim had just had his two pound ten and 'e took me to Whipsnade for the day. Very fond of animals, is Jim. And in the evening we went to the pictures – Anne Neagle in *Nell Gwyn* – a fair treat it was. But there was visitors on Friday.'

'On Friday?'

'Gentleman friend and an elderly female,' said Mrs Webster.

'Did you see them leave the house?'

'The woman was leaving just as Jim came 'ome. That would be at about six o'clock. He met her in the hall – funny old party, 'e said, with a nasty purple mark on her face.'

Martin's spirits rose. Miss Haslett had been brought to the flat by a man unknown on Friday, November 27th. She must have come to it immediately after registering at the Westmoreland Hotel. It was true that she had left it shortly afterwards, safe and sound, but, having come to it once, the presumption was that she had come to it again.

'You are quite sure, Mrs Webster, that you can tell me nothing further about these people. Think again.'

Mrs Webster appeared to be thinking and breathed hard at the unusual exercise.

'It ain't no use me thinking,' she said at last. 'I can't tell you no more than what I 'ave.'

'You don't know when the male visitor left the house?'

'Never set eyes on him again – not after 'e came to the 'ouse on Friday.'

'Thank you, Mrs Webster.'

Martin descended to the ground floor. Knocking and ringing had produced no response in Flat No. 1. He accordingly left

Sergeant Hitchcock and his two men on guard and made his way to the house-agents, Messrs Trussetter & Company in Grove Road. Messrs Trussetter confirmed the information already received. Mrs Carroll was the first tenant of the flat. The agents knew nothing about her except that they had frequently had trouble with her in regard to the rent. She had, however, visited them a week or ten days before – on Thursday, November 26th, to be exact – and informed them that she had let the flat furnished for a month to a Mrs Beck and had received the rent in advance. There was a clause in Mrs Carroll's lease permitting her to sublet; the matter was in order and Mrs Carroll had departed after paying the remainder of the rent due from herself. The agents had no idea of her present whereabouts.

A visit to the local post office revealed that Mrs Carroll had directed that letters should be forwarded to an address in Sutton.

Martin returned to the house, this time accompanied by a boy from the agents with a key. A thorough search of Flat No. 1, however, brought nothing whatever to light. The mysterious Mrs Beck and her gentleman friend had left not a wrack behind. There was no food in the larder and no evidence that the flat had been effectively occupied beyond the fact that one of the rooms, which contained a large roll-top desk, was cleaner and tidier than the rest.

Three-quarters of an hour later Inspector Martin gave instructions for instant inquiries to be made at Liverpool Street Station and at the Westmoreland Hotel after a man with a black patch over his eye and a brown beard.

He next paid a rapid visit to the address in Sutton in quest of Mrs Carroll. He found her living with a married sister, and he interviewed her at some length, but without any real result.

She had let the flat to an elderly and respectable gentlewoman.

She had received the rent in advance and the sum of ten pounds for instant possession. The gentlewoman had given her name as Mrs Beck and seemed to have been extraordinarily lacking in any really distinctive features – of middle height, greying hair, rather bright eyes which might have been blue or grey, quietly dressed. Mrs Carroll had no gift of description and Martin could form no definite picture of the elusive sub-tenant of Cadbury Road.

Mrs Carroll had seen no one else in connection with the letting of the flat.

Martin apologised for his intrusion and asked Mrs Carroll whether she intended to remain at Sutton. He might need her, perhaps, for identification purposes.

He left the house with the air of a man taking up arms against a sea of troubles.

For Mrs Beck would have to be found before she could be identified, and Inspector Martin had already formed a high estimate of the intelligence and resource of the persons unknown who had murdered Veronica Haslett.

3   *Friday, December 4th*

Inspector Martin, sitting with Crosby in his room at Scotland Yard, looked at his watch. It was five minutes to eleven. For the third time he turned over the leaves of the neat file in front of him. Chief Inspector McPherson had called for a report on the Brighton truck case at 11 a.m. There was to be a consultation.

The file which, with Crosby's assistance, he had that morning put in order, contained a great deal of evidence from many sources. Crosby had contributed notes on his trip to Paris. Martin had written a full account of his inquiries in Norwich and Brighton, of his examination of Throgmorton, of his discovery of the flat in Cadbury Road and of his interviews with Mrs Webster and Mrs Carroll.

The latest contribution to the file was in the form of a report from Sergeant Babbington. Sergeant Babbington had found at Liverpool Street a porter who at 4.31 on Friday afternoon, November 27th, had seen Miss Haslett leave the station in a taxicab with a man wearing a black patch over his right eye. He had further ascertained, on questioning the reception clerk at the Westmoreland Hotel, that the same man had come to the counter and stood beside her when she registered.

Other notes, placed upon the file, recorded the results of subsidiary inquiries which had been made at the office of Imperial Airways at Victoria and at Croydon aerodrome.

Crosby watched his colleague turning over the leaves. There was a look of malice in his eye.

'Cheer up, George,' he said. 'The chief will at least admire our industry.'

The telephone on Martin's desk rang sharply. He removed the receiver.

'Chief Inspector waiting to see you, sir,' came the message.

'Come along, Jimmy. Get it over.'

They walked together down the corridor.

Chief Inspector McPherson was sitting behind his desk as they entered the room.

'Sit down, Martin,' he said. 'You too, Crosby.'

He nodded at a couple of vacant chairs.

Martin placed the file in front of the Chief Inspector, keeping a duplicate for himself and handing one to Crosby.

'Well,' said the Chief Inspector, 'you seem to have been busy. How far have we got?'

'We've got a great deal of information, sir,' said Martin, 'but it all goes to show that this is going to be a difficult case. I suggest that we run through the facts together.'

The Chief Inspector nodded and sat back prepared to listen.

'Keep to the facts,' he said. 'I will look through the evidence later. Tell me first what you have discovered concerning the movements of Miss Haslett.'

'Miss Haslett left Norwich by train on the morning of November 27th. At Liverpool Street Station she was met on arrival at 4.31 by a man wearing a black patch over his right eye. She drove with him to the Westmoreland Hotel, where she registered. She left the hotel at once, still in his company, and she went with him to a ground floor flat at No. 147 Cadbury Road, Maida Vale. She stayed at the flat for about half an hour and left at about a quarter to six. She was then alone and there is no evidence as to when the man who had brought her to the flat departed. She called upon Throgmorton at his office in Shaftesbury Avenue shortly after six.'

McPherson nodded.

'I have read the report on Throgmorton,' he said.

'She stayed with Throgmorton for about an hour and returned to her hotel at about 7.15. She had sandwiches brought to her room and went early to bed. On the morning of November 28th she left the hotel at 7 a.m. in a taxi, took the Imperial Airways omnibus to Croydon, descended at Le Bourget and was delivered at her destination. She apparently went at once to the lottery ticket office, drew seven hundred and fifty thousand francs in notes and returned to London by air that same afternoon. She was last seen outside the office of Imperial Airways at Victoria shortly after five o'clock. There is no evidence as to how she spent her time in Paris between drawing the money and starting back to London, but it seems certain that she returned without the notes. She carried only a small suit-case which was opened by the customs at Croydon, and she could not have carried so large a sum concealed. She was to have lodged the money with the Norfolk and Suffolk Bank, but she did not call, as arranged, on their Paris agent. To me that is perhaps the most puzzling feature of the case.'

'I did all I could,' put in Crosby, 'to find out how Miss Haslett spent her time after leaving the lottery office, and the Paris police are still making inquiries. So far, however, we have failed to discover any trace of her movements. I tried the banks, the exchange offices and the tourist agencies. Nor could I find any clue as to what had become of the notes.'

'She was in London, you say, at five o'clock?' said the Chief Inspector.

Martin nodded.

'The rest is inference,' he continued. 'At some time on the Saturday afternoon or evening Miss Haslett must have returned to the flat in Cadbury Road. There she was murdered. Her body was stripped, placed in a sack and thrust into a truck stationed in the railway siding under the back windows of the house. The flat had been hired for the purpose only two days previously, and the murder was almost certainly committed by the man with the black patch over his eye who had met her at Liverpool Street on the previous day.'

Again he paused. The Chief Inspector was silent for a moment.

'Any general observations?' he asked.

'There were three main lines of approach, sir,' said Martin. 'Our first was from Norwich. It led us straight to Throgmorton.

There is nothing, however, to connect him with the crime, and he had a complete alibi for the night of the murder, which we have since confirmed. Our second line of approach was from the truck in Brighton. That took us to the flat in Cadbury Road and led us eventually to the man who met Miss Haslett at Liverpool Street and to the elderly woman, Mrs Beck, who had taken over the flat on Thursday, November 26th. These persons were seen on Thursday and Friday, but there is no direct evidence that they were still in the flat on Saturday, November 28th. This second line therefore stops short at a point before the murder was committed.

'Our third line of approach was through the lottery office in Paris. Chronologically it starts from the Westmoreland Hotel on the morning of Saturday, November 28th. We followed it successfully to Paris and back to London again, and it landed us finally at Victoria at five o'clock on Saturday afternoon.'

The Chief Inspector turned over the pages of the file.

'Thank you, Martin. I shall study the file in detail. I see you've gone pretty thoroughly into the situation of Throgmorton. What was your general impression?'

'There is nothing against him in the city except the usual prejudice of the licensed dealers against any man who sells stocks and shares and is not a registered member of the Stock Exchange. No one seems to know very much about him. He is only in a small way of business but is also a moneylender.'

'All fair and square so far as it goes?'

'Quite. His clients are mostly little people with fixed incomes. He travels about a good deal and is often absent. Do you think, perhaps, we should have him watched?'

The Chief Inspector shook his head.

'It would hardly be justified on the evidence,' he said. 'I suggest you concentrate on the clues which you picked up in Cadbury Road.'

'They are not promising, sir,' put in Crosby. 'I started the usual routine inquiries yesterday after my return from Paris. Mrs Beck obviously took care to be seen as little as possible. She did not call on any of the local tradesmen. Nothing was delivered at the house, and the only thing anyone seems to have noticed about her gentleman friend is that he wore a black patch over his right eye and a brown beard.'

'Which presumably he has since removed,' said the Chief Inspector.

'So that we are looking for a man whose only distinguishing features are that he will *not* be wearing a black patch over his right eye and that he will be clean shaven,' concluded Martin despondently.

'Well,' said the Chief Inspector, 'what are you proposing to do exactly?'

'Crosby is better on detail than I am,' said Martin. 'He will go over the ground again and maybe pick up something which I've missed. For myself, sir, I propose to get to work again in Norwich. This was a planned murder, and it was planned presumably by someone who had early information about Miss Haslett's intended journey to Paris. I can't help thinking that the person or persons who committed this crime may have had a confederate who was in close touch with Miss Haslett at the time she received news of her success in the lottery.'

The Chief Inspector pursed his lips.

'Possibly. On the other hand, she was herself in communication with Throgmorton before she went to London, and heaven only knows in how many other people she may not have confided.'

He paused.

'Besides,' he added, 'you have yourself alluded to the most puzzling feature of the case.'

'You mean, sir?'

'If Miss Haslett left her money in Paris, why on earth should she have been murdered on her return with empty pockets to London?'

Martin nodded gravely.

'That, sir, is a bit of a facer, and the going doesn't look any too good at the moment.'

The Chief Inspector held up a warning hand.

'There is just one thing I don't want you to tell me about the Brighton truck mystery,' he said. 'I've heard it too often of late.'

'Meaning, sir?'

'Don't come back and tell me that this is the perfect crime.'

CHAPTER IV

1 *Friday, December 4th*

Hermione, sitting with Throgmorton in the inner room at No. 153 Shaftesbury Avenue, looked up from her newspaper. She had heard in the outer office the sound of a door-knob turning.

'That will be Richard,' she said.

She rose to her feet, her heart thumping against her ribs. She passed quickly to the ante-room. As she did so the outer door opened and Richard Feiling stood upon the threshold. He came forward eagerly with outstretched hands.

Hermione gave him a warning gesture and jerked her head backwards. Richard, checked abruptly, turned and closed the door.

'Come along, Feiling.' Throgmorton's voice was quiet and friendly. 'We have been waiting for you for some time. Have a drink?'

'I will,' said Richard. 'How is everybody? Bearing up, Hermione?'

Throgmorton went to his desk. There was a clink of bottles as he pulled out the gin and the patent cocktail-shaker.

'Sorry I'm late,' Richard was saying, 'but there was a fog in the Channel and we were hours getting into Dover.'

'Take this,' said Throgmorton shortly, holding out a glass.

'Well,' said Richard, 'here's how.'

John drained his cocktail at a gulp. Hermione looked at the two men an instant.

'Hadn't we better perhaps talk over things to-morrow?' she asked. 'Dick must be tired.'

'Tired? Not a bit of it. Let's get down to it, what?'

Throgmorton was pouring himself out another drink. He sat down a little heavily behind his desk, while Richard perched himself on the arm of the chair in which Hermione was sitting.

How near he was to her. She had only to stretch out her hand to touch him. But Throgmorton's heavy face was turned towards them, and those light eyes of his behind the horn-rimmed spectacles saw a great deal, as well she knew.

'First of all,' said Richard, 'the money is all right.'

Throgmorton was leaning across his desk.

'All right, you say? No trouble?'

'None whatever. It is lodged in four separate banks: in La Banque de Paris et du Nord in Paris, in Le Comptoir du Midi in Lyons, in Le Nouvelle Banque des Agriculteurs at Rouen, and in La Banque Populaire Française at Bourges. You can have it whenever you like.'

'The sooner the better,' said Throgmorton. 'We have just been waiting to go ahead. What's the big idea?'

'Fifty thousand pounds,' said Dick lightly; 'that's the big idea. Fifty thousand of the best.'

There was a short silence.

'How soon?' asked Throgmorton.

'Soon as you like,' said Richard. 'All we have to do is to find someone who will deal with old Oswaldtwizzle.'

Hermione felt herself smiling. Oswaldtwizzle was the name invariably used by Richard in referring to his uncle, Sir Oswald Feiling.

'I don't quite understand.'

Throgmorton was speaking again.

'Then let me explain,' said Richard.

He began swinging his feet, making a thudding noise against

the leather chair. Hermione sat quite still. She ought, she felt, to be concentrating on Richard's plan, which was to make them all rich. But there was Dick, sitting so close to her and she had not seen him for weeks, except for that all too brief moment in Paris a few days before. Tap, tap, went Dick's heel against the chair.

'It's all quite simple,' he continued.

His tones were level, but there was a hint of excitement underlying them.

'Oswaldtwizzle is a collector, or, rather, the son of one. His house at Norwich is full of all sorts of stuff. Most of it is junk, but there are one or two pieces in his collection which are quite unique. There is an ivory virgin of the fourteenth century. I once found a buyer for that piece, but the old boy would not sell it. That is by the way. The other piece – the one that concerns us – is known as the Borgia reliquary.'

Richard paused, took a cigarette and lit it.

'It's not really a reliquary,' he continued. 'It's a sort of locket made of gold and it once belonged to Lucrezia, given to her, I believe, by d'Este, her third husband.'

'Well?'

'The South Kensington Museum offered him three thousand pounds for it some years ago, but he would not take it.'

'Three thousand?'

'Three thousand. But five thousand is his price, and he would not take a penny less. Consequently the reliquary is still in his possession – at least so Janet tells me. Useful old bird, Janet.'

Hermione nodded. Janet was Sir Oswald's housekeeper. She had always had a soft spot for Master Dick, and when Master Dick had thought it well to go abroad, she had continued to write to him and Dick had always answered her letters.

'Well?' said Throgmorton again, in his flat voice.

'That is all,' said Dick. 'We are going to buy the reliquary.'

'For five thousand pounds?'

'Five thousand pounds.'

'And what, may I ask, are we going to do with a reliquary worth five thousand pounds?'

'Sell it for fifty thousand,' responded Dick.

'But how? I don't understand.'

'Then let me explain. The reliquary is about an inch and a half long and is made of gold. It has a top and a bottom compartment inside. The top compartment is empty. That is why the experts from South Kensington refused to pay more than three thousand for it. The bottom compartment, however, contains an emerald carved as a cameo, and it so happens that no one but myself knows of it. The reliquary is a piece of trick work, very cunningly fashioned by a fifteenth-century goldsmith from Byzantium. I found the bottom compartment quite by accident. I was just fiddling about with the thing. You press various bits of ornamentation on the outer casing and you release the jewel with a probe. I discovered the emerald about a week before the old boy packed me off to the Continent because I thought he had left out a nought in one of his cheques. It was on the tip of my tongue to tell him about the emerald, but I'm a vindictive fellow and damnably hard up. Also I think it a mistake for Oswaldtwizzle to have too much money. Hoarding is bad for trade. The jewel, as I said, is in the form of a carved cameo, and it represents the sacrifice of Iphigenia. It must have come from some old Greek or Roman tomb.'

'How do you know that it is worth fifty thousand pounds?' Throgmorton demanded.

'Because I happen to have found a customer. I met him a fortnight ago in Paris – a rich American on tour and ready to buy the crown jewels if they were up for sale. I told him all about it – in confidence. A lovely story it was – old English family, priceless heirloom, publicity to be avoided at all costs. The man's palm is just itching for the thing – a Mr George P. Folliot of Michigan. Thank God for millionaires. There are still a few of them left – even in America.'

'Well?' he added, as the other two remained silent. 'Is it a go?'

Hermione found it difficult to speak. Fifty thousand pounds . . . equal shares . . . one-third each . . . nearly seventeen thousand pounds. Her own, with Dick's share, would set them up for life, and they would be able to fly to some warm, happy corner of the earth.

'Day-dreaming, both of you?'

Hermione found Dick looking from her to Throgmorton and back again with an amused smile upon his face.

Throgmorton was sitting inscrutably behind his spectacles, and Hermione saw the tip of his tongue as it passed slowly towards his full lips.

'All right,' he said at last. 'It's a go; though I must say that this is the queerest way of making money I ever struck, and we have yet to consider ways and means. Who is going to buy this reliquary, or whatever you call it?'

'That, my dear John,' replied Richard, 'I leave entirely to you. This is where I fade away. Oswaldtwizzle must not know that I have any hand in the business. He has a nasty suspicious mind, and, if he saw me anywhere about, he would jump straight to the conclusion that there was a catch in it somewhere. John himself must buy the thing or get some respectable dealer to do it for him.'

Hermione looked at Throgmorton. The heavy lips moved.

'Why not Hermione?' he asked.

Hermione shook her head.

'It is no good, John. I have met the old man.'

'Is that an objection?'

'Most certainly it is,' she replied. 'It was Dick who introduced us, and as Dick's friend I should be liable to suspicion.'

Dick nodded.

'No, John,' he said. 'You will have to do it yourself.'

'There are possible objections to that course,' said Throgmorton slowly. 'Sir Oswald may make inquiries about me, and I don't think this is the time for inquiries. Not at this moment. You will agree, I think, Hermione?'

Hermione sat still in her chair. She had again that sudden sensation at her heart which came so often now and set her apart in a world where she shared with Throgmorton the secret which Dick had yet to learn. How would Dick, so kind and easygoing, receive that revelation?

'Yes,' she heard herself saying, 'this is not the time for inquiries.'

The telephone bell rang sharply. Hermione crossed and picked up the receiver. To answer the telephone was part of the routine which she and Throgmorton had established.

'Is that Gerard 7004?' asked the operator.

'Yes.'

'Is Mr Throgmorton there?'

'Yes.'

'Ask him to come to the telephone, please. He is wanted on a trunk call from Norwich.'

Hermione handed the receiver to Throgmorton.

'It is from Norwich,' she said.

Throgmorton put the instrument to his ear. Hermione stepped back and, in doing so, brushed against Dick. For a moment their fingers touched.

'Yes,' Throgmorton was saying. 'I remember your visit. Will you hold the line a moment?'

He covered the instrument with his hand as he turned to Hermione.

'It's a man called Greening. He wants to see me to-morrow.'

Hermione gave Throgmorton a puzzled look.

'Don't you remember? He called some days ago and I lent him thirty-five pounds. There can be no harm in giving him an appointment.'

He spoke again into the telephone.

'Very good, then, Mr Greening. I can see you to-morrow morning . . . I beg your pardon . . . Not before six o'clock . . . That is a *little* difficult. It is after office hours, you know . . . Yes, I can manage it . . . Six o'clock, here in my office.'

He put down the receiver.

'He wants to see me urgently, but he cannot get here before six o'clock to-morrow.'

Throgmorton was silent a moment. What was he thinking about, wondered Hermione?

'Mr Greening is a respectable schoolmaster in Norwich, I believe,' Throgmorton said at last. 'He appears to be in difficulties. Make a note of the appointment, Hermione.'

Richard grinned.

'Still hoping to turn an honest penny?' he said.

'I'm still in business, Feiling. Also I have an idea that Mr Greening may be useful to us.'

2   *Saturday, December 5th*

Inspector George Martin, arriving at Norwich station on Saturday morning, decided to walk to St Julian's. A walk might clear his head. He was feeling tired and out of spirits, and even the prospect of seeing Elizabeth failed to restore him.

The Brighton truck mystery was wearing him down. So far, in all the cases he had handled, the difficulty had been to pick up initial clues, to get started upon a definite trail, to assemble the evidence. In this case there were a multitude of clues, many trails and too much evidence altogether. But the clues had broken in his hands; the trails ran easily to a point where they were lost; the evidence was contradictory.

So now he must begin again. The murder had been committed in London, but it had been planned on information received from Norwich before Miss Haslett had started on her fatal journey. The flat in Cadbury Road had been taken by persons unknown with intent to kill Miss Haslett, on Thursday, November 26th. Miss Haslett had left for London on Friday, November 27th. The murderer had been ready and waiting for his victim.

Miss Haslett had written to Throgmorton on Tuesday, November 24th, and had talked to his secretary on the telephone on Thursday, November 26th. Throgmorton, however, had been quite open about his dealings with Miss Haslett. She had left his office unharmed and he had a perfect alibi for the night of the murder.

What, then, of the man with the black patch over his eye? There was nothing to connect him with Throgmorton. Throgmorton, indeed, had been amusing himself with his friends on the very night when this unknown person who had met Miss Haslett at Liverpool Street the day before had presumably decoyed her back to the flat in Cadbury Road and murdered her. How had this man obtained his previous information concerning Miss Haslett? Was there not, perhaps, a link between Norwich and London which had yet to be discovered? Norwich at any rate was the only possible source of such information. There was a sister of Miss Haslett in Exeter and a nephew who had sent her the ticket, but it had been ascertained that neither of them had received any intimation of her good fortune in the lottery till the news of her murder had appeared in the newspapers.

Inspector Martin passed up the short drive, rang the bell at St Julian's and asked for Mr Hedlam.

The maid shook her head.

'Mr Hedlam has gone to London, sir,' she announced, 'and he will not be back till rather late this evening. But Miss Elizabeth is at home, if you would like to see her,' she added with a friendly smile.

'Thank you, Ruth,' he said.

The maid showed him into the drawing-room. It was a dreary apartment, reserved for prospective parents. On its walls were photographs of the Parthenon, of the Winged Victory and the Belvedere Apollo.

A minute later Ruth opened the door and Elizabeth came towards him.

'My dear,' she exclaimed, 'what a lovely surprise.'

The door closed softly behind them, for Ruth was a person of discretion and resource.

Martin, holding in his arms a rather breathless Elizabeth,

discovered that there were compensations even for a failure to solve the Brighton truck mystery.

'Lizzie,' he said, 'ten minutes ago I decided that life was a bad business. I'm feeling better now.'

'Sit down and tell me about it.'

She pushed him into a chair and sat herself upon the arm of it.

'The fact is,' continued Martin, 'this isn't a holiday. I'm working overtime. I came down to see Hedlam, but it seems he is away for the week-end.' He paused a moment. 'Can you lunch with me somewhere quickly? I suggest Prince's in Castle Street.'

Elizabeth looked at her watch.

'In ten minutes,' she said.

Luncheon was pleasant, but not as pleasant as it might have been. Martin could not throw off the problem oppressing him.

'I'm sorry, Lizzie,' he said, 'but you know how it is.'

She nodded.

'Get it off your mind,' she urged. 'It will do you good.'

He dived into his subject and spoke, to his astonishment, without consciously drawing breath for a quarter of an hour. All the time he looked at Elizabeth, who, in turn, was looking straight at him, not once interrupting him but nodding in silence.

'Tell me, Lizzie,' he said in conclusion, 'had Miss Haslett any special friends in Norwich? She lived here for many years.'

'There was Mrs Hampton and Miss Brown,' replied Elizabeth doubtfully.

'I must see them all,' said Martin. 'I can't help thinking that the man who murdered her in London had a confederate here in Norwich. Or there may be someone here with connections in London who, quite innocently, perhaps, conveyed to the murderer the information on which he acted.'

'But the poor old thing had no really intimate friends. The person she liked best was young Greening, and you have already talked to him.'

George nodded.

'I shall talk to him again,' he said.

'Then you will have to wait till Monday. Joseph is at Brancaster. He went off on his motor-bicycle about an hour ago.' She paused, and then added with a smile: 'If you want to get anything out of *him*, you had better get it quickly.'

'Quickly?'

'Before he breaks his neck. He rides that bicycle like nothing on earth. He very nearly killed me the other day.'

'You never told me, Lizzie. Where was this?'

'Just outside Ipswich. I went there to see Aunt Lucy, if you remember. It was just before you came down for the long week-end.'

'That was Friday, November 27th.'

'I dare say it was. But why so terribly precise? Joseph came sweeping round a corner and missed me by nothing at all. He was going all out.'

'Damn the fellow,' said George indignantly.

He extinguished his cigarette and beckoned to the waitress for the bill. But abruptly he paused in his gesture.

On Friday, November 27th, Greening had nearly run over Elizabeth in Ipswich. But Greening, questioned as to his movements during that week-end, had gone out of his way to make it perfectly clear that he had been staying at Brancaster.

Inspector Martin was thinking hard. Mr Joseph Greening, elaborately and of set purpose, had lied to him.

'What's the matter, George? Got a pain?'

Inspector Martin came to himself with a start.

'Sorry,' he said mechanically. 'I was thinking of our friend Greening. He's a danger to the public. He never even saw you, I suppose?'

'He was giving all his attention to the speed limit. Some day that young man will get into trouble.'

'Lizzie,' said Inspector Martin, 'I'm inclined to agree with you.'

3   *Saturday, December 5th*

Mr Joseph Greening, on his motor-bicycle, shot past the lorry which had held him up for at least three interminable miles, perceiving, as he did so, that a large car was meeting him from the opposite direction. Swerving to the left he missed the bonnet of the lorry by an inch and the right wing of the oncoming car by half as much.

'Quick reactions,' he muttered.

It was the third time that morning he had missed death more by good luck than management. But that only showed that he was worried.

There was no avoiding the fact. He was in the devil of a mess. He had written a cheque for thirty-five pounds, and the cheque would be presented the day after to-morrow. That would be Monday. And he had not got thirty-five pence in the bank to meet it.

Throgmorton must see him through – jolly old Throgmorton, who had not, however, seemed on the telephone quite so jolly as he might have been. But it was difficult to be jolly on the telephone. Anyhow, here he was, buzzing up to London, a trip which he could ill afford. Desperate situations required desperate remedies.

Then, of course, there was that other complication. Not so long ago Phyllis had been a bright spot, a redeeming feature. But of late she had become a problem – perhaps the most urgent of all his problems. Her last letter had conveyed a suggestion that, if he did not comply with her very reasonable request for a meeting, there would be 'consequences'.

'Consequences' was a nasty word – vague but definitely unpleasant.

First, however, he had to straighten out this business of the post-dated cheque. He had also to get to London without breaking his neck. Life might be difficult at times, but he had no real wish to leave it untimely.

There was another small matter that worried him not a little. He had given Inspector Martin to understand that, during the week-end in which poor old Hazelnut had met her death, he had been at Brancaster. There had been no avoiding that small decep-tion, but it had involved withholding from Inspector Martin a vital piece of information. On Saturday, November 28th, in the Wilton Road he had seen a woman who was not Miss Haslett wearing Miss Haslett's clothes and bearing on her face a port-wine mark, obviously intended to give to a casual observer the impression that this was Miss Haslett herself. He thoroughly appreciated the significance of this encounter, and he knew that, in keeping this fact from the police, he was helping to defeat the ends of justice. But what could he do? It was impossible for him to come forward and openly confess that he had been within a hundred miles of Victoria Station on that particular afternoon.

> Oh, what a tangled web we weave,
> When first we practise to deceive.

Greening reached Shaftesbury Avenue shortly before six o'clock. He went at once to his appointment, leaving his bicycle in the street and not even removing his overalls.

It was Throgmorton's secretary who opened the office door – an attractive woman, but he was not in a mood to notice an attractive woman. Women were a delusion and a snare. They began in fun and ended in fury.

The secretary had her hat on and was evidently on the point of leaving the office.

'Please come in,' said Throgmorton.

Greening followed a broad back into the inner office.

'Well,' said Throgmorton, affable but severe, 'what's the trouble?'

The financier sat down behind his desk and motioned Greening to a leather chair. The man of means was smiling, but it was a bleak sort of smile, and Greening doubted very much whether it extended to his eyes, which were invisible behind the horn-rimmed spectacles. It was also to be noted that he was suffering from a severe cold in the head. He spoke in a voice that was hoarse and thick, and he was obviously in a state of great physical discomfort.

Greening perched himself on the chair and for a moment there was silence.

'Come,' said Throgmorton at last in the encouraging tone of voice peculiar to dentists and bank-managers discussing an over-draft, 'what can I do for you?'

'The fact is,' said Greening, 'I was wondering . . . that is to say, I have come to inquire . . . to suggest in short . . . I mean to say . . . would it be possible for you to make another – er – arrangement.'

Throgmorton, who had waited very patiently, sat back in his chair.

'How much?' he asked briskly, but without enthusiasm.

Greening licked his lips.

'Shall we say forty pounds?'

He had meant to be casual, to assume that the transaction he proposed was a mere matter of routine – one man of the world to another, a question of mutual profit and accommodation. But the dreadful reflection occurred to him: Why should Mr Throgmorton say forty pounds, and he could not think of any reason why he should.

The financier leaned a little forward over his desk.

'May I ask, Mr Greening, what security you have to offer?'

'No *security*,' said Greening, slightly emphasising the word, as who should say: I am prepared to offer you anything else you like.

'You told me at our last interview,' continued Throgmorton, 'that you were a school-master?'

Joseph nodded eagerly.

'St. Julian's,' he said. 'It is a good school.'

'No doubt, Mr Greening, but I imagine you can scarcely offer it as a pledge.'

'I am not a partner, Mr Throgmorton. I receive a salary. I have received it regularly now for three years.'

'May I ask how much?'

'Two hundred and fifty a year,' said Greening. 'But all found, you know, all found.'

'And you want forty pounds?' said Throgmorton at last. 'You borrowed thirty-five pounds from me a week or ten days ago. That makes seventy-five pounds.'

Throgmorton was slowly shaking his head.

'Frankly, Mr Greening, it isn't good enough. Not unless you can provide some guarantee. Have you, for instance, a substantial friend who would back a bill for you?'

Greening shook his head.

'Not a *substantial* friend,' he admitted.

'You see,' said Throgmorton, 'I should have no guarantee whatever.'

'But I should be absolutely compelled to pay you back,' Greening persisted. 'St. Julian's is a highly respectable establishment. My integrity has to be above suspicion – like Caesar's wife, you know.'

Mr Greening smiled wanly upon the money-lender.

'You appear to suggest, Mr Greening, that I should be able to bring rather strong pressure to bear upon you in the event of your finding it difficult to meet your obligations. But I should be very sorry to put you or any of my clients in such an unfortunate position. I am indeed not a little surprised by your suggestion. It is the first time in my experience, Mr Greening, that a client has offered himself, so to speak, as a potential victim of blackmail.'

Throgmorton rose from the table.

'I fear it is useless to prolong this conversation,' he said.

Greening stared miserably in front of him. This was the end. On Monday his post-dated cheque would be presented and on Wednesday, at the latest, he might expect to receive it back again marked R.D. Then good-bye to his integrity.

'I had hoped you would be more accommodating, Mr Throgmorton,' he said.

He, too, was now on his feet. He must pull himself together. It was no good showing the white feather. He squared his shoulders and moved towards the door.

His hand was on the knob when the voice of Throgmorton arrested him.

'One moment, Mr Greening.'

Greening turned.

Throgmorton had sat down again. The electric light was shining on his horn-rimmed spectacles. He pointed to the chair.

'One moment, Mr Greening,' he repeated. 'I think perhaps the matter might be arranged.'

Greening felt himself going weak at the knees. He was thankful to feel the solid chair beneath him once more. There was a short silence.

'Have a cigarette?' said Throgmorton, pushing a box across the desk.

Greening took a cigarette and lit it, pleased to note that his hand was steady again.

'It has just occurred to me, Mr Greening, that you might be of use to me in a little matter of business.'

'Only too happy,' said Greening eagerly. 'Always provided that you can also be of use to *me*.'

That was a good one. Greening smiled as he delivered it. But there was no answering smile on the face of the financier.

'Of course,' said Throgmorton coldly. 'Business is necessarily a mutual transaction.'

There was a slight pause.

Throgmorton took a cigarette for himself and lit it deliberately.

'I am looking for someone,' he continued, 'who will make a small purchase on my behalf. Curiously enough, the person from whom the purchase is to be made lives not far from Norwich, and it has for that reason occurred to me that you might be willing to act for me.'

Throgmorton leaned farther forward across his desk.

'Please understand,' he went on, 'that the matter is strictly confidential. Do you by any chance know Sir Oswald Feiling of Tenby Hall?'

'I know him by name and I have seen him,' answered Greening. 'But I have never spoken to him. I've often passed his place near the Aylsham Road.'

'It has come to my knowledge,' Throgmorton continued, 'that Sir Oswald has in his possession a fifteenth-century reliquary which I am anxious to acquire. I do not, however, desire to appear in the transaction myself. In business, as you know, it is often necessary for the principal in a transaction to keep in the background.'

'Er – yes,' said Greening.

'I must therefore make the purchase through an agent, and it has occurred to me that you might be willing to act for me in that capacity.'

'What exactly do you want me to do?'

'I want you to see Sir Oswald at your convenience one day early next week and to make him an offer on my behalf.'

'An historic piece?'

'It is supposed to have belonged to Lucrezia Borgia – a tradition which adds immensely to its value in the market. I can authorise you to go up to five thousand pounds.'

Greening sat back in his chair stunned.

'Five thousand pounds,' he found himself repeating.

'I am not purchasing the reliquary for myself,' Throgmorton went on. 'I, too, am only an agent in this matter. But, frankly, if I were to approach Sir Oswald direct, the price would be considerably higher, and I do not want my client to pay more than is necessary. Do you understand?'

Greening nodded.

But he did not understand very well.

'Then you will act for me in this matter?'

'Certainly,' said Greening steadily.

Throgmorton pulled open a drawer and produced a cheque book.

'As soon as you have seen Sir Oswald,' said the smooth voice above the scratching of the pen, 'and have his consent to the sale of the reliquary, please inform me by telegram and I will place the money at your bank.'

'Eastern Counties,' said Greening eagerly.

Throgmorton made a note of the bank and then resumed his writing of the cheque.

'I have reason to believe,' he continued, tearing out the cheque with a rasp, 'that Sir Oswald is prepared to part with the reliquary for the price I mention. He has been offered three thousand by the South Kensington Museum. He appears to be of the "take-it-or-leave-it" type, so I don't advise you to bargain with him, Mr Greening.'

He pushed the cheque across the table.

'Here is part of your commission in advance on the transaction.'

Greening looked at the cheque in amazement. It was for a hundred pounds.

'You will receive the remainder of your commission, less the sum that you owe me, when you hand me over the reliquary. I hope that will be satisfactory, Mr Greening.'

'Extremely generous, if I may say so,' Greening stammered.

'Then perhaps you will kindly sign this receipt,' said Throgmorton.

Greening bent over the desk and signed his name rapidly at the bottom of a printed form.

Three minutes later he was in Shaftesbury Avenue.

It was only on the run back to Norwich that night that he began to have doubts. Assuredly it was a queer business. Why should Throgmorton pay him a considerable sum of money to avoid appearing in the matter? There must be something here not entirely above-board. Beggars, however, could not be choosers, though the more he thought of the business the fishier it seemed.

He reached Norwich at about eleven o'clock, stabled his motor-bicycle and began to walk back to his rooms. He was full of evil presentiment, frightened, out of spirits. Life was proving too much for him. To add to his troubles, there would certainly be a letter from Phyllis awaiting him, reproachful, perhaps even menacing.

Thank heaven that he would at least be able to cover his cheque on Monday.

'I beg your pardon,' he said suddenly, on finding that he had walked rather forcibly into a girl coming from the opposite direction.

'You're very absent-minded, Joseph.'

'Hello, Lizzie. Sorry I bumped.'

'Habit of yours,' said Elizabeth. 'You nearly killed me a week ago on Friday.'

'Where was that?'

'In Ipswich.'

Greening stared at her in consternation.

'In Ipswich?' he echoed. 'What was I doing in Ipswich?'

'Driving in a manner dangerous to the public,' said Elizabeth. 'To London, apparently.'

'Impossible,' said Greening.

Elizabeth shook her head at him.

'I suppose I oughtn't to have seen you,' she said.

Greening grinned sheepishly.

'That's all right,' he mumbled. 'But don't give me away.'

'Sorry, Joseph, but I was lunching with George to-day, and it slipped out.'

'Oh, Lord,' said Greening and hoped that he did not look as sick as he felt.

Elizabeth gazed at him in surprise.

'Nothing to worry about,' she said lightly. 'George will have forgotten all about it by now. Good night, Joseph.'

Joseph Greening mechanically lifted his hat and walked forward.

Inspector Martin had been informed that he, Joseph Greening, had nearly killed Elizabeth in Ipswich a week ago last Friday. But Joseph Greening had informed Inspector Martin that on that day he had been spotting birds at Brancaster.

He stood at his gate. What should he do? Elizabeth thought that by now George would have forgotten all about it. But George would not forget. George was much too wide awake.

Mr Joseph Greening had lied to the police and the police would want to know the reason why.

'There's no doubt about it,' said Greening as he let himself into the house, 'I'm in the devil of a mess – the very devil of a mess.'

CHAPTER V

1   *Saturday, December 5th*

Hermione Taylor, approaching Piccadilly Circus, suddenly pulled up short.

Now, at last, she remembered. The man who had seen her at Victoria dressed in Miss Haslett's clothes, the man whose face had been vaguely familiar, but which she had not at the moment been able to identify, was the man who had just called at the office to see Throgmorton. He had borrowed thirty-five pounds on November 27th and was probably borrowing a further sum at that identical moment.

She stood on the pavement watching with unseeing eyes the swaying motor-buses that roared round the circus. Should she return to the office? Was the man dangerous or was she merely beginning to give way to unnecessary panic? He might well be dangerous, for he had only to recognise her as the woman he had seen wearing those dreadful clothes and bearing upon her cheek that tell-tale mark to be in a position to destroy them all. She must turn back and warn John Throgmorton at once.

Yet should she?

Was she not perhaps giving way needlessly to a fear which existed only in her imagination. It all depended whether the man who had met her at Victoria had seen in her the money-lender's secretary who had shown him into the office on the day previous to their encounter in the Wilton Road. He had noted her appearance at Victoria, but had he recognised her as the woman he had met in Shaftesbury Avenue.

She tapped her heel against the kerb, trying to make up her mind.

After a moment's hesitation she came to the conclusion that at Victoria he had not realised her identity. He had not even glanced at her when passing into the office a few moments ago.

What was it, then, that had attracted his attention at Victoria?

If he had not recognised her as Throgmorton's secretary, he must have been struck by her clothes and the mark on her face. Was he, then, a man who had known Miss Haslett? And if he had known Miss Haslett had he mistaken her for the dead woman or had he seen through her disguise?

She walked on thoughtfully round the Circus. It was not much use returning to the office. Throgmorton was himself leaving London that day and Richard was waiting for her at Warwick Avenue. The man Greening might be dangerous, and she must certainly warn Throgmorton to have no further dealings with him. But the matter could wait.

This was a small black shadow lost in a swift blaze of happiness which sprang alive as her thoughts carried her forward.

Richard was waiting, and all of the day that remained and of the day that followed would be their own.

2   *Sunday, December 6th*

Mr Joseph Greening, about to lather his chin, stared into the mirror. He had always understood that people who suffered from sleepless nights looked unpleasant in the morning. Now he knew.

He had never before endured such a night. Hour after hour he had brooded and sweated over his predicament. Now, in the grey light of morning, he must somehow pull himself together. He must be ready to face the music – discordant though it might be.

He had lied to Inspector Martin and he would have to satisfy the police that his lie had nothing whatever to do with the crime which was under investigation. That, of course, would be an easy matter. He could prove that he had often before pretended to be at Brancaster when, in actual fact, he had been in London, and on these former occasions nobody had been a penny the worse for his misdemeanours. Admittedly he had deceived the police and with-held from them information which might be vital to their inquiry. But that was the head and front of his offending.

If the police were sceptical and insisted on investigating his movements during the fatal week-end, he would be driven, of course, to produce his witnesses, and it was distinctly unfortunate that they should include the manager of a gambling hell and a young lady who was obviously no fit companion for the assistant-master of a preparatory school.

One thing was pretty clear. He would find it difficult to keep from Hedlam the true facts of the case. Inspector Martin would be indignant and suspicious – not at all inclined to help him cover his traces. Besides, there were complications which made it impossible for him to take Martin altogether into his confidence. What, for example, was he going to do about the business with which Throgmorton had entrusted him? Either he must execute the commission or forfeit the money, and he could not afford to do that.

Gradually, as he shaved, his resolution was formed. Hedlam would sooner or later come to know of his conduct. Then why not go to Hedlam at once and make a clean breast of everything?

Hedlam was the only person to whom he could tell the whole story. Hedlam would be shocked, of course, but he might not be harsh or vindictive. He would go to Hedlam as a soul in trouble.

Thus it happened that immediately after morning chapel Mr Joseph Greening found himself confronting his employer across the study table.

'Sit down, Greening. What can I do for you?'

The old man looked especially benevolent this morning. Or was that merely an illusion – the effect of Sunday and the wish to find him so. Or perhaps it was because his ankle was mending so nicely, though he still had need of the rubber-shod stick.

Greening swallowed hard and took the plunge.

'I have come to consult you, sir, about myself,' he said.

'Yes, Greening.'

Hedlam's tone was kind but non-committal.

'The fact is, sir,' Greening continued, 'I am badly in need of advice. I am in rather a difficulty and I would like to tell you about it.'

The quiet brows beneath the bald scalp rose in gentle astonishment.

'By all means, if I can be of any help.'

'I don't know what you will think of me, sir, but the fact is I have made a perfect fool of myself. I shouldn't be at all surprised if you decided to give me notice – throw me out. Yes, sir – throw me out, neck and crop. That is what I should be tempted to do, sir, if I were in your position.'

'Suppose you tell me what it is all about, Greening. Then I will see whether I can resist the temptation.'

'Well, sir, as you know, sir, I told Inspector Martin last week that I spent the long week-end at Brancaster.'

'Yes, Greening. You go there quite often, I believe.'

'Well, sir, I wasn't at Brancaster.'

Hedlam looked at him, mildly expectant rather than reproving.

'I went to London, sir.'

'To London?'

'I am in the habit of going to London, sir.'

'But, my dear Greening, why shouldn't you go to London? I often go to London myself.'

Greening grinned nervously, visited by a sudden incongruous picture of old Hedlam loose in Piccadilly.

'The purpose of these visits,' continued Hedlam with a smile, 'is presumably to enjoy yourself.'

'Precisely, sir. To enjoy myself, to see the town a bit.'

'I'm sorry you should have felt it necessary to practice a deception, Greening. I am not a narrow-minded man, and I can make allowances for young people. I suggest that you go straight to Inspector Martin, who, I understand, is in Norwich, and tell him the truth. That will put you right with the police, and, in consideration of the fact that you have taken me into your confidence, I am prepared to overlook your previous – er – reticence.'

'Thank you, sir. But I haven't finished yet.'

Greening gulped like the Russian hen that swallowed a bean.

'Then you had better perhaps continue,' responded Hedlam dryly.

'Well, sir, the police, for one thing, may want to know what I was doing in London, and I suppose I shall have to tell them.'

'I suppose you will, and I infer from your manner that what you were doing was not what a schoolmaster at St Julian's ought to have been doing. Is that it?'

Joseph nodded.

'I met a friend and – we . . . I lost a large sum of money.'

'How did you manage to do that?'

'Very easily, sir. Just a little flutter – if you know what I mean.'

'Gambling? Was that it?'

Again Greening nodded.

'How much money did you lose?'

'Seventy pounds, sir.'

'That is a considerable sum, Greening. How did you come to have so much money in your possession?'

'I – er – borrowed it, sir – from Mr John Throgmorton of Shaftesbury Avenue.'

Hedlam looked at him keenly.

'The man who sent the circulars to poor Miss Haslett?'

'Yes, sir. I originally borrowed thirty-five pounds from him, but I lost all that and as much again. So I signed a cheque for another thirty-five. It will be presented to-morrow.'

'Have you funds to meet it?'

'As a matter of fact I have, sir. I went to see Throgmorton yesterday.'

'A second time?'

'Yes, sir, and he gave me money to cover the post-dated cheque.'

'I see. What else did you do during your week-end in London?'

Greening repeated his impersonation of the Russian hen.

'I – er – met a girl, sir.'

Hedlam nodded.

'But nothing much happened.'

Greening coloured.

'Except,' he added hastily, 'that she caused me to spend what was left of my salary.'

'I see; and of course all this will come out when the police begin to make inquiries.'

'Exactly, sir. That's why I'm telling you now.'

There was a short silence. Greening raised his head and ventured to look at his employer. Hedlam was sitting quiet and collected behind his desk.

'It was very right and proper of you, Greening,' he said, 'to come to me. Your conduct is of course very reprehensible, but you are young, and that circumstance explains and, to a certain degree, excuses your conduct. There is another and to my mind even graver side to the matter. I have heard rumours about your conduct here in Norwich.'

Joseph's heart sank like a stone.

'Rumours,' he echoed.

'I am given to understand that there is a young lady in the town to whom you are more or less engaged.'

Greening nodded miserably.

'More or less,' he confessed.

He raised his head. The old man was looking at him sternly.

'Well,' he asked, 'what are you going to do?'

'I put myself entirely in your hands, sir.'

Hedlam nodded slowly.

'Very well, Greening. If you take my advice you will go at once to the police and put things right in that quarter.'

'Tell them everything, sir?'

'Everything. Just as you have been telling me.'

Joseph was silent.

'Are they likely, do you think, to take – er – proceedings?'

'Why should they take proceedings? It is true that you misinformed Inspector Martin concerning your movements over the long weekend. But I have yet to learn that a false statement to the police, except when you are on oath or in a witness-box, is an actionable offence. Of course they will check your alibi very carefully.'

Again Greening was silent.

'It's rather more complicated than that, sir,' he said at last. 'Having misled the police as to my movements, I was obliged to withhold from them a vital piece of information concerning Miss Haslett.'

'Indeed?'

Hedlam leaned forward over his desk.

'This,' he said, 'may be rather more serious.' Greening stared at his employer, scared and silent.

'It may be very serious indeed,' continued Hedlam. 'Technically it makes you what I believe is called an accessory after the fact.'

Still Greening was silent.

'Hadn't you better tell me the particulars?' prompted Hedlam.

'Well, sir, when I was in London, I went to Victoria to meet a friend. That was on Saturday, November 28th. As we were walking away from the station I saw a woman dressed in Miss Haslett's clothes. She wore a veil and there was a mark on her face, but I am not quite sure that it *was* Miss Haslett.'

Hedlam was smiling now, faintly contemptuous.

'Are you quite sure it was *not?*'

'Not absolutely sure, but fairly certain. You see how important it is. If the woman was not Miss Haslett, it was someone impersonating her, and in that case it seems fairly certain that Miss Haslett was not alive on the Saturday evening, as the police assume.'

'Do the police assume that she was still alive?'

'They are working on the theory that Miss Haslett went to Paris on the Saturday and was murdered on her return to London.'

'How do you know that the police are working on that theory?'

'I have discussed the case with Miss Orme. Inspector Martin makes no secret of his line of inquiry.'

There was a short silence.

'I appreciate your point, Greening. But everything depends on your being quite sure that the woman you saw at Victoria was *not* Miss Haslett.'

He paused a moment and added: 'Incidentally, Greening, what was your condition at the time?'

'My condition?' stammered Greening.

'I understand that you had rather a troubled week-end.'

'I was stone-cold sober, sir, if that is what you mean.'

Hedlam appeared to be considering the matter.

'Well,' he said at last, 'you must decide for yourself what you will tell Inspector Martin.'

Once more there was silence.

'Meanwhile,' continued Hedlam smoothly, 'what is your position financially? You say that you have received money to cover the cheque which will be presented to-morrow?'

'Yes, sir.'

'On what terms, may I ask?'

'Throgmorton gave me the money.'

'*Gave* you the money? That is an odd expression. What exactly do you mean?'

'He gave me the money on condition that I would undertake a small commission.'

'What sort of commission?'

'He asked me to buy from Sir Oswald Feiling an antique which he was anxious to obtain. It is on behalf of a client and he does not wish to appear in the transaction himself. He gave me a cheque for a hundred pounds on account of my services.'

Hedlam's eyebrows went up.

'Didn't that strike you as rather strange?'

'I must own it did, sir, but in the circumstances it was a little difficult for me to refuse.'

'Have you cashed Throgmorton's cheque yet?'

'No, sir. I only had it yesterday and to-day is Sunday.'

'Then if you will take my advice, Greening, you will return that cheque to Throgmorton immediately and have nothing whatever to do with the business. If Throgmorton wishes to buy antiques from Sir Oswald Feiling, or from anyone else, he should do it himself. You are almost certainly being employed to cover some underhand and presumably illegal transaction.'

'But what can I possibly do, sir? I am in debt to Throgmorton and there is also my own cheque to be covered.'

Hedlam put a hand beneath his desk. There came a click and a drawer opened. Joseph sat back, his eyes round with astonishment. Out from the drawer came a cheque-book, and the silence that followed was broken by the scratching movement of a pen as it moved across the paper and a rasp as two slips were torn away.

Hedlam held the slips out.

'Pay the top cheque into your bank to-morrow morning and give the other one to Throgmorton. You will see Throgmorton first thing on Monday morning. Return him the cheque for a hundred pounds and say that you wish to have nothing more to do with him.'

'Yes, sir,' stammered Greening. 'I don't know how to thank you, sir. It is most kind of you . . . most generous.'

Hedlam held up his hand, looking very stern and practical.

'I shall deduct fifteen pounds a term from your salary until the advance is paid off,' he said. 'I am giving you another chance,

Greening. You have had your lesson, and I don't think it will be altogether lost on you. We will not refer to this matter again. Is that clear?'

'Yes, sir,' answered Greening and turned towards the door.

'One moment,' said Hedlam.

Greening turned.

'You had better go up to London some time to-day. The first thing is to get clear of this entanglement with Throgmorton. Then you will be able to face Inspector Martin with clean hands and a quiet mind.'

'Yes, sir,' said Greening, and left the room.

3 *Sunday, December 6th*

'Of course I think it is perfectly lovely. But where are we going and why are you taking a rest from your labours? I thought you would be nosing about at St Julian's this morning.'

Elizabeth settled herself back in the two-seater car. They were driving through the flat country just outside Norwich. The road was narrow and winding. Tall elms stood leafless in the fields looking over the high hedges. It was an unexpectedly soft day for December and Elizabeth was feeling happy. George had hired this very comfortable car and was driving her into the country. What more could a loving heart desire?'

'Nosing about,' protested Martin. 'That isn't a very nice expression.'

'Sorry, George. It's a nice nose, but I'm glad you are giving it a rest this morning. This is better than putting our little Joseph through the third degree, or whatever you call it. I don't hold with cruelty to the feeble-minded. There ought to be a law against that sort of thing.'

'I hope it will not be necessary,' said Martin shortly. 'That is why we are driving in this jolly little car along this jolly little road.'

'It *is* a jolly road,' said Elizabeth. 'Where are we going?'

'We are going to Brancaster.'

Elizabeth sat up suddenly.

'Why Brancaster?'

'It is a pleasant spot and there will be lunch and woodcock and a bottle of Chambertin 1911 – so he says.'

'Who says?'

'Man called Blossop.'

'Friend of yours?'

'He sounded friendly. I rang him up this morning. You will be surprised to hear that on Friday 27th and over the long week-end he had the pleasure of entertaining our friend Joseph. Blossop is an innkeeper.'

'Did he say that Joseph was there on the 27th?'

'That is what he said. He asserted, in fact, that Joseph, at the very moment he was trying to kill you in Ipswich, was lunching at the King's Head. What is even more surprising, Joseph sent a post card from Brancaster to his landlady during the week-end, saying that he would be back in Norwich on Monday.'

Elizabeth looked coldly upon her lover.

'I should never have told you about seeing Joseph in Ipswich if I had thought it would be used in evidence against him. Why can't you leave the poor lad alone? You can't possibly suspect him of having a hand in the murder. Joseph is incapable of killing even a fly.'

'I must know why he lied to me.'

'There may be a thousand reasons. Joseph is like that – always takes the line of least resistance.'

'One good reason will be quite enough, my dear. But I intend to have it.'

Elizabeth drew away from him and sat back in her corner of the car.

'I think it is very mean of you,' she said, 'to make use of a casual remark that I made to you in order to hound down one of my personal friends.'

Martin looked in surprise at her angry face.

'Lizzie,' he pleaded, 'don't be so unreasonable.'

'You think I am unreasonable?'

'I do.'

Even in her anger Elizabeth could not but appreciate the firm set of his jaw as he stared out through the wind-screen.

'I'm only doing my duty,' he pointed out.

'Very well, George – as long as you don't expect me to admire you for it. I suppose you'll get an extra stripe for this, or whatever it is they give to a policeman.'

They drove on in silence to Brancaster and Martin pulled up at the King's Head.

'Are you going to be long?' inquired Elizabeth.

Martin gazed at her sadly.

'What about lunch?' he asked.

'You can cancel the lunch,' said Elizabeth.

'But look here—' he began.

'It's no use, George. I see the idea. It was to combine business with pleasure; but your business and my pleasure don't happen to combine very well.'

'All right,' said Martin. 'I'll just be as quick as I can.'

She sat in the car and through the open door of the inn heard in snatches what was passing inside.

'Frederick Blossop, sir, that's my name.'

'You told me on the telephone that Mr Joseph Greening was here on November 27th.'

'Yes, sir.'

'You are quite sure?'

'Yes, sir.'

'Show me your books, please.'

'I beg your pardon, sir?'

'Your register.'

There came a shuffle of feet. Silence followed and then the heavy steps of the landlord returning.

'I don't seem to be able to find the entry, sir.'

'Give me the book, please.'

There came a rustle of pages.

'It does not appear that anyone stayed here on the 27th, 28th, 29th or 30th,' said George.

'Could I have a look, sir?'

Elizabeth imagined the book passing from one pair of hands to the other.

'You are quite right, sir. I must have made a mistake.'

'An odd mistake, landlord. I don't understand it. You may like to know that Mr Greening was seen in Ipswich on Friday, November 27th.'

'Indeed, sir. But that is no business of mine.'

'Then why did you tell me he was here?'

'It was a mistake, sir. Anybody can make a mistake.'

'Perhaps you can also explain how Mr Greening, who wasn't here during the week-end in question, contrived to send a post card from Brancaster to his landlady in Norwich.'

'Begging your pardon, sir, but that is not for me to say.'

'Begging your pardon, Mr Blossop, I mean to know.'

There came the sound of heavy breathing. Mr Blossop was apparently becoming indignant.

'And who may you be, I should like to know?'

'Inspector Martin from Scotland Yard, at your service.'

There was a pause.

'Well,' said Mr Blossop at last, 'that alters things. If I'd known it was the police. Such a 'armless, affable young man, too. Not you, sir, Mr Greening.'

'Come, Blossop, tell me the truth. No good comes of obstructing the police in the performance of their duty.'

'Well, sir, if you want to know, I sometimes oblige Mr Greening. He is a good friend of mine and I have known him for years. So when he goes up to town for a bit of fun, which 'appens every now and then, I'm in the 'abit of providing him with an alibi.'

'Do you often accommodate Mr Greening in this way?'

'Once in a while.'

'This week-end starting on November 27th was not the only occasion on which he has made use of you in this way?'

'Lord, no, sir. Many is the time.'

'Thank you, Blossop.'

'Don't mention it, sir.'

Elizabeth looked expectantly at the inn door and her eyes were surprisingly kind when in due course George appeared.

'Poor George,' she said unexpectedly and gave him a loving smile.

He came forward eagerly.

'Lizzie, darling, is this an olive branch?'

'You forgot to cancel the lunch,' she reminded him.

'So I did,' he admitted.

'It would be a pity to waste it – such a fine morning as it is; and I'm feeling better now. So I will help you to bear your disappointment like a man.'

'My disappointment?'

'I heard everything you said to Blossop and all that he said to you, and it means, of course, that poor Joseph is as innocent as an April lamb. One such alibi might have been dangerous for the silly mutt, but not a whole lot of them – unless you can prove that he committed a murder every time.'

Inspector Martin, leaning over the edge of the car, drew her close.

'Clever girl,' he said. 'But all the same I shall want to know what he was doing in London on the 27th.'

'Leading a man's life, I shouldn't wonder.'

'Perhaps you're right. I'll have a word with him after lunch – just a friendly word. You don't mind?'

'Not if you promise to be tactful.'

'I won't breathe a word to old Hedlam, if that's what you mean.'

Elizabeth squeezed his arm.

'Thank you, George. I'm glad you don't feel like a policeman all the time.'

Mr Blossop's lunch was a success and the Chambertin proved to be authentic. The afternoon, moreover, ended in a glorious winter sunset, and it was seven o'clock before Inspector Martin, having deposited Elizabeth at St Julian's, inquired for Mr Joseph Greening at his rooms.

Mr Greening, however, was not at home, having left for London at four o'clock on his motor-bicycle. His landlady stated that he would be returning to Norwich on the following day.

Surprised and inclined to be thoughtful Inspector Martin made his way back to his hotel.

He was by that time beginning to feel more like a policeman.

4   *Monday, December 7th*

Hermione Taylor looked across the desk at her employer. He was reading a letter dated Sunday, December 6th, which she had handed to him a moment ago. It was from Mr Joseph Greening of St Julian's Preparatory School, Norwich, and it stated briefly that the writer was proposing to call at the office on the morning of Monday, December 7th at ten o'clock precisely.

Throgmorton looked at his watch.

'He will be here in ten minutes,' he said. 'You had better not be seen again.'

He paused and added:

'I wish I had known of this before, Hermione. You are sure it was Greening who noticed you at Victoria.'

'Quite sure.'

'I shall have to get rid of him – send him about his business.'

'Why is he coming to see you?'

'How should I know? Perhaps he has already approached Sir Oswald Feiling and is ready to complete the transaction. Otherwise I shall break the connection and find another agent.'

Hermione took up her hat from the desk.

'I will make myself scarce,' she said, 'though I don't think he has any idea that it was me he saw in the Wilton Road. He knew Miss Haslett and was merely struck by the clothes I was wearing. I can't think why on earth you employed him. You knew he was a master at St Julian's.'

Throgmorton shook his head.

'There was no risk in employing a man who knew Miss Haslett. I did not know he had seen you wearing her clothes. You ought to have told me. That alters everything.'

'Well, it's no use arguing the matter. The man must be a perfect fool, or he would at once have realised the importance of his evidence. I can't think why he didn't go immediately to the police.'

'Perhaps he has gone to the police already. We simply don't know. It's a bad business, Hermione.'

There was a pause. Hermione stood uncertainly at the door.

'What are you going to do about it?' she asked.

He stretched out his hand and took her gently by the arm.

'Leave it to me, my dear. You may rest assured that I shall not lose sight of Mr Joseph Greening till I am satisfied that he isn't really dangerous.'

5   *Monday, December 7th*

Mr Joseph Greening, brushing his hair in front of the small looking-glass in his room at the Lowestoft Hotel, paused to pick up the note-case which his elbow had knocked from the dressing-table. From between its leaves a folded piece of paper had fluttered, and, retrieving this also from the floor, he read it again.

There was no real need for him to read it, for he had it already by heart. But always he hoped to find something which perhaps he had missed – something between the lines which might indicate what the writer really meant to do.

He finished brushing his hair and began to put on his coat.

The letter was from Phyllis Bateman and it was in the following terms:

'DEAR JOE,

'Why do you treat me like this? What have I done? If you are tired of me, why haven't you the courage to say so?

'Meet me to-night, *without fail*, at the cricket pavilion. Make it nine o'clock sharp, and if you don't come, Joe, there are going to be consequences. It is time we came to an understanding.

'Your loving
'PHYLLIS.'

The letter was typewritten. Phyllis always typed her notes, even down to the signature.

Greening frowned into the mirror. He supposed he would have to go and there would be further complications just as things were setting themselves right.

He glanced at his watch. Ten o'clock. In half an hour he was to see Throgmorton and he would have the satisfaction of paying the money-lender every penny he owed him. That at any rate would be an enormous relief. He would not now, of course, handle that commission for the purchase of the reliquary. But what was a commission, even if it amounted to a couple of hundred pounds, compared with a safe job? To that he must cling with both hands. He had no illusions about his value in the labour market. It was pretty well nil, and if he lost his position he would be on the streets within the year.

He had done wisely and well to go to Hedlam. Who would have thought the old man would be so kind and generous? Now he would be able with a light heart to tell the police everything that had happened. He would go to Inspector Martin as soon as he returned to Norwich. That would look better than waiting for Inspector Martin to come to him. He was glad of the opportunity to make the first move. He had expected to be approached before leaving Norwich on the previous day. Luckily, however, Inspector Martin had taken a day off, and no blame to him for that. Lizzie was a nice girl – a bit too ladylike for his taste, but young Martin was a serious fellow. Every man to his kind. Lightly come, lightly go was more to the liking of yours truly. Unfortunately, however, the formula did not always complete itself. Phyllis had come lightly enough, but showed no disposition to go, lightly or otherwise.

Phyllis was still a problem. To make things worse, she had evidently been talking – airing her grievances in the town. How else had Hedlam heard of the affair? Hedlam, perhaps, would help to deal with this difficulty as well. Hedlam was a man you could trust. It was a pleasure to be upheld and guided by such a man.

'You will see Throgmorton first thing on Monday morning,' Hedlam had said.

At one moment he had thought that Hedlam was going to suggest that they should travel together, for the old man was spending Sunday night with his mother as usual. Fortunately, however, there had been no such suggestion as to this. Hedlam always travelled first class, and Greening, with fifteen pounds a term off his salary, could less than ever afford such a luxurious form of locomotion.

The motor-bicycle must continue to serve his turn and not too efficiently at that. This time, on the way up, it had broken down at Ipswich. He had thought it was only a choked jet, but it had soon appeared that there was something seriously wrong with the ignition. Luckily the garage people had been unexpectedly accommodating. They had lent him a bicycle, not much of a machine, but in good running order, and he had reached London by nine o'clock in the evening.

Greening completed his toilet, descended for breakfast, and a little later started from the hotel.

He called at a bank on the way, and it was just ten o'clock when he entered Throgmorton's office.

The financier rose eagerly to greet him.

'Good morning, Mr Greening. This is quick work indeed. Have you seen Sir Oswald Feiling?'

'I have not,' answered Greening shortly. 'Nor do I intend to see him. I have decided, Mr Throgmorton, that I cannot act for you in this matter.'

Feeling very firm and brave he faced the man of means. For once in his life he had the whip-hand of his masters. But there was no movement in the heavy face or any gleam behind the horn-rimmed spectacles. The cold in the head seemed slightly better, but it still affected the vocal chords.

'I am sorry,' continued Greening with dignity, 'but I am afraid it does not suit my convenience.'

There was a short silence.

'As you please, Mr Greening,' said Throgmorton at last. 'But in that case I must inform you that it does not suit my convenience that you should continue to remain in my debt. You will therefore make arrangements to repay me in full by midday and you will, of course, return me the cheque I gave you on Saturday.'

Joseph smiled. He was enjoying himself.

'Set your mind at rest, Mr Throgmorton.'

He thrust a hand into his pocket as he spoke and pulled out his note-case.

Throgmorton sat still and impassive as a Chinese idol.

Greening opened the note-case. A paper fluttered down to the desk and lodged itself on the blotting-pad, wide open, under Throgmorton's eyes.

It was the letter from Phyllis.

Throgmorton was staring fixedly at the blotting-pad, but it was impossible to say whether the eyes behind the spectacles rested on the paper or were alive to what they saw.

'Allow me,' he said quietly, and picking up the paper he handed it across the desk to Greening.

Greening thrust it back into his pocket. He then handed to Throgmorton the cheque for a hundred pounds and began counting out the notes from his case. He had obtained them from Hedlam's bank only ten minutes ago. It went to his heart to see them pass so swiftly from his possession.

Throgmorton counted the notes carefully. Then he bent down and Greening heard the whine of a drawer.

'Your agreement,' said Throgmorton, laying it on the table. 'But I would remind you, before you destroy it, that you have forgotten the interest.'

'But I only borrowed the money ten days ago,' protested Greening.

'Ten days' interest at twelve per cent on thirty-five pounds,' said Throgmorton, 'that will be two shillings and fourpence, please.'

Greening, boiling inwardly, put the money on the desk and turned to go.

'Good morning, Mr Greening,' said the impassive voice. 'If at any time you require accommodation, you have only to let me know.'

'Thank you,' said Greening, and hoped that the bitter sarcasm in his voice would be appreciated.

A few minutes later he was walking down Shaftesbury Avenue towards the Circus. He had decided that he would not leave for Norwich until after lunch and it was still only eleven o'clock. At the bottom of Shaftesbury Avenue was the Revudeville. He had heard about it from Barton – a continuous show starting at eleven in the morning and ending at eleven in the evening. He paid a half-crown and entered. It was warm and comfortable and some of the turns were good.

He lunched at his hotel, packed his dispatch-case and started back to Norwich at about three o'clock. He reached Ipswich two and a half hours later, and there once more fortune refused to smile. His own machine was not yet ready. Would he wait for half an hour?

He waited for half an hour. He waited for an hour. At last the machine was ready. It ran exactly a hundred yards and then it stopped again.

He pushed it back to the garage and demanded to speak with the foreman. The foreman was apologetic. The connection had given way again. Would he wait for a couple of hours?

'I can't wait for a couple of hours,' protested Greening.

He was uncomfortably aware that, if he waited in Ipswich for a couple of hours, he would miss the appointment with Phyllis. He must meet Phyllis at nine o'clock, and, if he missed Phyllis, there would be consequences.

'May I go forward on your machine?' he asked.

'Certainly,' said the foreman. 'We will have this one ready for you to-morrow, sir. We shall make no charge for the substitute, of course.'

Greening clambered once more upon the borrowed bicycle.

It was ten minutes to nine as he passed the dark mass of Norwich Cathedral. The roads from Ipswich had been wet and greasy. He was cold, damp and miserable. But Phyllis was waiting and must be met.

He garaged the bicycle and walked in his overalls down the Aylsham Road. The cricket pavilion of St Julian's stood at the end of the field which lay at the back of the school, and it could be approached by a narrow lane. Greening walked up the lane.

'I must take a firm line,' he said to himself.

The cricket pavilion loomed in front of him, a dark shadow against the dark.

Greening left the path, pushed open a little gate and walked across a small strip of grass. His hand rested a moment on the wooden balustrade.

It was past nine, but where was the girl?

He halted a moment and listened.

'Phyllis,' he called.

There came a rustle from above and in front of him. She had apparently climbed the steps and was standing on the veranda.

Greening set his feet on the steps and began to mount.

'Phyllis,' he called again, as he reached the veranda.

There came a vague movement forward in the darkness and he leaned towards it.

Hands were touching his throat!

He recoiled and the hands shifted. He was gripped as in a vice. Thumbs were pressing low down on his neck beneath his ears.

He opened his mouth to scream but found he had neither voice nor breath – only an intolerable pain that filled the night and a sudden burst of stars.

Then darkness and an abrupt release from his agony.

CHAPTER VI

1 *Tuesday, December 8th*

Inspector Martin was worried. He had spent a sleepless Sunday night at the Maid's Head. Not all the comforts of that admirable house, one of the many in England where Queen Elizabeth was reputed to have slept, though they included a warm bed with a hot-water bottle between the sheets and a fire in the grate, had sufficed to soothe his troubled mind.

It was all very well for Elizabeth to assume that Greening's false alibi in Brancaster had no real bearing on the case. But the fact remained that Greening had lied as to his movements over the long week-end.

And now he had disappeared.

He had gone off to London and no one at St Julian's – Hedlam being also absent – could tell him why he was making the journey from Norwich to London a second time almost within twenty-four hours.

Early on Monday morning Martin had called again at the school. Still no news of Greening. Thereupon he had communicated with Scotland Yard and an all-stations' call had been sent out, giving a description of Greening with the number of his motor-bicycle and ordering his detention for inquiries.

In the evening had come a message from the school: Hedlam was back again and would speak to him on the telephone. The conversation with Hedlam, so far as it went, had been reassuring.

Greening, it seemed, had made a statement to his employer. As a result of that statement he had, on Hedlam's advice, gone to London to settle some urgent private business. He was expected back at St Julian's at any moment and he would then probably wish to make a further statement to the police.

Martin had inquired as to the nature of the statement. Hedlam had replied that Greening intended, among other things, to give a true account of his movements during the long weekend.

In response to Martin's inquiry whether Hedlam himself had anything of importance to communicate, the proprietor of St Julian's had represented that it would be better for Greening himself to put matters right with the police. Would Inspector Martin therefore come round to the school as soon as Greening returned, either that night or first thing in the morning?

To this arrangement Martin had rather doubtfully consented, and his doubts had been justified when, at 7 a.m. on Tuesday, he had found, on ringing up Hedlam, that Greening had still not returned. He had promptly informed Hedlam that he was coming round at once to the school.

He pushed open the painted gate with the brass plate and rang the bell. The front door opened and he walked down a corridor in the wake of a maid. A moment later he found himself in Hedlam's study. Hedlam was sitting, his rubber-shod stick beside him, under the bust of Socrates on the rosewood pedestal.

'No, Inspector. It is as I said. Greening has not yet returned.'

Mr Hedlam's tone was formal and rather weary.

'Then we must find out where he is,' said Martin promptly. 'It is essential that we get on to his traces as soon as possible.'

'I thought the police in this country had ample means at their disposal for that purpose,' said Hedlam dryly.

'The ordinary means are being used,' Martin hastened to assure him; 'but we are losing time. You alluded yesterday to a statement which he had made to you. Have you any objections to repeating it?'

Hedlam sat back and reflected a moment.

'I have no objections,' he said at last. 'Greening came to me in confidence, but I know that he meant to be equally frank with you on his return from London. As I said last night on the telephone, I would rather he spoke for himself, but in the circumstances . . .'

Hedlam broke off as a sound of hurried steps came from the corridor outside. The door of the study was flung violently open. Martin rose to his feet and turned to find Elizabeth on the threshold. Her eyes were very wide and large. One hand gripped the lintel of the door and the other was at her breast. Her mouth was trembling and, though she made to speak, no word came for the moment as she swallowed in her throat.

'What is it, Elizabeth?'

There was more than a touch of irritation in Hedlam's tone.

Elizabeth shook her head slowly like a swimmer breaking the surface.

'It's . . . it's . . . Greening,' she said. 'He has been found.'

'Found?'

'In the pavilion . . . swinging. He's . . . he's dead.'

Martin started forward. Her weight lay heavy against his shoulder and her face was chalk white.

'Hold up, Lizzie,' he urged.

Out of the corner of his eye he saw Hedlam dive beneath his desk. His bald head flashed a moment and then he was up again like a humpty-dumpty. In his hand was a bottle of sherry and a glass.

He moved round the desk as Martin supported Elizabeth to the arm-chair. Martin put his hand on the back of her head and pushed it forward, as he had been taught during the course in first aid which he had attended at the beginning of his career in the police force.

Hedlam limped to the other side of the chair, glass in hand. Martin took the glass and put it to Elizabeth's mouth. She drank a little and made a quick face of disgust.

'No, no,' she said.

Hedlam was patting her shoulder.

'A terrible shock, I am sure. But you can leave her to me, Inspector.'

Martin stood back a moment. He was reluctant to abandon Elizabeth.

'The school doctor is coming,' she said, and, even as Martin turned to the door, a tubby little man with pince-nez and a merry face, Fountain, the school practitioner, bustled into the room.

'What's all this?' he demanded. 'What is the matter?'

He pushed past Martin and went to Elizabeth, now lying back in the arm-chair.

'I'm all right, Doctor,' she said quietly. 'I have had a bit of a shock, but I'm better now.'

'Shock?' repeated the Doctor, feeling Elizabeth's pulse and producing a gold watch from his pocket. 'What's the trouble?'

'The trouble is in the cricket pavilion,' said Hedlam. 'Perhaps you had better go. Inspector Martin, this is Doctor Fountain.'

The doctor, still busy with Elizabeth, nodded at Martin, but with an urgent gesture she shook her wrist free of his grasp.

'I'm all right, Doctor – really I am. Please, Doctor . . . George . . . Go. Go at once, or someone may walk into the pavilion as I did.'

'Then sit quiet,' said the Doctor. 'Finish the sherry if you can. It won't do you any harm. I will see you again before I leave.'

The doctor quitted the room. Martin was waiting for him just outside.

'She found Greening in the cricket pavilion – dead, apparently,' he said as they walked down the corridor. 'Is it all right to leave her?'

'Nothing to worry about,' said the Doctor.

They turned to the left into a hall, beyond which, through long glass windows, appeared the cricket field streaming with mist. The doctor led the way and they passed across a stone yard to the wet turf, making for a small black and white pavilion backed by a group of tall elms. Together they mounted the wooden steps. Together they pushed open the door, which was slightly ajar.

Then they stopped.

A man was hanging from the metal strut, one of half a dozen that ran across the top of the single large room of the pavilion. He twisted slightly. His face was congested and terrible to look upon. His shoes were perhaps two feet from the ground, and near at hand lay an overturned chair.

Martin set the chair on its feet, pulled a knife from his pocket and cut the thin cord which was fastened to the strut. Together they lowered the body of Greening to the floor. The doctor bent over it, loosening the cord, which was tight about his throat.

'Not much doubt about this,' said Martin sadly. 'Hanged himself by the neck till he was dead, poor devil. Perhaps you will examine him, Doctor, while I telephone for the local police.'

Martin left the doctor in charge and moved to the door.

2 *Wednesday, December 9th*

Inspector Martin looked disconsolately at Chief Inspector McPherson, who leaned back in an office chair which creaked under his vast weight. Winter sunshine, streaming through a window above the Thames Embankment, gave an almost ethereal aspect to the big red face.

'Well,' said the Chief Inspector, 'accidents will happen. I'm not blaming you, but I should at least like to know why, after exploding Greening's alibi on Sunday, you didn't succeed in having him detained immediately. Something wrong there, surely?'

'Greening was expected back on Monday, and I was given to understand that he intended to make a statement. When he failed to turn up on Monday morning I sent out the usual instructions, but we were defeated by the merest fluke. Greening always used a motor-bicycle. He went up to London on Sunday afternoon, but his bicycle broke down and he left it at Ipswich in a garage there. He borrowed another machine on which he continued his journey to London and back again. The police were looking for the wrong number and one man on a motor-bicycle is very like another.'

The Chief Inspector grunted.

'Hedlam, you say, made an important statement?'

Martin looked at the open pages of his notebook, though he already had the story which Hedlam had told him clear enough in his mind. 'Greening, it seems, had been borrowing money from Throgmorton.'

'Throgmorton again?' interrupted Chief Inspector McPherson.

'Precisely, sir. Throgmorton lent him thirty-five pounds on November 27th and gave him a cheque for a hundred pounds on Saturday, December 5th. The second sum was apparently to cover a cheque which Greening had made out to the proprietor of a gambling establishment off the Tottenham Court Road. He was also having trouble with a girl, a Miss Phyllis Bateman, typist, employed by a firm in Norwich. Greening poured all this out to Hedlam on Sunday morning, and I must say that Hedlam was pretty decent about it. He gave the young man a good dressing down, but lent him enough money to pay his debts on the understanding that it would be deducted from his salary. He then packed him off to London to settle up with Throgmorton.'

'You have seen Throgmorton, of course?'

'I had a long interview with him this afternoon. Again he had nothing to conceal. He told me all about the loans to Greening. He states that on Monday morning Greening called on him at about ten o'clock; Greening repaid him the sum of thirty-five pounds plus two and fourpence interest, and returned him the cheque for a hundred pounds which Greening had received on Saturday. There is nothing to connect Throgmorton with the suicide.'

'Except that his name keeps cropping up,' grumbled the Chief Inspector.

'Greening,' continued Martin, 'went up to London on Sunday. He returned to Norwich on the following day and arrived some time during the afternoon or evening. The doctor reckons he must have been dead for roughly twelve hours when we found him, which would mean that he committed suicide round about nine o'clock on Monday evening last.'

The two men looked at one another.

'Odd,' said McPherson at last. 'Very odd indeed. Here is a young man who has just paid his debts and been given a second chance by his employer. Then, just as all his troubles are over and he should have been thanking his lucky stars, he runs into the cricket pavilion and hangs himself.'

Martin nodded.

'Well,' said the Chief Inspector, 'what does it all suggest?'

'It suggests very forcibly, sir, that we haven't yet got to the bottom of the affair. I can't believe that Greening had any hand or part in the murder of Miss Haslett. I knew him pretty well and he is not that sort of man. Nor was he the man to commit suicide unless he had been absolutely driven to it – and I should say that even then he would need a helping hand. I'm pretty sure in my own mind, however, that the murder of Miss Haslett and the death of Greening are somehow connected.'

'You can't get round the fact of suicide,' commented the Chief Inspector. 'Greening took his own life. There is no getting away from it.'

He paused.

'There will, of course, be a post-mortem?' said Martin thoughtfully.

'Naturally.'

'I should like someone from the Home Office to be in charge,' said Martin.

The Chief Inspector looked at him dubiously.

'What's this bee in your bonnet?' he asked.

'I want a copper-bottom verdict,' said Martin firmly.

'Why not the local man?'

'There is no harm in having a second opinion,' responded Martin.

'Very well,' said McPherson, 'If you insist. When is the inquest?'

'On Friday, sir, the eleventh.'

'Very well. Fix it up with the people over the way.'

'Thank you, sir.'

Thus it came about that Sir Wilfred Higgins of the Home Office received instructions that same evening to take an early train to Norwich on the following day.

3   *Wednesday, December 9th*

Hermione looked uneasily from one to the other of the two men. They were sitting in the office at 153 Shaftesbury Avenue. Throgmorton was in his accustomed place at his desk. Richard was striding up and down the small room holding in his hand a copy of the *Evening Standard*. It contained a paragraph which reported the suicide at Norwich of one Joseph Greening. Hermione lay back in the leather arm-chair.

'It was a mistake to employ a third party,' Richard was saying. 'I can't imagine why you are so scared of taking a hand in the business yourself. But if you must employ an agent, why give the job to a silly mutt who goes straight away and hangs himself?'

'Not a bad thing, as it happens,' said Throgmorton.

Richard paused in front of the desk and stared at Throgmorton resentfully.

'Are you suggesting that this suicide is going to help us to buy the reliquary? We shall now have to start again. Every day counts and we've wasted nearly a week.'

'I admit that Greening was a mistake,' said Throgmorton, 'and it might have had serious consequences. Greening has now been removed and I can make other arrangements.'

'What in God's name are you driving at? You sit there looking grim and mysterious when you ought to be getting on with the job.

Are you suggesting that the end of this poor devil is a blessing in disguise?'

'That,' said Throgmorton, 'is exactly what I do suggest.'

'Leave it alone, John,' Hermione begged. 'All this has nothing to do with our plans.'

Throgmorton turned upon her heavily.

'Limited liability for Richard – is that what you mean? No, my dear. He has been flinging his weight about long enough. He wants to know why it is a fortunate thing for us that Greening should have removed himself. I'm going to tell him.'

'No, John.'

Hermione, forlorn and terrified, stared at Throgmorton. Richard went to her and put an arm round her shoulder.

'What's all this about?' he demanded angrily. 'I've felt ever since I came back that something was wrong.'

'Richard, do please leave it alone.'

'I insist on knowing,' said Richard.

'I am telling you now,' said Throgmorton bluntly. 'Greening, as it happened, was a dangerous person. He had it in his power to give us all away.'

He paused.

'Ever heard of the Brighton truck murder?' he demanded suddenly.

Richard was standing very still. He had not yet realised the significance of the question, but there was no mistaking the heavy threat implied in the manner of the other man.

'What has the Brighton truck murder to do with us?' he asked.

Hermione noticed how white he had gone. What would he do when he realised the truth?

'Only that I am a principal and that you are an accessory after the fact,' said Throgmorton.

Hermione, sick at heart, looked in fearful astonishment at Throgmorton. Why should he be saying these things almost with satisfaction? Had he divined her interest in Richard?

'Fact?' stammered Richard. 'What fact?'

'Hermoine handed over to you in Paris the sum of seven hundred and fifty thousand French francs. How do you imagine she came by them?'

'Hermione told me that she had collected the money in Paris on your behalf. She did not go into details.'

'That was most considerate of her. I also was prepared to be considerate, but, since you seem disposed to underrate our difficulties, I think it time you assumed your full share of responsibility. You shall have the details, Feiling. Some of them are unpleasant. They happen to include among other things the Brighton truck murder. The money handed to you in Paris was obtained by cashing a lottery ticket which was once the property of Miss Haslett of Norwich.'

Richard put his hands on the desk to steady himself.

'The woman who was murdered?'

Throgmorton nodded.

Richard wavered a moment. Then he stiffened and thrust a hand out towards Throgmorton.

'Don't tell me. I don't want to hear it,' he muttered.

Silence fell between them.

Richard, fighting for self-control, gradually lost his pallor. The blood flooded back into his face. He seized Throgmorton by the arm.

'You blackguard!' he raged. 'You've let Hermione in for this.'

Throgmorton sat stolid in his chair.

'Nothing of the kind,' he said calmly. 'She came into it of her own free will and with her eyes wide open.'

Richard turned to her incredulously.

'Is this true, Hermione?'

Hermione, without looking at him, bent her head.

'So now,' said Throgmorton, 'you know how we stand.'

'God,' said Richard. 'Then it was murder. Is that really what you mean?'

He was leaning against the wall. His voice was low now but controlled.

'That's precisely what I do mean,' said Throgmorton. Abruptly he leaned forward. 'Now look here, Feiling,' he continued. 'Are you with us in this business or are you going to quit? You can please yourself. But pull yourself together and give me a plain answer.'

Throgmorton stooped to a drawer as he spoke and there came the clink of a glass.

Hermione felt something snap in her head. She reached forward, spreading out her hands.

'For God's sake,' she implored, 'I cannot bear any more of this.'

She was trembling violently. She thrust out a shaking hand.

'It is horrible . . . all this talking. It is done now . . . finished. Can't you stop talking about it? Can't we leave it alone? Richard . . .'

She felt a hand on her shoulder. Richard was holding to her mouth the gin and vermuth intended for himself.

'Take it easy, old girl,' he said. 'I'm standing by you in this business now to the end. Here, drink this.'

Hermione gulped. It was a strong mixture and she nearly choked as the liquor ran down her throat. She felt tears on her cheeks and dabbed them uncertainly with her handkerchief. She shrank back in her chair as she felt a fat but well-shaped hand on her other shoulder. Throgmorton had risen and was leaning over her from the opposite side. She made a violent effort.

'I am perfectly all right now,' she said. 'But for heaven's sake don't begin all over again. John . . . tell Richard some other time.'

Throgmorton was looking at her intently.

'All I want to say now is that I have good reason for not wishing to advertise my personal connection with the purchase of the reliquary. Greening seemed to me to be an ideal person for the task. He owed me money and he lived on the spot. I did not know that he had seen Hermione at Victoria. . . .'

Hermione gripped the fat hand on her shoulder.

'Very well,' he said. 'I will explain all that some other time. Our job now is to get the reliquary.'

'And without loss of time,' added Richard. 'Folliot will be sailing at the end of the week, or on Monday at latest.'

Throgmorton sat silent a moment in his chair.

'I will see your uncle myself,' he said at last.

'Good,' said Feiling. 'And now about ways and means.'

'You can leave all that to me,' said Throgmorton. 'I shall go to Norwich to-morrow morning.'

Hermione surveyed him doubtfully. Why was he looking at them both so strangely? She felt herself beginning to tremble again. Her nerves were all to pieces.

'Hermione!'

Richard was speaking to her and his hand was outstretched.

'Put your hat on,' he said. 'I'm going to give you a bit of dinner.'

Hermione felt herself gripped and pulled to her feet. Throgmorton made no sign.

'No objection?' Richard asked.

'None whatever,' said Throgmorton quietly.

'Anything we can do?' Richard continued.

'I can make my own arrangements,' responded Throgmorton.

Hermione took her hat from a peg on the wall. She gazed blankly into the small mirror below it, adjusting the hat with mechanical gestures. She felt drained of all feeling. This was not Hermione Taylor but a figure in a play. It was a rather terrible play and no one knew how it would end. That was Richard whose hands, oddly comforting, were helping her with her coat.

She turned back to the chair and picked up her gloves as Richard moved to the door. He smiled at her as she went towards him. Richard was her friend. There was safety in Richard.

'See you later,' said Richard to Throgmorton, as he pushed open the door.

Hermione looked back. Throgmorton was sitting again at his desk.

He looked towards them and nodded heavily.

CHAPTER VII

1   *Wednesday, December 9th*

Robert Hedlam, sitting at his mother's occasional table in her tiny flat in the Addison Road, surveyed his cards. He was not doing very well this evening – a fact which was due partly to bad hands but more especially to an irritating absence of mind.

Mrs Hedlam – Mrs Seymour Hedlam as her visiting cards still insisted – looked at him with a touch of disapproval. She liked her opponents to be keen and anxious to win, for the indifference of a losing gamester dulls the spice of victory.

It was Bobby's major, but she had a sixième and fourteen aces as well and Bobby would be rubiconed a second time – a sixième in spades. She discarded a small club, the knave of diamonds and the eight of hearts and received two tens and a knave in exchange. Decidedly she was in the vein, and she gently negatived Bobby's suggestions relative to a carte major or three kings.

Her mind went back to the early days when she had taught Bobby piquette in the bleak house in Camden Town, where they had lived when Robert Hedlam, senior, had been a clerk in a shipping office before he had successfully diverted his attention to the tea trade.

Since then they had played how many hands together? Young Robert, like his father before him, had always been ready to give her time and attention – a good son who, though he lived so far away in distant Norwich, never failed to visit her at least once a week in the little flat which she ran so neatly and comfortably on her small but adequate annuity.

Bobby to-night played the cards mechanically.

'I have rubiconed you, Bobby,' she declared with a satisfaction which was only marred by his evident lack of attention.

'So I observe,' he said quietly.

She found him looking a little yellow as she bent down and added up the score.

'That's four and ninepence you owe me, Bobby,' she said.

He fumbled in his pocket.

'Bobby, come here.'

He came obediently.

'Bobby,' she said, 'you've been overeating again and you've been drinking, too.'

She sniffed for confirmation.

'My dear mother, I am not a child,' he protested.

'Fifty in a month,' she said, 'but you still have no idea how to look after yourself. No tobacco and none of your filthy spirits for a fortnight, Bobby – and meat only once a day. Do you understand?'

Hedlam rose from the card-table and moved across to the fire. Fumbling in his pocket she watched him pull out a pipe and pouch.

'Now, Robert,' she said warningly.

Obediently he put them away. Mrs Hedlam sat back more comfortably in her chair.

'You are not worried about anything, by any chance?' she inquired after a short silence.

Hedlam turned his head.

'No, mother. It must be as you say. I must go slow for a bit on the eatables and – er – drinkables.'

'And a little syrup of Californian figs, I think,' said Mrs Hedlam, nodding her head.

Hedlam did not answer for a moment. Then he turned away from the fire.

'I shall be taking the early morning train to Norwich,' he said abruptly and moved towards the door.

2   *Friday, December 11th*

'Rolfe! Rover! Come on now.'

The two Gordon setters came obediently to heel. Sir Oswald Feiling winced as he turned to go home. He had felt a warning twinge of lumbago. He must get back to the fireside and a hot-water bottle in the small of the back.

He looked about him as he climbed a little stiffly over the stile. The flat fields belonging to Tenby Hall stretched away from him on either side, bounded by high hedges from each of which rose clusters of tall elms. There was much moisture in the air. The morning was repellent – distinctly repellent. So was life. Poachers had been reported in the five-acre wood and the Saxbys were due in a couple of days for a week's shootin'. Saxby was a spoiled sports-man and was apt to be critical. It was therefore distinctly annoying that Maggs, the head keeper, had been so discouraging. Birds were not plentiful this year. The weather in the spring had been vile and there had been serious depredations in the covers.

Sir Oswald strode disconsolately across the field. The pain in the middle of his back was becoming steadily worse. To his right the country rolled imperceptibly towards Gunton. Tenby Hall, his Palladian mansion, unnecessarily large and very costly to maintain, was still a good mile away. Who would be a member of the oppressed class of English landowners?

Sir Oswald pulled out his old-fashioned watch and whistled. Already it was noon and he had an appointment at 12.30. But why should he hurry? Let the fellow wait. Who was this Mr Bannister anyway? He was coming from London to discuss the purchase of an antique. He had seemed civil enough on the telephone, but that only meant, very probably, that the man was expecting to get something for nothing.

Well, business was business, and in these hard times it was advisable to lose no opportunity of turning an honest penny. Bannister was probably a dealer, and, though Sir Oswald knew next to nothing about antiques, his experience with dealers was extensive and he remembered just what value his father had set on his inherited collection of jewels, intaglias and mediaeval ornaments. Each one of them had its price, from the onyx carved with the representation of Hercules slaying the Hydra to the silver Communion cup said to have been used by Archbishop Laud.

Sir Oswald grunted as his lumbago gave another twinge and Rolfe, trotting at his heels, pushed a wet nose into his master's hand.

'Good boy,' said Sir Oswald gently, but his mind was far away.

He was thinking how different he was from his father. The old man had been a great collector and a great traveller in foreign parts in the 'sixties of the last century when collecting had been easy and even profitable. But all that was years ago. His father had been dead getting on fifty years, and there was no good reason to think about him this morning except to thank God, times being hard, that he himself had no particular interest in antiques except as being now and then conveniently marketable. The old man had known he would have to sell the stuff sooner or later, so there was no need to feel any qualms of sentiment in disposing of things which his father had spent his life in getting together.

'I'm not leaving you a fortune in cash, Oswald,' he had said on his death-bed, 'but if ever the Hall needs money, there is money enough locked up in the collection. But don't forget this, my boy. Never sell it as a whole. Offer it piecemeal or, better still, wait till you get an offer and stand out for your price. A keen collector will usually pay twice as much as he ought for a thing he really wants.'

The collection was still almost intact. Sir Oswald had done pretty well during the war out of his timber, and there had been no death duties to pay for many years, not since the old man had died. But there was no doubt that the shoe was beginning to pinch. He had been obliged to sell that Spanish monstrance in '30, or was it '31? He had clapped two thousand on to the price offered and got it. And now this dealer Bannister was coming along. What was he after, Sir Oswald wondered? Some of the rugs, perhaps. The old man had taken up with Eastern carpets towards the end of his life. There were stacks of them – some of them from Bokhara.

Bannister, perhaps, was one of those bandits from the South Kensington Museum. Sir Oswald's mouth set grimly. He had met those gentry before. They had tried to beat him down. They had even appealed to his public spirit. But nobody had any public spirit these days. It was as much as one could do to get a really satisfactory sentence from the bench on a notorious poacher caught red-handed among the pheasants. If the public funds did not run to paying a good price for a genuine article, then the public must go without.

He pushed open an iron gate and crossed the lawn in front of his house. A ramshackle taxi was waiting in the drive. So this fellow had arrived and was keeping his cab. That meant he would not be staying to lunch. Good!

Sir Oswald was met at the entrance of the french windows to the drawing-room by Jenkins, the butler. Jenkins had a salver in his hand and upon it lay a visiting-card.

'I have put the gentleman in the morning-room, Sir Oswald.'

Sir Oswald passed into the small hexagonal room known as the morning-room. It was a famous room, added by Sir Oswald's grand-father in the later days of the Regency and was intended to represent the inside of a parrot's cage. The walls were entirely covered by a most elaborate Chinese paper of golden bars through which could be seen exotic tropical foliage. The ceiling was a dome and there were sham recesses in the walls to hold seed and water, all elaborately painted to maintain the illusion. Old Sir Brutus Feiling, responsible for this work of art, had been a highly eccentric friend of Brummell and the Prince.

But the person awaiting him inside the cage bore little resemblance to a parrot. He was a broad-shouldered man wearing a grey suit. The face was round and colourless. Big horn spectacles covered the eyes. A brown leather brief-bag lay on a small table beside his chair.

'Sorry to have kept you waiting,' said Sir Oswald.

The stranger rose from the chair and bowed.

'Not at all, Sir Oswald. I hope I shall not have to detain you long.'

Mr Bannister, Sir Oswald noted, spoke with a city accent, a twang which his own stockbroker, Turton, used and which had always prevented Marian, his wife, from asking Turton to Tenby Hall.

Sir Oswald shook hands and motioned the other to sit down.

'Well, Mr Bannister, what can I do for you?' he said, seating himself at the ridiculous little Chinese lacquer writing-table at which his wife occasionally conducted her correspondence.

'I am a busy man, Sir Oswald, and, if you will forgive me, I will come straight to the point.'

'By all means,' assented Sir Oswald.

'I understand from the authorities at South Kensington that you have in your possession an interesting reliquary which once belonged, it is said, to Lucrezia Borgia.'

'That is so,' Sir Oswald warily admitted.

'I am anxious to purchase it, that is, of course, if it corresponds to the description which has been given to me.'

'Sharks,' said Sir Oswald.

'I beg your pardon.'

'Sharks,' repeated Sir Oswald firmly. 'I am alluding to your friends at South Kensington. They know already what I think of them.'

The stranger raised a plump hand and smiled.

'There I think we agree, Sir Oswald. I am aware of your dealings with those people. I understand they refused to go further than three thousand pounds.'

Sir Oswald looked at his visitor a little blankly. These business people were so very direct. And what did the fellow mean by agreeing with him so easily? There must be a trap somewhere.

'Believe me,' continued the stranger, 'I am not acting for the South Kensington authorities. I appear, on the contrary, for a rival collector.'

Sir Oswald stared with his air of habitual indignation at his visitor. He felt it was up to him to show that he could be as direct as anybody else.

'Five thousand pounds,' he said aggressively. 'That is my price.'

'A fair price,' said the other with the air of a man about to produce a cheque-book.

'Not a penny less,' said Sir Oswald.

He liked the sound of all this – two direct and hardy men of business getting together.

'One moment,' said the stranger. 'Would it be too much if I asked you to show me the reliquary?'

'Of course,' said Sir Oswald. 'Never buy a pig in a poke.'

Sir Oswald rose.

'If you would not mind coming this way,' he added.

The stranger also got to his feet. Sir Oswald led the way across the room and opened a door flush with the wall, painted to represent a door of the parrot's cage. It gave on to a small corridor which ended in a landing and a winding stair going up and down.

'The servants' stairway,' said Sir Oswald. 'The collection is in the corridor above.'

'After you, Sir Oswald.'

Sir Oswald climbed the stairs briskly. He had almost forgotten his lumbago. The gallery in which his father's treasures were displayed was dark, for Marian kept the blinds drawn in the winter. Sir Oswald snapped various switches and a long row of glass cases was flooded with light.

The stranger looked about him. Sir Oswald saw his glance stray to the Crivelli at the far end, but the Crivelli was not for sale, not until Tenby Hall was bankrupt.

Sir Oswald approached one of the glass cases and touched another electric switch, which lit the interior. In the centre of the case, on a cushion of white silk, lay the reliquary.

'A very fine example of the goldsmith's art of the fifteenth century,' said Sir Oswald, and hoped that he had got it right, having learned it by heart from the catalogue.

The stranger gazed at it for some moments in silence. He took a photograph from his pocket which Sir Oswald recognised – a picture of the reliquary which had appeared some years previously in the *Studio Magazine*, devoted to art and *objets de virtu*.

'You would like to handle it, I expect,' said Sir Oswald.

He produced a bunch of keys, unlocked the case and handed the reliquary to his visitor, who studied it. The man even produced a small magnifying glass. Finally he nodded briskly and turned to Sir Oswald.

'Yes,' he said, 'that is what I have been instructed to buy.'

'You are not buying it for yourself then?' said Sir Oswald.

'I thought I had made that clear, Sir Oswald. I am acting for a collector – an American gentleman. You must forgive me, but I am not at liberty to reveal his name. I was to offer you four thousand pounds and to go up to five thousand if necessary. I tell you this quite frankly as I realise that you are not prepared to take a penny less than you say. I'm afraid my client will not think very highly of my business capacity, but I know when I'm beaten.'

'Five thousand pounds,' repeated Sir Oswald firmly.

'Then may I regard it as a deal?' asked the stranger.

He produced, as he spoke, his brown leather note-case from his pocket.

'If you are ready to complete the transaction, I am prepared to pay here and now for the reliquary in notes. My client requires immediate delivery, and it would hardly be possible, if I gave you a cheque on London, for you to clear it in time.'

The stranger laid on the top of the adjacent case a small pile of one-hundred-pound notes. Sir Oswald picked up a bundle and inspected them carefully.

'If you will be good enough to count them, Sir Oswald.'

Sir Oswald was good enough. He was feeling slightly dizzy. He had never done business quite so rapidly before and never seen so many notes within his reach. Almost of their own motion they seemed to find a way into his pocket.

He picked up the reliquary.

'Come,' he said, 'I will give you a receipt.'

He led the way down the spiral staircase to the parrot's cage. There he sat down at the lacquer writing-table, pulled a sheet of paper towards him and began to write. As he finished and was blotting the sheet, a small cardboard box half full of cotton-wool was placed beside him.

'I ventured to bring this box,' said his visitor, 'in case you had nothing suitable.'

Sir Oswald placed the reliquary on the cotton wool and handed over the box with a little bow to Throgmorton.

'A glass of sherry,' he suggested, 'or perhaps you would stay to lunch?'

'Very kind of you, Sir Oswald,' said the stranger, bestowing the little cardboard box with great care in his waistcoat pocket. 'A glass of sherry, by all means, but I hope you will forgive me if I do not accept your invitation to lunch. I must return to London at once.'

He paused.

'Business,' he sighed.

Sir Oswald's hand wandered to his breast pocket. He nodded, as one man of affairs to another.

'Business,' he echoed. 'I quite understand.' Still feeling slightly stunned, Sir Oswald Feiling crossed the room and rang the bell.

3   *Friday, December 11th*

Inspector Martin sat to his desk in Scotland Yard and squared his shoulders. He slit the long, buff-coloured envelope awaiting him. Here at last was the report from Sir Wilfred Higgins of the Home Office on the body of Joseph Greening.

He skimmed the formal opening sentence and came to a sub-heading:

'Condition of the Body. – Well nourished male of approximately 27 years of age; no distinguishing marks or evidence of external violence other than those mentioned on page 7 of this report.'

He passed to a more important item.

'Post-mortem Appearances, External.'

This should be interesting.

He settled down in his chair and began to read:

'The face was congested. A shallow groove passing an inch and a quarter beneath the lower jaw ran obliquely towards a position behind the ears and was lost in the occipital region. This mark was caused by the rope, which had abraided the epidermis.'

'Damaged the skin,' translated Martin.

'The mark was pale with reddened edges.'

This concluded the post-mortem appearances external, a section followed by 'Post-mortem Appearances, Internal.' Here the learned doctor had spread himself. There were several pages of it.

'No dislocation or fracture of the upper cervical vertebrae, *but*' (and Higgins had underlined the conjunction) 'the inner and middle coats of the carotid arteries had been ruptured.'

Martin ran his eye further down the page.

'The lungs were normal. The trachea, but not the larynx, was injected. I found the condition of the brain to be highly congested. This led me to make a microscopic examination of the tissues of the neck, from which I drew the conclusion that death occurred from extreme pressure on the carotid arteries. Under the microscope the skin covering them showed distinct traces of punctiform haemorrhage.'

'Does that happen when a man hangs himself?' wondered Martin. He passed on to a section headed: 'Conclusions.'

'It is my opinion,' he read, 'that death was caused by pressure on the carotid arteries, and that the body was suspended after death to suggest the appearance of suicide by hanging. I am confirmed in this view by the complete absence of any signs of asphyxia and by the congested appearance of the brain.'

Inspector Martin drew a deep breath and read these words again. Then he suddenly woke up and pulled the telephone towards him, dialling a number.

'Is that Chief Inspector McPherson?' he asked. 'This is Martin speaking. May I come and see you at once, sir . . . Yes, most important.'

4 *Friday, December 11th*

'Sweetheart,' murmured Richard and kissed her again.

He held her back at arm's length and looked at her.

'Hermione,' he said, noting in a curiously detached manner that his voice was trembling, 'I believe you have the secret of eternal youth. Or are you growing backwards? You are more lovely every time I look at you.'

'Look as much as you like, if that's the effect it has. But you create for yourself illusions, as the French say. Or perhaps it is my pyjamas?'

'I adore you in black,' said Richard, and drew her again towards him.

She gave a sudden wriggle.

'That tickles, Dick.'

Her voice was low, husky with happiness. She turned suddenly, took his head in her two hands and kissed him passionately. How bright were her eyes.

'I love you, Dick, you understand?' she said. 'I have never loved anyone but you in my life. You won't ever let me go, will you?'

'Never,' he found himself saying. He slid his hands down her sides till they gripped her waist.

'Never, you sweet, precious idiot!'

He bent forward and kissed her throat as her head went back and her eyes closed. She put her hands on his shoulders and pushed herself away.

'I must go and make myself respectable, darling,' she said. 'John will be back at any minute now.'

'Honest John,' he groaned. 'I had almost forgotten.'

That, as she knew, was an exaggeration. They neither of them ever forgot honest John. John was quiet, stolid and ruthless. They never knew what he was thinking, but they knew there were no limits to what he might do.

Hermione rose to her feet and Richard also stood up, holding her hands.

'Just one more,' he said.

Their lips met. God! What was that? The door was opening. He governed an instinctive impulse to spring too suddenly away from her and moved quietly to the mantelpiece.

'That you, John?' he called evenly as the door opened.

Hermione, in her black pyjamas and dressing-gown, was already sitting in the arm-chair which he had quitted and lighting a cigarette.

The door of the sitting-room was now fully opened and Throgmorton stood on the threshold. He was in his overcoat, open down the front. There was a cigar in his mouth and a bowler hat on his head. His spectacles glinted in the electric light. Hermione stopped lighting her cigarette, rose from the chair and went to welcome him.

'Back already, John. Tell us what you have been doing. Richard and I have been mooning here for hours, wondering how you were getting on. I've been too worried even to dress myself properly.'

Throgmorton did not speak at once but produced from his waistcoat pocket a small white cardboard box with a lid secured by an elastic band.

'I have got it,' he said at last.

'Good man,' said Richard heartily.

'Well done,' said Hermione. 'I feel now that I can bear to put on a decent frock.'

She moved with a swift grace to the door and kissed Throgmorton lightly as she passed. Richard took a cigarette and lit it, furious to find that his hand was trembling.

'So you have got it, John?' he said. 'Any trouble at all?'

'None whatsoever.'

'How did you find the old boy? Huntin', shootin' and fishin' as usual?'

'He was quite civil,' answered Throgmorton.

He stood, oddly heavy and forlorn, in the middle of the room, with his bowler hat still on his head.

'What about a drink?' suggested Richard.

'Damn it,' he thought, 'I shall give myself away if I'm so confoundedly agreeable.'

'I don't mind if I do,' responded Throgmorton. 'I think I deserve it.'

He turned, as he spoke, to the oak cabinet where the drinks were kept and bent to the door.

'I will get some glasses,' said Richard.

He went from the room, leaving the door wide open. He was not going to steal a word with Hermione. That must be quite clear. Standing in a wooden cupboard in the kitchen he found glasses and brought them back. Throgmorton had set the gin and vermouth on the top of the gramophone cabinet, already marked with many rings.

Richard bustled forward with the glasses and set them down. Throgmorton poured out the gin with a steady hand.

'The whole thing didn't take ten minutes,' he said, as he added the vermouth. 'I didn't haggle over the price and your uncle seemed a little bewildered at my business methods. He keeps some very good sherry.'

'That would be the Amontillado '93,' said Richard.

He had drunk half his vermouth at a gulp and was feeling better.

'The old boy always produces it on special occasions,' he continued.

'Very dry, very pale and very old,' said Throgmorton. 'Chin-chin!' he added, lifting his glass.

'Sorry,' muttered Dick.

He never could get used to Throgmorton's old habit of waiting till everyone's glass was filled before starting to drink.

'Have another one?' he suggested.

'Mix it for yourself,' said Throgmorton. 'I'm going to get an evening paper. I thought we might go to a show to-night.'

He turned and a moment later came a sound from the front door.

Richard poured himself out another drink and wandered round the sitting-room. He was feeling better now. Throgmorton did not seem to have noticed anything, and there, at last, on the mantelpiece was the reliquary.

He set his glass down and opened the box. Then he moved away and, standing beneath the light, pressed the two little knobs which, as he alone knew, were concealed in an intricate pattern of the foliage. The bottom half of the gold case fell apart and he found himself looking once more, after a lapse of many years, at the carved emerald inside. He gazed at it a moment.

'I will show it to Hermione,' was his first thought, but he pulled himself up on his way to the door. Better wait till she was dressed. Throgmorton had noticed nothing, but there was no need to run any further risk. He shut the case and put it back in the cardboard box.

As he did so he glanced at himself in the mirror hanging above the mantelpiece. There was a mark on his cheek? He bent his head forward, tilting it a little so that the light fell directly upon it. Only too plainly there was a red mark and quite unmistakably it was where Hermione had kissed him. He felt his heart beginning to flutter again and, pulling out his handkerchief, made as though to rub his cheek. At that same moment, however, the door opened.

Throgmorton was back again. He held an evening paper in his hand and his face had a curiously tense expression.

'What's the matter?' inquired Richard sharply.

Without a word Throgmorton pointed to a headline which ran right across the front page.

'INQUEST ON NORWICH SCHOOLMASTER
VERDICT OF MURDER.
SUICIDE THEORY REJECTED.
EVIDENCE OF SIR WILFRED HIGGINS.'

Richard stared at Throgmorton, who nodded slowly.

'Yes,' he said, 'I killed Joseph Greening. He was not the man to kill himself and he obviously had to die.'

Richard felt that his bones were melting within him.

'But why?' he demanded. 'And how?'

'I killed Greening,' said Throgmorton heavily. 'Leave it at that. It is better, perhaps, for you and Hermione to know nothing whatever about it.'

CHAPTER VIII

1   *Saturday, December 12th*

'Just step in here, sir. The Chief Inspector will see you in a moment.'

'Thank you,' murmured Throgmorton.

Constable Butterworth, indicating one of the waiting-rooms at Scotland Yard, looked at Throgmorton respectfully. It was not usual for persons summoned to an interview with the Chief Inspector to seem quite so obviously at their ease. This was undoubtedly a cool customer.

Constable Butterworth left the waiting-room and tapped upon a door on the opposite side of the corridor.

'Throgmorton is here, sir,' he announced.

'Bring him along when I ring,' said the Chief Inspector, who was busy writing at his desk.

Chief Inspector McPherson ran his eye over the typed letter before him and signed his name with a flourish. Then he picked up the telephone and summoned Inspector Martin.

Waiting for Martin to arrive, he crossed to the window, holding in his hand the report of Sir Wilfred Higgins on the body of Joseph Greening. But he did not read it. He stood a moment, looking down at the Embankment and the river beyond. It was a dull, misty day and he could not see the Surrey side. Fog was driving up the river.

There came a tap at his door.

'Come in,' said the Chief Inspector, moving away from the window as Martin entered.

'Anything new?' demanded the Chief Inspector.

'There is a letter from a girl. Calls herself Phyllis Bateman. It seems she was to have met Greening at the cricket pavilion at 9 p.m. on the night of the murder, but that she received a telephone call in the morning from a man unknown cancelling the appointment.'

'We must get a statement.'

'Yes, sir. Sharpen of Norwich is seeing to that.'

The Chief Inspector nodded.

'Sit down, Martin,' he said. 'Throgmorton is waiting to see us.'

He moved across the room and sat down at his desk. Martin took a chair to his right.

He glanced at the paper in front of him.

'It is pretty certain, I see,' he said, 'that the murder was committed round about 9 p.m. on Monday.'

'Yes, sir. Certainly not earlier than eight and not later than ten, if the medical evidence is to be believed. Greening was last seen alive by the man who keeps the garage where he houses his motor-bicycle.'

'That was about half-past eight,' noted the Chief Inspector. 'We must ask Throgmorton exactly what he was doing on that evening. He will probably produce an alibi. The moment you are clear as to its general lines, I want you to slip out and check it. I'll give you the usual signal and I will keep him here till you return.'

'I understand, sir.'

'Good. Then we will have him in at once. Fill your pipe, Inspector. It is as well for us not to look too formal. After all, there is nothing against him so far.'

Inspector Martin produced his pipe and began to fill it. There came a sound of heavy boots in the corridor. The door was pushed open and Constable Butterworth stood aside to let Throgmorton pass.

Throgmorton was dressed in city clothes with a light grey overcoat over his short black jacket and striped trousers. He carried a bowler hat, which he set down carefully on the floor beside the leather arm-chair to which Chief Inspector McPherson was pointing.

Martin had seen many visitors in that special chair. It was placed so that anyone sitting in it should be facing the light and should also be on a lower level than the person at the desk. This was a small detail, but every little helped.

'We are sorry to trouble you, Mr Throgmorton,' the Chief Inspector began, 'but you will, of course, have seen in the newspapers an account of the inquest on Joseph Greening.'

'One could hardly miss it,' said Throgmorton quietly. He spoke with some difficulty, and Martin noted that he was still suffering from a severe cold in the head. The eyes behind the spectacles could not readily be seen.

'Greening,' continued Chief Inspector McPherson, 'was murdered. The medical evidence is quite conclusive. We are obliged, as a matter of routine, to question everyone who saw anything of Greening on the day of the crime.'

Throgmorton nodded.

'That includes myself,' he said without hesitation. 'Greening came to see me on Monday morning. I cannot tell you the exact time, but, if you will allow me, I will ring up my secretary and ask her to look it up in my engagement-book.'

The Chief Inspector waved his hand.

'There is no necessity to do that,' he said, 'provided you are sure that you saw him in the morning.'

Throgmorton nodded again.

'He came to see me at about ten or half-past, if I remember rightly, and stayed for about half an hour. He came on business. He left me as soon as the business was settled.'

'Will you tell us the nature of the business?'

'Certainly. He came to repay me some money which I had lent him.'

'And you did not see him again?'

'I did not see him again,' repeated Throgmorton quietly.

There was a short silence. Chief Inspector McPherson began to play with a paper-knife on his desk.

'Have you any objection, Mr Throgmorton, to telling us how you spent the rest of the day? I'm sorry, but it is a routine question, you know.'

Throgmorton gave a quick smile. The muscles of his mouth barely revealed his even teeth and contracted again.

'I quite understand, Inspector. You have your duty to perform. I am, of course, under no obligation to give an account of my movements on that or any other day. On the other hand, I have nothing to conceal. You may ask me anything you like, and I think I shall be able to show you that there is no occasion whatsoever to hold me under suspicion.'

Again he smiled, displaying his teeth.

'That will be very satisfactory to both of us,' replied Chief Inspector McPherson dryly.

'On Monday, December 7th,' continued Throgmorton, 'I left the office at about four o'clock. My secretary will probably be able to tell you the exact hour, or, at any rate, within ten minutes or so. I went by tube to my flat in Warwick Avenue, Number 219. I had intended to go that evening with my secretary to the cinema. There was a new film at the Marble Arch which we wanted to see. But I had a slight cold and my secretary went to the pictures with a lady friend. I myself stayed at home and listened to the radio. *Fledermaus* was being broadcast from Vienna and my secretary, who is musical, wanted me to hear it. But it was all Greek to me, though I must own there were some pretty tunes.'

'Your secretary,' interpolated the Chief Inspector, looking at the ceiling, 'was she with you any part of the evening?'

'Yes,' answered Throgmorton. 'My secretary . . . lives with me.'

'Lives with you?'

'We have lived together for several years. But we are not married. I feel it would not be wise – not in these hard times. But if things take a turn for the better . . .'

He waved his hand vaguely.

Martin felt a sudden violent dislike for this smooth creature.

'So you spent the whole of Monday evening listening to the radio?' said the Chief Inspector.

'Till midnight,' confirmed Throgmorton.

'Alone?'

'I was alone most of the time. My secretary, as I have said, went to the cinema with a friend. I had bought the tickets and I thought it would be a pity to waste them.'

Chief Inspector McPherson was tapping his front teeth with a pencil. It was the agreed signal and Inspector Martin obediently left the room.

In the yard outside waited a flying-squad car about to start on morning patrol. He begged a lift and the car dropped him twenty minutes later at the top of Warwick Avenue. Thence he made his way to No. 219.

Throgmorton's flat was, he discovered, on the third floor of an old-fashioned block, built, he judged, just before the war. There was no lift and the porter sat in a cubby-hole under the stairs.

Martin approached the porter and represented himself to be the agent of a wireless firm with a new machine to put on the market. Tactful inquiries soon revealed that at No. 219 Mr Throgmorton and one other family, a Mr and Mrs Chase, who also lived on the third floor, were the only tenants who owned a wireless set.

'You will be wasting your time here,' said the porter. 'The folks in these flats don't fancy the wireless. Between you and me, they are a bit behind the times. Some of them is even what you might call 'ostile. There is old Mr Prendergast, for instance, who is always complainin'.'

Inspector Martin pricked up his ears.

'Of what exactly does he complain?'

'He complains regular whenever Mr Throgmorton or the married couple play their wireless late at night. It's a bit 'ard on 'im, too, I will say. 'E lives between 'em, you see. Retired corn merchant, I 'ave 'eard, and keeps 'imself very much to 'imself, except when 'e talks to me. "Jenkins," 'e said to me only the other day, "that there wireless will be the death of me. I'll 'ave to move as soon as my lease is run out. Mornin', noon and night it goes on. Drives a man distracted."'

'Has he been complaining lately?'

'He's always complainin',' responded Jenkins. 'But 'e's not a bad old stick. Always comes out proper at Christmas.'

'Thank you, Jenkins,' said Martin, and came out proper with half a crown.

'Thank *you*, sir,' said Jenkins.

'I wonder if I could have a word with this Mr Prendergast?' said Martin.

Jenkins looked doubtfully at the man who was supposed to be selling wireless machines.

'Well,' he said, 'you could have a word with him, of course. But I shouldn't try to convert 'im, if that's what you 'ave in mind. That would only be givin' 'im a chance, and there's nothin' what would please 'im more. 'E would tell you exactly what 'e thinks. Pests. That's what 'e calls you wireless men. Licensed pests. 'E would be delighted to meet you, I'm sure. It would make 'im 'appy for a week.'

'You never can tell,' said Martin hopefully. 'I'll put it to him that if he buys a wireless set himself it will enable him to drown the others.'

'Well, if 'e bites your 'ead off, don't blame me, mate. And I should warn you, perhaps, that 'e's a gentleman in the prime of life, as you might say, and that 'e's six foot 'igh and uncommon muscular.'

'I'll chance it, Jenkins,' said Martin and set his foot upon the stairs.

Mr Prendergast, wearing a pair of grey felt slippers, himself opened the door of his flat. He was tall. He was powerful. He had the air of a man who might be easily moved to indignation.

Martin decided to drop his impersonation of a wireless agent. He produced instead his warrant card.

'I'd like a word with you, if I may, Mr Prendergast,' he said.

Mr Prendergast's eyes opened wide.

'Come in, Inspector,' he said.

Martin entered the flat.

'Sit down,' said Mr Prendergast.

Martin sat down.

'I have been sent to make a few inquiries,' he began, and looked at Mr Prendergast shrewdly. 'There have been complaints lately about the number and noise of the wireless sets installed in these flats.'

Mr Prendergast started. His eyes gleamed. He opened his mouth and the floods were loosed. His life was one long, lingering hell. Only his embarrassing financial situation – he was a retired corn merchant and his investments were far from what they should have been – had prevented him from long ago quitting this pandemonium. Besides, where could he find a refuge? Everywhere was the same infernal hubbub. What was coming over the world? You couldn't drink a cup of tea or take the simplest meal at a restaurant without somebody banging a piano or scraping a fiddle at you, and when one went home for a bit of peace and quiet this damnable crooning and tumtumming went on without stop or intermission. Mr Prendergast grew Biblical in his denunciation. He was encumbered. He was compassed about on every side.

With difficulty Martin finally checked the flow. He flicked the pages of his note-book and made a pretence of consulting it.

'We have had various complaints about specific dates,' he said. 'Can you, for example, cast your mind back, Mr Prendergast, to Monday, December 7th?'

'That I can,' said Mr Prendergast promptly. 'It was the night on which I so far forgot myself as to thump upon the wall, but it didn't do any good. The noise went on till well after midnight.'

'Who was the offender?' asked Martin casually.

'Tenant on the right,' said Mr Prendergast. 'Throgmorton he calls himself.'

'Thank you,' said Martin, closing his book. 'I take it, Mr Prendergast, that, if anything comes of this inquiry, you would be prepared to give evidence?'

'Most certainly I should be prepared.'

Mr Prendergast leaned forward and grabbed at the top button of Martin's waistcoat.

'I don't mind telling you, Inspector, that if there is no legal remedy for this nuisance I may one of these days lose control of myself, and take the law into my own hands. I'm a law-abiding man, Inspector, but when I lose control—'

'Quite so, Mr Prendergast. But I hope things will be better soon.'

Martin rose to go.

'A little drop of something,' suggested Mr Prendergast.

Martin shook his head.

'I am sorry, Mr Prendergast, but I have still a number of inquiries to make and very little time to make them. Very good of you, all the same.'

They shook hands and Martin descended the stairs. In the hall below Jenkins the porter was waiting.

'Any luck?' he inquired.

Martin shook his head.

'It was just as you said. Mr Prendergast is not at all partial to wireless.'

Martin paused a moment.

'He complained, by the way, that on Monday last his neighbour on the right was using his set right up to midnight.'

Jenkins nodded.

'That would be Mr Throgmorton.'

'Mr Throgmorton was at home on Monday evening?'

Jenkins, a little astonished by the question, nodded.

''E came 'ome with the lady what ought to be Mrs Throgmorton in the afternoon and passed me in the 'all. At five o'clock his wireless was in full blast and after that it never stopped till "Good night, everybody." It was all 'is doing, too, for 'is lady friend went to the cinema that night with *'er* lady friend, if you know what I mean, Mr Throgmorton 'aving a cold in the 'ed, as she told me in passing.'

'Then Mr Throgmorton spent most of the evening alone listening to the wireless?'

Jenkins nodded. Then his face lit up.

'You're not the police, by any chance?' he inquired.

'Scotland Yard,' said Martin briefly.

'You don't say?'

'Just making a few inquiries,' said Martin.

'I see, sir. Well don't be too 'arsh. I likes to 'ear a bit of music myself when I'm sittin' in the 'all, but I don't 'old with a man bein' a nuisance to 'is neighbours.'

Martin stood a moment with Jenkins at the corner of the street. A glance at the thin, spidery iron stairs which crept up the back of the block of flats showed him that the fire-escape was under repairs and that a large section of it had been removed at about twenty feet from the ground. Jenkins informed him that it had been in this condition for more than a fortnight.

Throgmorton's alibi for Monday evening seemed sound enough, and Martin, returning to the Yard somewhat discouraged, heard from Sergeant Babbington, who had been simultaneously dispatched to interview Miss Hermione Taylor at 153 Shaftesbury Avenue, that she had confirmed in every particular Throgmorton's account of how they had spent the evening of Monday, December 7th.

Chief Inspector McPherson shrugged his shoulders.

'I don't like Throgmorton,' he said. 'And I like still less the way he keeps cropping up. But we have nothing whatever against the man ... We shall have to let him go with apologies.'

2 *Saturday, December 12th*

Elizabeth looked up wearily from her desk. The task of combining her own duties with those of the late Miss Haslett was no light one, and she was beginning to feel the strain. From the half-shut window came the clamour of the school at play, shrill, incessant and meaningless. Elizabeth felt that if she stayed much longer at St Julian's she would hate all boys for ever.

There came a tap on the door and Mrs Simpson, the cook, who was very large and very clean in a blue-and-white check apron, appeared before her. Her massive face was expressionless.

'Yes, Mrs Simpson?'

'It's for the meenew, miss,' she said.

'Miss' was an afterthought, and Mrs Simpson looked with definite disapproval at a smudge of ink on Elizabeth's sleeve.

Mrs Simpson resented a world which, according to her standards, was irremediably a dirty place.

'You can eat off the floor in my kitchen any day,' she would often say, and there was no reply to this declaration except to retort that you were unlikely to be pleased with what you ate if Mrs Simpson had prepared it. Mrs Simpson advertised herself as a good plain cook and confined herself to dishes which she described as nourishing.

'Here you are, Mrs Simpson,' said Elizabeth, handing to her a typewritten sheet.

Mrs Simpson took the sheet and wrinkled her brows in an affected effort to decipher it.

Elizabeth had at first made out the weekly bill of fare by hand, but Mrs Simpson had pretended not to be able to read her writing.

Elizabeth had then resorted to type, but still Mrs Simpson went through the same irritating motions. Mrs Simpson did not love Elizabeth. She had hoped, on the death of Miss Haslett, to inherit the position of housekeeper, and she ascribed it to the shameless wheedling of a younger woman that she had been baulked of her expectations.

Mrs Simpson, breathing rather heavily, was running down the list with a forefinger.

'Rissoles on Wednesday,' she said, and it sounded like an accusation. 'Wouldn't 'ash be better for the boys?' she inquired.

'Rissoles,' insisted Elizabeth firmly.

Mrs Simpson's hash was not popular. The boys made rude remarks about it and Elizabeth could not find it in her heart to blame them.

Mrs Simpson tossed her large head.

'The Doctor,' she affirmed, 'is partial to 'ash.'

'The Doctor,' retorted Elizabeth, 'doesn't care in the least what he eats.'

'Lucky for you,' she almost added.

There was a silence while Mrs Simpson sought vaguely and unsuccessfully for some crushing rejoinder. Elizabeth, awaiting developments, looked from the florid figure in the apron to the grey, drab field seen through the window. At its farther edge was the cricket pavilion. The dull horror, which hardly ever left her now, returned. In that wooden shanty – it was scarcely anything more – Joseph Greening had died, not by his own hand, and she had been called upon to face the whole wearisome business of trying quite unsuccessfully to conceal the facts. The days following his supposed suicide had been bad enough – with the boys whispering in knots and parents telephoning every hour. The verdict of murder published in the newspapers of the evening before had provoked a further crisis, and her frayed nerves were stretched to breaking point. She had urged Uncle Robert to close the school for the rest of the term and start with a clean slate in January. But Uncle Robert was obstinate.

'And the accounts, miss?' interjected Mrs Simpson.

The words brought Elizabeth back with a shock. Mrs Simpson held in her hand a sheaf of bills and a small bundle of tradesmen's books.

'Just put them on the table, please,' said Elizabeth. 'That will be all this morning, thank you, Mrs Simpson.'

Mrs Simpson laid the bills down and left the office.

Elizabeth, looking through the books, noted that the total would be fourteen shillings less than the week before. That would please Uncle Robert.

But Uncle Robert had gone to Town to spend a few days with his mother. That, she felt, was in the circumstances, inconsiderate. Moreover, he had forgotten, in the flurry of his departure, to sign a cheque, or, rather, she had forgotten to remind him. The bills would accordingly have to wait till he returned, and she did not know when that would be. Uncle Robert's week-ends with his mother were apt to extend well beyond the limits of Saturday to Monday.

Uncle Robert was faddy about his bills. His cheque was normally drawn on Saturday morning and the bills paid promptly on Saturday afternoon.

Elizabeth sighed and then smiled. Here was an excuse to get away herself for a few hours. If Uncle Robert did not return before Monday morning she would go up to Town with the cheque-book. It was not a very good excuse, but it would serve. She would have a few quiet hours in the train, and she might be able to fix up a lunch with George, and do some useful shopping for Christmas. She would also be able to visit her dentist. There was a tooth which had been troubling her for some time and was really hurting at last.

Uncle Robert would think her journey to Town extravagant and unnecessary. He might even chide her for neglecting her responsibilities.

'But I shall go,' said Elizabeth firmly, 'for what you need, young woman, is a change of scene.'

3   *Saturday, December 12th*

Richard Feiling, sitting in the office at 153 Shaftesbury Avenue, looked at his watch. He rose from his chair and walked across to Hermione.

'Nearly one o'clock,' he said. 'Come along and have some lunch.'

Hermione did not seem to hear.

'Come,' he said sharply. 'I'm sick to death of this infernal office.'

Hermione raised a white face.

'Don't bully me, Dick. I have had about as much as I can stand.'

He bent over the chair and put his arms about her, but she did not respond. It increased his uneasiness to find her in the grip of a torment for which he had no remedy.

'It is going to be all right,' he urged.

Hermione turned towards him, and Richard perceived that she was far away in some secret hell of her own.

'Come, sweetheart, it is one o'clock and I am hungry.'

He tried to sound convincing but his mouth and tongue were dry.

'It's over two hours since he went to Scotland Yard. Why are they keeping him?'

At that moment the telephone bell rang sharply. Richard made a movement towards the receiver, which stood on the desk beside him, but Hermione pushed him aside.

'No,' she said, 'this is my job. You are not supposed to be here.'

She seized the instrument.

'Maitland Investment Trust,' she said, her voice taking on as by magic an impersonal business note.

A long pause followed.

'Very good,' she said at last. 'I will be back in the office by two o'clock. Yes, the letters are ready for signature. Good-bye.'

She hung up the receiver and turned to Dick, a slim figure in a black business frock. But Richard saw only the fear in her eyes.

'They are detaining him,' she said.

Richard felt as though a hand had closed about his heart.

'It was John who telephoned. He told me to carry on as usual, and even asked whether the letters were ready.'

'Probably he was not alone,' answered Richard. 'Did he say when he would be back?'

Hermione shook her head.

'Probably,' continued Richard, 'they are still checking his movements.'

'We must assume in that case that the police sergeant didn't believe what I said to him just now.'

Richard passed his hands over his front hair. It was damp at the roots. He must somehow pull himself together.

'Hermione,' he pleaded, 'it's no use upsetting ourselves in this way. If the police hold on to John they will presumably send for us; and, if they don't hold on to him, he will be back soon and tell us all about it. That is all there is to it. So, for God's sake let's get away and have a spot of lunch.'

He made a dreadful effort to end upon a light note and walked brightly to the door. Hermione seized her hat and joined him on the stairs. Instinctively his arm went round her and she leaned a moment heavily against him.

He thought he caught the words 'Oh, Dick!'

It was very dark on the stairs, for the offices were old-fashioned and had no lift.

Suddenly he saw over her shoulder the figure of a man standing on the floor beneath. Instinctively he drew back.

'Had lunch yet?'

It was Throgmorton's voice, very cold and steady.

'No,' said Richard. 'We were just thinking about it.'

'Then come along,' said Throgmorton. 'I'm starving. I refused to lunch at the Yard.'

'John!' – it was Hermione's voice – 'John, what has happened?'

'I'll tell you at lunch.'

'No, John, tell us now.'

They stood a moment on the dark stairs. Then Throgmorton made a movement towards the office.

'Very well,' he said, 'but there is nothing much to tell.'

Was this man a murderer? Had those hands, one of which was gripping Richard's elbow and pushing him lightly up the stairs towards the office which they had just left, crushed the life out of Miss Haslett and Joseph Greening?

They stood all together in the office. Throgmorton was hanging up his hat and coat. Richard glanced at Hermione. She was standing – very pale – by the little typewriter desk in the corner. Throgmorton moved across the room. He bent down and there came the inevitable clink of bottles.

'A little drink,' he suggested.

His face was smooth, but there was no smile on his lips nor presumably in his eyes behind the heavy tortoise-shell glasses.

'John, for God's sake, what has happened?'

Throgmorton deliberately set the bottles of gin and vermouth and the glasses upon the table before him and as deliberately began to pour their contents into the patent cocktail-shaker.

'Nothing has happened yet,' he said quietly.

Richard looked at him, and again he tried to believe that this man had twice committed murder. There was nothing alive about him except those hands that poured the liquid slowly and carefully into the shaker.

Hermione, looking at him, was shaken with a gust of rebellion.

'Why did you kill him, John? What on earth possessed you?'

The head with the yellowish-white hair turned slowly in her direction.

'Greening had it in his power to destroy us.'

'You had no reason to believe he would go to the police,' said Hermione, 'and I don't believe he knew it was me that he saw at Victoria. Probably he never gave the matter another moment's thought.'

Throgmorton looked at her coldly.

'It is true that he might never have gone to the police,' he said. 'It is also probable that he did not realise that it was you whom he met at Victoria. But we are not going to risk our lives on assumptions and probabilities. Greening had it in his power, if his evidence ever came into Court, to hang us both – you, Hermione, as well as me. He may not have recognised you at Victoria, but he most certainly perceived that some woman unknown was masquerading as Miss Haslett. The police would at once have seen that my alibi for the 28th was valueless. I should have had to account for my movements on the 27th. They would not, in that case, have had far to look for my accomplice.'

Richard drained his glass and set it down unsteadily on the table.

'Why didn't Greening go to the police at once?' he demanded.

'Greening was a respectable schoolmaster. He was afraid that, if he went to the police, his escapades would come to the knowledge of his employer.'

'Escapades?'

'He contrived, while he was up for the weekend, to spend at least seventy pounds and to sign a worthless cheque for part of the amount.'

'But in that case,' put in Hermione, 'we had nothing to fear from him. He would never have gone to the police.'

'On the contrary,' said Throgmorton. 'I feel pretty certain that he had made up his mind to do so. He had somehow got free of his complications. He came to me with money to pay his debts, and he refused to act for me in the matter of the reliquary. This could only mean that he intended to put himself right with the authorities. It was necessary to act at once, and I followed him that day to Norwich.'

'Had you any definite plan in your mind?'

The voice of Hermione was low. To Richard she seemed at once frightened and fascinated.

'You can't make up your mind to murder a man in the morning and carry out your intention in the evening without running a terrible risk,' she added.

'I am coming to that,' answered Throgmorton quietly. 'I was enabled to carry out my intention by an almighty stroke of luck. Greening paid me in notes. He was careless in handing them over, or perhaps he was nervous. Anyhow, he dropped his note-case and a slip of paper fell from it on to this desk. It was a typewritten letter and I could read it easily, for it was right under my nose. It was an urgent appeal from one Phyllis telling him to meet her at the cricket pavilion that night at nine o'clock without fail or – I remember the exact phrase – "there would be consequences". After Greening had left I thought the matter over. It seemed to me that if I could contrive to side-track the girl, whoever she might be, I could take her place at the rendezvous. I made my way as fast as I could to Norwich by car. The note had been typed on headed paper, the address of some solicitors in the London Road. I did not even know the girl's surname, but I went to a telephone-box, rang up the office and asked to speak to Miss Phyllis. There again I had a bit of luck, for she answered the telephone herself, which, after all, was natural enough since she was secretary to the firm. I said I was a friend of Mr Greening and told her that Mr Greening had gone to Town and would not be back till the following day. I was a little mysterious. I said that he had told me the whole story and that I had spoken to him very strongly about the matter. The unknown girl appeared to be pleased with this development. I went on to say that she would shortly hear from Greening without fail. Then I rang off. My ruse was successful, and, when I reached the cricket pavilion, which was easy enough to locate, there was no Phyllis. Greening was only a few minutes late, and the rest you know.'

There was silence as he finished speaking. After a moment Richard turned his head slowly and looked at Throgmorton. Were the eyes dead or alive behind the spectacles? To Richard he had become a figure of doom, inhuman and mysterious.

'What are we to do now?' he asked.

Throgmorton turned slowly towards him.

'Henceforth,' he said, 'I must regard myself as under suspicion, and I shall assume that the police will have me shadowed. How long will it take you to get rid of the reliquary?'

'I telephoned to Folliot this morning,' answered Richard.

'Folliot?'

'The American who is buying it. He is starting for Norway a day earlier than he expected and he sails from Hull on Tuesday afternoon.'

'That is all to the good,' said Throgmorton. 'We will go to Hull together in the car. Is he certain to buy the reliquary?'

'No doubt of that,' said Richard.

'Fix an appointment with him at Hull on Tuesday morning. He must give us a draft on New York. Meantime, Hermione, you will book three passages on the *Ile de France*. It is a French boat and it leaves Southampton at 2 p.m. on Wednesday. We will pick up another boat at Cherbourg.'

'Do we book in our own names?' asked Hermione.

'Certainly not,' said Throgmorton. 'Book for Mr and Mrs Anderson accompanied by Mr Pritchard. You can leave your passports with me. I will see that they are in order.'

He ceased and looked at them both. There was a moment's silence.

'You said you were likely to be followed,' said Richard at last. 'Wouldn't it be better for me to go alone to Hull?'

Throgmorton looked at him steadily.

'I think not,' he said. 'I believe that you intend to play fair with me, Richard, but you might take fright and bolt from so dangerous a couple as Hermione and myself.'

He laid a gentle hand on Hermione's wrist as he spoke, and Richard noted the effort it cost her not to flinch from the contact.

'We have committed murder, you see,' he said softly.

'But what in God's name do you intend to do?' Richard stammered. 'The police will be trailing us every inch of the way.'

Throgmorton smiled.

'I had not forgotten that,' he said. 'I shall not see either of you again till Monday. On Monday afternoon you, Richard, will kindly arrange to be at the Norfolk Hotel, Charing Cross, at half-past four. Have the car outside ready for the journey to Hull. I shall telephone and tell you where to pick me up. Meanwhile Hermione will get the steamer tickets and come to the office here on Monday as usual.'

'What will you be doing in the meantime?' demanded Hermione.

'In the meantime,' said Throgmorton, 'I shall disappear.'

'Disappear?'

Throgmorton raised his glass.

'A very necessary precaution, is it not? Between now and Monday morning the police must lose sight of Mr John Throgmorton of the Maitland Investment Trust. I think it may even be unwise for you to be seen again to-day in my company.'

He paused.

'Here's luck to us,' he said, and drained his glass.

CHAPTER IX

1 *Monday, December 14th, 3 p.m.*

Inspector Martin sat disconsolate in front of a heaped basket of letters. Another three or four hundred correspondents were claiming to have seen the mysterious Mrs Beck, tenant of Mrs Carroll, and her equally mysterious friend with the black patch over his right eye and the brown beard. Crosby would be distinctly annoyed when he saw what the weekend post had brought to hand. He had already sifted thousands of similar communications and returned only that morning from Coventry on the last of many fruitless errands of confirmation.

Inspector Martin was beginning to doubt whether Mrs Beck had ever really existed. 'Like Mrs 'Arris, there's no sich person,' was his dawning conviction. Hundreds of clues had been examined, but all to no purpose. That was what came of advertising for public assistance.

All this was discouraging enough, and, to crown all, Sergeant Babbington, instructed on Saturday morning to keep Throgmorton hence-forth in view, had promptly lost sight of him on Saturday afternoon. It seemed that Throgmorton, on leaving the Yard, had gone straight back to his office. Thence he had emerged about an hour later and walked down to Piccadilly Circus tube station. Babbington had followed him down the moving staircase, but Throgmorton, instead of continuing on his way to the trains, had, at the bottom suddenly crossed from the descending to the ascending escalator. The Sergeant had followed hard upon him, but had lost his quarry in the press. He could not even say whether Throgmorton had deliberately thrown him off the scent or had merely in all innocence changed his mind and his direction in that abrupt and disconcerting fashion. Martin, addressing harsh words to Sergeant Babbington, had sent out a number of men in search of Throgmorton, but all these efforts had been so far unavailing. Throgmorton had disappeared as from four o'clock on Saturday afternoon and he had not yet returned to the office in Shaftesbury Avenue, though his secretary Miss Taylor, it seemed, was there as usual.

There was nothing to associate Throgmorton directly with the Norwich murders. But indirectly he had been connected with both victims, and the two murders were themselves obviously linked. Veronica Haslett and Joseph Greening had both been killed in the same fashion and presumably by the same hand.

Miss Haslett had been murdered for her money, though nobody knew what had become of it. Why had Greening been murdered? Probably because he knew something about the previous crime. But what had Greening known? His movements during the long week-end had been most minutely investigated, the only result of it all being the suppression of a gambling club off the Tottenham Court Road, a most inadequate return for all the time that had been expended.

Inspector Martin turned over the file in front of him. At that moment, however, the telephone sounded sharply. He picked up the receiver.

'Mr Robert Hedlam to see you, sir,' said a voice. 'It's by appointment, he says.'

'That's all right. Send him up.'

Martin had for the moment forgotten this engagement. Hedlam had rung him up that morning from his mother's house in the Addison Road, asking if he might call, and Martin had agreed, fixing the interview for three o'clock. What Hedlam wanted with him at Scotland Yard he could not imagine.

Martin turned to receive his visitor – a shabby apparition in the afternoon sunlight. He looked old and worried. That, perhaps, was only the effect of his bald head and the crumpled over-coat, neither grey nor black, smudged and sprinkled with tobacco ash. He came in, leaning on his rubber-shod stick.

'Good afternoon, Mr Hedlam, how is the ankle?' Martin inquired.

'Better, thank you, Inspector,' said Hedlam and sat down in the leather arm-chair.

Martin raised his eyebrows at the word 'Inspector.' It seemed that this was to be a formal interview.

'Well, Mr Hedlam, what can I do for you?'

Hedlam did not reply for some moments. What was the matter with the old boy? He seemed nervous and ill at ease.

'Inspector,' said Hedlam, twisting in his chair, 'I am afraid I have a confession to make, and I fear, when you hear what I have to say, that you will conclude that I am not a little to blame.'

He paused.

'I must hear what you have to say first,' said Martin with a smile.

Hedlam leaned forward.

'It is this, Inspector,' he said earnestly. 'I'm afraid I have been concealing from you, quite unconsciously, a fact which has an important bearing on the cases you are investigating.'

It was Martin's turn to lean forward.

'Yes?' he prompted eagerly.

'You will remember,' continued Hedlam, 'that on the morning

of Tuesday, December 8th, when we discovered poor Greening in the pavilion, I made a statement to you concerning his movements during the long week-end. I was, in fact, repeating to you a confession which he had made to me on the previous Sunday morning.'

Martin nodded.

'A very useful statement,' he said. 'We acted upon it at once and we found, on questioning Throgmorton, the moneylender, that it was correct in every particular.'

'Yes, Inspector, but by an incredible lapse of memory I omitted to tell you something which I have since come to realise may lead you to a solution of all your problems.'

Martin looked unbelievingly at the shabby old man in front of him.

'In that case,' he said dryly, 'the sooner you repair the omission, the better.'

Hedlam swallowed hard and continued.

'Greening stated in his confession to me that outside the station at Victoria on the afternoon of Saturday, November 28th, he ran into a woman wearing Miss Haslett's clothes and bearing on her face and neck the port-wine disfigurement which was perhaps the most distinguishing characteristic of the dead woman.'

Martin stared at his visitor.

'Say that again,' he said.

'He ran into a woman wearing Miss Haslett's clothes and bearing on her face—' began Hedlam obediently.

But Martin interrupted him.

'Miss Haslett, as we know, returned from Paris on that Saturday afternoon. We need no further confirmation as to her movements.'

Hedlam shook his head.

'You do not understand me, Inspector. Greening did not say

that he had met Miss Haslett. He said that he had met a woman wearing Miss Haslett's clothes.'

Martin half rose from his chair. His arm brushed the desk and a file in front of him fell unheeded to the floor.

'You don't mean—'

'That is just what I do mean, Inspector. The woman was not Miss Haslett.'

'Was Greening sure of that?'

'He was practically sure. The matter worried him considerably. You see, Inspector, if the woman he saw was not Miss Haslett, it would follow that Miss Haslett, whom you assume to have been murdered later that very day, was already dead. How, otherwise, could another woman have been wearing her clothes? You see that, Inspector?'

Inspector Martin, beyond speech, stared at his visitor. His mind was working rapidly. Already he had begun to reconstruct the whole case. Meanwhile, here was an old gentleman who had withheld this information for nearly a week asking him whether he *saw*.

'Yes, I see that,' he said at last, his indignation suddenly aroused. 'But there is one thing I do not see. I do not see why you did not yourself realise that this evidence was vital. Why on earth didn't you tell me about it when you made your statement to me in Norwich last Tuesday?'

Martin, in his vexation, had almost forgotten that Hedlam was Elizabeth's employer.

'Really, Mr Hedlam,' he continued. 'I can hardly believe it possible. You make an official statement and you omit the most significant part of it. I am sorry I express myself so warmly, but I hope you will realise how exasperating this must be to me and to my colleagues.'

Hedlam blinked his pale blue eyes and swallowed nervously.

'I'm very sorry, Inspector. I fully realise that from your point of view the evidence which I am placing before you this morning is most important. But everything in life depends on the point of view. I am not a policeman, Inspector. Consider my state of mind on the morning in question. Poor Greening had just been found, killed, as we thought, by his own hand. Naturally I was thinking almost entirely of *him*. I told you of his troubles and difficulties and of his association with Throgmorton. I suppose it is not easy for you, as a trained investigator, to believe that I entirely forgot to mention this other circumstance.'

Martin, moved by the evident distress of the old man, nodded slowly.

'That's all right, Mr Hedlam,' he said. 'I must be thankful that you did at last remember. When did the evidence first recur to you?'

'It was the verdict on poor Greening that set me thinking. As you know, Inspector, I am partial to a quiet game of chess in the evening. It stimulates the faculties. Your opponent makes a move. You ask yourself why he made that move. You study all its implications. I began to think of this problem of yours in the same spirit of detachment, and I came at last to certain conclusions. You may think it very strange, Inspector, but it was only when I had worked the whole problem out for myself that I realised with a shock that you yourself were still in ignorance of the very fact on which my own solution was based. I remembered only then that I had not told you of poor Greening's encounter with the woman at Victoria. The human mind works curiously at times.'

'Very curiously,' said Martin dryly.

He paused and added:

'What *is* your solution, Mr Hedlam?'

'The two crimes were committed in the same way and therefore by the same hand. They were committed by a man who knew that Miss Haslett was in possession of the lottery ticket. The same man had also an intimate acquaintance with poor Greening and his financial difficulties. This man had a female accomplice who went to Paris on November 28th, wearing Miss Haslett's clothes. She assumed Miss Haslett's characteristic disfigurement so that, when inquiries were made, strangers would identify her as Miss Haslett both in Paris and during the journey there and back. This woman unfortunately ran into Greening at Victoria, and Greening thus had it in his power to connect her with the crime. Presumably she reported the fact to her male confederate, who was thus obliged to commit the second crime in order to cover the first.'

Martin was nodding rapidly.

'Admirable,' he said with conviction, and looked in all the greater astonishment at his visitor, who sat on the edge of his chair very earnest and pink in the face. The old man certainly had his wits about him, but why on earth hadn't he made use of them before?

'Throgmorton is the only person who fills the bill,' continued Hedlam. 'Greening, moreover, mentioned a female secretary, and she, if I mistake not, was his accomplice. She saw Greening on his first visit to the office and she would naturally assume that he had recognised her at Victoria.'

'Capital,' said Martin grimly. 'They ought to make you Public Prosecutor.'

Hedlam waved a plump hand.

'These, of course, are merely assumptions,' he continued. 'But you have at least one definite fact which will enable you to renew your investigation on altogether different lines. You have always assumed that the first crime was committed on the evening of

November 28th in the belief that it was Miss Haslett herself who made the trip to Paris. You may now assume that the crime was actually committed on the previous day. You have examined Throgmorton, and he was probably able to account for his movements on the night of the 28th. But what was he doing on Friday, November 27th?'

Martin had ceased to listen. The facts of the case were rearranging themselves in his mind well in advance of their orderly exposition by the proprietor of St Julian's. Miss Haslett had been murdered not on Saturday, November 28th, but on Friday, November 27th. She had been taken to the house in Cadbury Road by no less a person than Throgmorton himself, thinly disguised with a beard and a black patch over his right eye. There were, as he had begun to suspect, no such persons as the mysterious Mrs Beck or her bearded companion who had been sought in vain over the length and breadth of England. Mrs Beck, who had taken the house in Cadbury Road a day or two before the murder, could be none other than the female accomplice who had cashed the lottery ticket in Paris.

He could not but admire the brutal cunning of it all. Nothing, as he well knew, was so difficult to bring home as a crime misdated, and in this case the criminals, with little risk to themselves, cleverly using the port-wine disfigurement on the cheek and neck of Miss Haslett, had arranged deliberately for the victim to be reported alive and well on the day following the murder. They had only to count on the false Miss Haslett being seen only by persons who had never met Miss Haslett in real life, such as the officials of Imperial Airways and the lottery clerk. These people would, of course, easily remember the tell-tale mark, and had in fact done so. It had been sheer bad luck that the woman, in the course of her impersonation, should have run into Joseph Greening at Victoria Station.

But Hedlam had finished speaking.

'Exactly,' said Martin, 'what was Throgmorton doing on the night of November 27th?'

Hedlam leaned forward eagerly.

'And the secretary,' he said. 'We must not forget the secretary.'

Martin, eager to be at work again, rose from his chair.

'No, Mr Hedlam,' he said. 'On the other hand, we must not take too many things for granted. All we can infer for the present is that the murderer, whoever he may be, had a female accomplice.'

Hedlam blinked rapidly as he, too, rose from his chair. He seemed disappointed that so little should be made of his masterly exposition.

'Well,' he ventured, 'I can only hope that what I have said may be of some assistance to you.'

'I'm sure it will,' responded Martin a little absently. 'I'm sure it will,' he repeated more heartily as he accompanied Hedlam across the room.

'Still limping, I see,' he added as he stood with Hedlam at the door.

'As you observe,' said Hedlam plaintively, 'though I must admit that the new treatment is really most satisfactory.'

'New treatment?' echoed Martin politely.

'My Norwich doctor recommends me not to lie up with it but to use the foot, which should, of course, be suitably bandaged, as much as possible. But it's a slow business.'

Martin opened the door.

'Well, good-bye, Inspector,' added Hedlam. 'I hope we shall see you again shortly at St Julian's. Elizabeth will, I am sure, be delighted.'

'I shall hope to run down at any rate for Christmas,' said Martin. 'Thank you, Mr Hedlam and good afternoon.'

He closed the door and moved swiftly to his desk.

He picked up the telephone.

'That you, Babbington?' he said. 'Go straight round to 153 Shaftesbury Avenue. Detain for inquiries and bring to me here anyone you find on the premises. Take a couple of men with you. I want in particular Throgmorton's secretary, Miss Taylor. If she is not at the office, go round to the flat in Warwick Avenue.'

Martin hung up the receiver, dialled a number and spoke again.

'Emergency call to all stations,' he announced. 'John Throgmorton is to be detained wherever found for the murder of Veronica Haslett.'

But where *was* Throgmorton to be found? Had this evidence of Hedlam come too late? What on earth had possessed the old man that he should have remained stone-blind to the significance of his revelation for nearly a week?

Martin rose from his desk. He must see Crosby and report these developments to the Chief Inspector.

With an angry gesture he swept into the wastepaper basket a pile of letters all purporting to have come from correspondents who claimed acquaintance with the mythical Mrs Beck and a mystery man with a brown beard and a black patch over his right eye.

2   *Monday, December 14th, 3.45 p.m.*

Elizabeth left Harrod's with a guilty mind. When she came to think of it, the excuse which she had given herself for coming to London was pretty thin. The Norwich tradespeople could perfectly easily have waited a day or two for their money in spite of the fact that Uncle Robert was usually so punctilious in these matters. The tooth, of course, had been trouble-some, but, after all, there were good dentists in Norwich.

The truth of the matter was that, in escaping to Town, she was, in effect, kicking over the traces. She was being monstrously over-worked, and this was an act of rebellion. Uncle Robert would prob-ably read her the Riot Act, but, if he was at all unpleasant or grieved about it, she intended to be perfectly frank with him. It was time he was made to realise that his poor little orphan girl was fed-up, and she must make it clear that a successor would have to be found for poor Miss Haslett. She could not continue indefinitely doing the work of two.

'I was unjust to that woman,' reflected Elizabeth as she boarded an omnibus. 'I used to think she did nothing but fuss about. But I know better now.'

There were a hundred and one small but exasperating details. Jones minor had only four pairs of socks instead of eight and all were in holes; Lethridge never remembered to go to the dispensary for his cod-liver oil; Ponsonby major must go to the dentist; Harris had torn his trousers and, by the same act, run a splinter into his nether parts.

So thank God for Christmas and the prospect of a week at Cromer with George!

But George, poor darling, was worried too. He was making no progress. It would mean a great deal for him if he solved the mystery of the Norwich murders. But, alas! he had confessed to being no nearer a solution than he had been at the start.

Elizabeth descended from the 'bus a little beyond Olympia and began to walk down Auriol Road towards the block of flats in the

Gwendwr Road, where old Mrs Hedlam lived. There, if you like, was a lucky old lady, parked comfortably in London with a small but adequate annuity and refusing gently but firmly to live in Norwich. Elizabeth found it difficult to blame her. She frankly marvelled at the old lady's interest in life, and hoped that, when she reached that age – for Mrs Hedlam must be at least seventy – she, too, would have interests, like bridge or the movies, that would enable her to have so firm and vivid a hold on life. So many old people died of sheer boredom, having survived their friends and watched their children depart from their lives.

Not that Uncle Robert had departed from his mother's life. On the contrary, a more devoted son it would be difficult to find. Not a weekend passed without his going to see her. But Uncle Robert, however, could afford all this devotion. The routine of St Julian's he could safely leave to his staff. All Uncle Robert had to do was to collect the fees, supervise the details of management and pay the bills – when he remembered to do so.

Elizabeth found herself ringing the front-door bell. Maggie opened the door. Maggie was almost as old as Mrs Hedlam and had been with her for forty years.

'Good afternoon, Maggie,' said Elizabeth.

'Well, I never!' exclaimed Maggie. 'I didn't know you was in Town, miss.'

'I came to do a bit of Christmas shopping,' answered Elizabeth, 'and I wanted to see Mr Robert. Is he at home?'

'Yes, miss. He came in a few minutes ago, but I think he is having a bath. Come in, miss, and I will tell the mistress you are here. You would like a cup of tea, I expect.'

Elizabeth passed into the small sitting-room, glancing at the watch on her wrist as she did so. It was already a quarter to four. She would have to hurry if she was to be at Liverpool Street to catch the 4.32.

But she could scarcely pursue Uncle Robert into his bath. She had a swift vision of him sitting there, his bald head gleaming like a large egg in a cup.

At that moment Mrs Hedlam came briskly into the room, her jet ornaments, of which she wore a large number, rustling pleasantly on the black silk of her dress.

'Elizabeth, my dear, how nice,' she said, kissing her warmly. 'What a pleasant surprise.'

Elizabeth hastened to offer her the half-pound box of expensive chocolates which she knew the old lady liked.

'Christmas shopping,' she said.

'Thank you, my dear, how lovely!'

The old lady's eyes lit up as she perceived the name of the makers.

'Charbonnel and Walker! How naughty of you!'

'I'm afraid I cannot stay for tea, Aunt Lucy. I must go back to Norwich by the 4.32. I was just hoping to catch Uncle Robert.'

'I thought you had come to see *me*,' said the old lady archly.

'And you, too, of course,' added Elizabeth.

'Robert came in only a few minutes ago,' continued Mrs Hedlam. 'I think he is having a bath. Is it business, Elizabeth?'

'He has forgotten to make out the weekly cheque and I have no money at the school to pay the tradesmen.'

'Dear me, how careless of him. I will go and ask him at once. Where would he keep the cheque-book?'

'It would be in his dressing-room, I suppose,' said Elizabeth. Where did men keep their cheque-books?

The old lady bustled out of the room and returned a moment later with a leather brief-bag.

'Robert is in his bath,' she said, 'but the cheque-book would be here, I expect.'

She handed the bag to Elizabeth.

'Sit down at my writing-table and make out the cheque. I'll get him to sign it at once.'

Elizabeth took the bag. There were, she noticed, two marks of burning in the leather, one of which was a real hole. How careless of Uncle Robert. He must have got some acid on it somewhere. Mechanically she slipped the catch and opened it.

But the bag was empty.

'I am afraid the cheque-book isn't here,' she said.

'Wait,' said Mrs Hedlam. 'I'll tell him you have called.'

Elizabeth waited. The bathroom was at the end of the passage in full view of where she sat.

Mrs Hedlam knocked.

'Robert, Elizabeth is here.'

She could not hear Uncle Robert's reply, but Mrs Hedlam briefly explained the situation. There were further murmurs from behind the door. Then she heard her name called.

'Elizabeth, dear, Uncle Robert has his cheque-book. Have you a fountain-pen? He will sign a cheque in blank and you must fill in the amount yourself later.'

Elizabeth produced a fountain-pen from her bag and took it to Mrs Hedlam. A bare arm came through a gap in the door as she turned away.

Elizabeth, while the cheque was being signed, powdered her face in the Queen Anne mirror in the hall.

'Here you are, dear,' said Aunt Lucy at her elbow. 'And now, if you are to catch your train, you must run. Next time I hope you will find time to stay a little longer.'

'Yes, Aunt Lucy. Sorry to run away. Good-bye.'

'Good-bye, dear.'

Elizabeth, thrusting the cheque into her bag, moved quickly down the stairs.

She was secretly relieved at having missed her scene with Uncle Robert. She had screwed herself up for the delivery of an ultimatum, but felt no great eagerness for the battle.

She had vowed to herself to have it out with the old gentleman next time she saw him, but this afternoon didn't count, for she had not seen him at all – nothing but a bare arm through a gap in the door.

'Crisis adjourned,' she said to herself as she hailed a taxi in the street outside.

3   *Monday, December 14th, 4 p.m.*

'An actress, you say?' said Martin thoughtfully.

Crosby nodded.

'When she can get a shop,' he responded.

'Suggestive, isn't it?'

The two inspectors were sitting in their room at Scotland Yard. Babbington had just reported on the telephone that Miss Hermione Taylor had been brought from the office in Shaftesbury Avenue and was waiting below.

'No news yet of Throgmorton's car?' Martin asked.

'Sergeant Hutchins has just returned from the garage where he keeps it in the Harrow Road. It seems it was removed on Saturday by a man called Feiling. I'm already after *him*. It seems he's a nephew of Sir Oswald Feiling of Tenby Hall, Norwich. I'm trying to get Sir Oswald on the telephone.'

'Norwich again,' commented Martin.

'I got Feiling's description from the man at the garage and there is now an all-stations' call out for him as well as for Throgmorton, and we have also sent out a full description of the car. Here it is: Morris Oxford 1928, dark blue saloon, number XZ 4063.'

'Did you fix up that arrangement with the BBC all right?'

Crosby nodded.

'The descriptions will be broadcast to-day in the news bulletin.'

'I wonder how Feiling comes into it.'

'It was probably Feiling who handled the money in Paris. The woman impersonating Miss Haslett went over to Paris and cashed the lottery ticket. Feiling came to London later with the goods. That hypothesis fits in with the fact that the customs officials at Croydon found no notes in the woman's suit-case on her return from Paris.'

'I suppose we are right in assuming that it was *not* Miss Haslett who cashed the ticket.'

'Quite. I've just put a call through to the lottery office. The clerk on being informed that the port-wine mark was not sufficient to establish the identity of the woman who cashed the ticket was able to give us further particulars. In particular he remembers thinking that the port-wine mark was unfortunate for her, as she was quite young and would not, he said, have been bad-looking at all but for her disfigurement. That impression doesn't tally with Miss Haslett, but points to a younger woman. If necessary, we will have the man over and confront him with Miss Taylor.'

Martin touched a bell and two minutes later Hermione Taylor entered the room in the company of a constable.

'Sit down, please,' said Martin.

He signed to the constable to leave them and looked with interest at the woman in front of him.

She was pale but outwardly composed. She was undoubtedly good-looking, with a face full of character and eyes of a hazel brown. The addition of a port-wine mark would serve, perhaps, to emphasise her comeliness.

'Miss Taylor,' Martin began, 'I think you already know why we felt it necessary to ask you to come here, and I would first inquire whether you would care to make a statement?'

She looked at him, raising her head slightly.

'Tell me, Inspector, am I under arrest?'

'No, Miss Taylor. The position is that you are detained for inquiries.'

He paused a moment, but she did not offer to speak.

'I will be quite frank with you,' he continued. 'It will depend on what you tell us this afternoon whether or not we shall find it necessary to obtain a warrant. It is my duty to add that anything you may say may be taken down and used in evidence.'

There was a short silence. The woman in the chair was looking him fully in the face.

'In that case,' she said, 'I would prefer to consult a lawyer.'

A hard, wary look had come into her eyes.

'Certainly, Miss Taylor, but I would point out that technically we are asking you to assist the police, and that for such a purpose you would not normally require legal assistance.'

The woman looked at him appealingly.

'Is that really fair to me?' she asked. 'You are trying to have it both ways. If I refuse to answer your questions now without legal advice you will regard me as suspect. If, on the contrary, I do answer them here and now and you are not satisfied, my position will be even worse.'

'It is not for me to advise you,' said Martin shortly, 'but in your own interest I should say that you can have nothing to lose by being entirely frank with us.'

She considered this a moment.

'Very well,' she said at last. 'I will answer your questions. What is it you want to know?'

Martin opened the file in front of him.

'I want you, if you will be good enough, to give me an account of your movements and those of your employer, Mr Throgmorton, on Friday, November 27th, and Saturday, November 28th.'

Miss Taylor wrinkled her forehead a moment.

'Mr Throgmorton has already, I believe, made a statement?'

'Mr Throgmorton,' said Martin, glancing at the file, 'has made a statement which covers his movements on the evening of November 28th. I would ask you, however, to begin, shall we say, from the evening of November 27th. I see from my file that Miss Haslett called at the office in Shaftesbury Avenue at about 6.15 on that day.'

'I was not present at her interview with Mr Throgmorton,' answered Miss Taylor. 'I showed her into the office and I showed her out again afterwards.'

'That would be at what time precisely?'

'Somewhere about seven o'clock or a little later.'

'I see. Did you ever see Miss Haslett again?'

'No.'

'How did you spend the rest of the evening?'

'It is some time ago and I am afraid I cannot remember, but I think I went to the cinema. It was a Friday night and I often go on Friday.'

'Did you go with anyone?'

'Yes, with Mr Throgmorton.'

'I see. Which cinema was it?'

'The New Gallery in Regent Street.'

'Do you remember the film?'

Miss Taylor again wrinkled her forehead.

'Now that I come to think of it, I do remember,' she replied. 'It was an American film. *Lady for a Day* I think it was called.'

'And afterwards?'

The pale face of Miss Taylor suddenly flushed.

'Afterwards we went home.'

'To the flat in Warwick Avenue?'

'Yes. I live with Mr Throgmorton, as I think you know.'

The flush had left her cheeks, leaving them dead white again. Martin nodded.

'We come now to Saturday, November 28th.'

'I worked in the office all day with Mr Throgmorton. He gave a party in the evening. But he has told you about that.'

Martin again made a pretence of consulting the file.

'Yes,' he said. 'Then you simply confirm Mr Throgmorton's statement?'

'Certainly.'

Martin leaned back in his chair.

'Have you any idea, Miss Taylor, where Mr Throgmorton is at present?'

'Not the slightest idea,' answered Miss Taylor.

'You parted on friendly terms?'

'Is that of consequence?'

'I am only thinking it a little strange that he did not give you any indication as to how he intended to spend the week-end.'

'He gave me no indication whatever.'

'Is it usual for him to leave you without letting you know where he is going or what he is doing?'

'I know nothing of his private life except for that part of it which he devotes to me.'

'Am I to infer that he is in the habit of disappearing without your knowing in the least how he spends his time away from you?'

'It is part of the understanding between us that I shall not inquire into these matters.'

'Then you cannot help us to discover his whereabouts?'

'I am afraid not.'

'Are you acquainted with a gentleman of the name of Feiling – Richard Feiling, nephew of Sir Oswald Feiling of Tenby Hall?'

Inspector Martin noted the start she made on hearing the name and an increase in the sullen reserve of her manner.

'Mr Feiling is a friend of mine.'

'Can you tell us where we are likely to find him this afternoon?'

'I know nothing of his movements.' She added as though involuntarily: 'Why do you ask?'

'We are anxious to find Mr Throgmorton, and Mr Feiling is at present in possession of Mr Throgmorton's car. Is it possible that they may be motoring together somewhere?'

'It is possible.'

'But you have no idea where they would be likely to go?'

'I have no knowledge whatever of their movements.'

'Thank you, Miss Taylor.'

Martin nodded at Crosby, who sat with pencil poised over his note-book, taking down a shorthand report of the interrogation. Crosby closed his book.

'Will you sign this statement when it is typed?' Crosby asked.

She turned to Crosby.

'Of course I will,' she said.

'Thank you, Miss Taylor.'

She looked back at Martin.

'May I go now?' she asked.

'Not just at present,' he replied. 'I am afraid we must request you to remain here a little longer.'

Miss Taylor made a slight and rather helpless gesture with her hands.

'Very well,' she said quietly.

CHAPTER X

1   *Tuesday morning, December 15th*

Jacob Crawley, agricultural labourer, plodded steadily through the dawn to his work. He was heavy with sleep and not even the cold air of the morning sufficed to enliven his senses.

First he must turn the ewes into the five-acre field. Then Farmer Higgins would expect to find him back in the barn. It was a dog's life, but he thought himself lucky to have a job at all at his age. It was all very well for young Bill Harris to talk of the old making way for the young, but what was the use of talking like that if the old had nowhere to go except to the 'House'?

He was not going to the 'House' yet, not as long as he had the use of his arms and legs.

He turned his weather-beaten face to the morning mist. His huge boots, studded with nails, battered the hard tarmac of the London-Cambridge Road. Stiffly he climbed a stile and set out across a dun-coloured field. This was a short-cut and it would save him half a mile. He made steadily for the corner of High Tree Wood and the clearing where the sheep were penned.

Running into the wood was a low hedge and beyond it a little by-road deep in mud.

Jacob Crawley fumbled in the pocket of his old corduroy coat.

'Dang it,' he muttered as he approached the wood. There was his tobacco all right, twisted up in a screw of paper just as Wilcox had handed it to him over the counter the night before, but he had forgotten his pipe – a splendid new pipe which the young gentleman who had stood a round of drinks at the Green Man two nights before had left behind him. Jacob, who had pocketed the pipe as soon as the departing rear light of the young gentleman's car had vanished up the dark road, had now left it behind himself on the second shelf of the kitchen dresser. The day had begun badly for Jacob Crawley. Not ten yards away, on his right, was the gloomy wood, leafless and with moisture dripping from bough and twig.

He set his foot upon another stile. Half-way over he paused and sniffed the air. There was an odd smell somewhere about. It was probably one of those dratted motor-cars. Jacob had no use for motor-cars, not since the day one of them had knocked him down in the High Street. No bones had been broken, and all he had got out of that business was five shillings and a quart of beer.

Jacob turned to his left in the mud and came to an abrupt halt. A couple of yards away from him was a twisted mass of metal. Once it might have been a motor-car, but it had passed through the fire – and a pretty fierce fire it must have been.

Jacob moved forward and laid a cautious hand on the wreckage. It was quite cold.

The car had not been there yesterday. It had come there during the night.

Jacob looked round.

The car was hidden from the main road by the wood, and hidden also from the village. It must have been a rare old blaze, he said to himself, but there had been no one to see it except the sheep a hundred yards away. He moved alongside the car, walking to the front of it. Here would be a fine story to be recounted at the Green Man, and worth, he should say, two or three pints to him.

Suddenly, in stepping forward, he held his foot arrested in mid-air, and then moved backwards like a pulled horse. For he had seen something at the wheel of the car – a dreadful mass, blackened and unshapely, but still to be identified as the body of a man.

2   *Tuesday evening, December 15th*

'Here goes,' said Elizabeth to herself. 'It's now or never.'

Uncle Robert was sitting back in his leather arm-chair beside the fire in the room known as the Doctor's parlour. She glanced at him resentfully. He had just remarked that she was looking tired. That gave her an opening and it was too good an opportunity to lose.

'Naturally I am tired, Uncle Robert,' she said.

She tried to speak in an objective tone of voice. She wanted to seem quite dispassionate. But she sounded inevitably a note of protest. The note was aggravated by her sufferings. The dentist in London had not made a success of the failing tooth. Sometimes it hurt a little less and sometimes a little more.

'After all,' she continued, 'I am doing the work of two strong women, and I find it exhausting to be with the boys all day.'

Uncle Robert leaned forward and re-lit his pipe. His pipe was always going out and he was mainly a smoker of matches. Perhaps it was because he could not hold it in his teeth – the gaps being so awkwardly placed.

'I'm sorry, Uncle,' went on Elizabeth, 'but I think it's time we considered finding a successor to Miss Haslett. The present arrangement cannot continue indefinitely. Besides, it isn't really good for the school.'

Uncle Robert turned his head and nodded kindly.

'Of course,' he said. 'We will see about it presently. I was wondering whether to advertise or perhaps we might ask Tabetha and Jones to recommend us a suitable woman for the post.'

Elizabeth, with her decks cleared for action, was disconcerted by this bloodless victory.

'We should not want her, of course, until after the holidays,' Uncle Robert continued. 'It's only ten days now to Christmas. You will be going to Cromer, won't you, my dear?'

Elizabeth felt herself flushing slightly.

'I have been invited,' she said, 'but it isn't certain.'

Hedlam raised his bushy brows, which contrasted so oddly with his gleaming skull.

'I thought it was all arranged,' he said.

'It all depends on George,' Elizabeth pointed out. 'He is working day and night on that dreadful case.'

Hedlam was lighting his pipe again.

'The case can hardly keep him beyond Christmas,' he said reassuringly, flinging his match into the grate, a habit of his which was a perpetual annoyance to Emily, the housemaid. 'He has only to lay his hands on Throgmorton, and that broadcast message last night cannot fail to lead to his arrest.'

He paused and puffed a moment silently.

'Criminals make odd mistakes,' he said reflectively. 'It was surely most foolish of the man, knowing himself to be under suspicion, to run away in his own motor-car. It's bound to be traced sooner or later. This wireless, my dear, must be of great assistance to the police in the exercise of their profession.'

Elizabeth glanced at the clock.

'We shall get the second news bulletin in a few minutes,' she said. 'Perhaps there will be another call to-day.'

'No need to worry,' said Hedlam. 'George will get his holiday, never fear.'

He smiled and for a moment there was silence.

'By the way,' he added, suddenly removing his pipe, 'what would you like for a Christmas present? What about some silk stockings?'

Elizabeth nodded gratefully. She was feeling contrite. Uncle Robert was not a bad old boy, really. He always asked what you wanted for Christmas or birthdays instead of buying at random the last thing in the world that was either suitable or pleasing.

'I should like silk stockings enormously,' she said. 'And I think I shall buy you a brief-bag.'

'A brief-bag?' echoed Uncle Robert.

'Yes, Uncle, it's time you had a new one. I had a look at that shabby old thing of yours the other day in London. There were nasty holes in the corner. You must have spilled some acid on it from the lab.'

Hedlam looked at her very gravely and nodded. He smiled a moment and his lips closed reluctantly upon his ruined teeth.

'A brief-bag,' he repeated slowly. 'That will be a most acceptable gift, Elizabeth.'

'This is the national programme,' came a silken voice from the polished oak cabinet in the corner. 'I am sorry that we are a little late with the news to-night. The time is now 9.37. Before we give the news, there is a police message which we have been asked to broadcast from all stations. The message is as follows: "Listeners are informed that the car with police number XZ 4063, Morris Oxford, dark blue saloon, 1928 model, for which they were asked to keep a sharp look-out last night, was found at an early hour this morning burnt-out beside High Tree Wood near the village of Little Missett on the London-Cambridge Road. The driver of the car, his body charred beyond recognition, was recovered from the wreckage. In connection with this discovery the police are anxious to ascertain the whereabouts of Richard Feiling, a man of thirty-five, height five feet eight or nine inches, grey eyes, brown hair, and, when last seen, wearing a blue macintosh trench coat, grey soft hat and dark trousers. Any listener who has knowledge of his whereabouts is requested to communicate with the nearest police station or direct with New Scotland Yard, telephone number Whitehall one two one two."

'We now begin the second news bulletin, copyright reserved.'

But Elizabeth was not listening.

'The driver,' she said thoughtfully. 'That would be Throgmorton.'

Hedlam nodded.

'Yes, my dear. It looks as though he had met his deserts.'

Elizabeth gripped the arms of her chair.

'What can it mean?' she asked. 'Will this make things more difficult for George? Or is it the end of the case?'

Hedlam removed his pipe.

'No doubt George will tell you all about it during the Christmas holidays,' he said. 'And now, if you don't mind,' he continued gently but firmly, 'I should like to hear the rest of the news.'

The silken voice resumed control: 'A census taken to-day of the animals in the Zoological Gardens, Regent's Park, showed that the population in that part of London has almost doubled during the past twelve months. This remarkable result . . .'

3   *Wednesday, December 16th, 10 a.m.*

Inspector Martin, as he sat to his desk, noticed with mortification that his hands were trembling. He thanked Heaven that for once he was alone. It was bad enough to feel as he did. The curiosity or sympathy of Crosby would at that moment have been harder still to bear.

Chief Inspector McPherson had good reason to be dissatisfied, but he had allowed himself a liberty, not to say a licence of expression, which far exceeded the limits of what one gentleman should say to another. He had, in fact, spoken very sharply to George. Throgmorton had been suspected of murder. Throgmorton had been released, on the strength of an alibi inadequately checked. Throgmorton had been shadowed, but most incompetently lost in Piccadilly Circus tube station. From that moment until the discovery of his burnt-out car at Little Missett on the London-Cambridge Road he had been invisible. Now, apparently, he was dead. There would be no arrest, no solution of the mystery surrounding him, nothing to placate the public or gratify the Press which had been flaming over the week-end with headlines about the Norwich victims and attacking the police for their lack of sagacity and resource.

Such had been the tenor of the Chief Inspector's long and vehement declamation.

He had alluded, peevishly and with irritation, to the sudden appearance in the case of the man Feiling. Why had Martin and Crosby, who were supposed to combine the solid competence of the old dispensation with the nimble wits of a younger generation, failed to light upon this obviously important personage until the eleventh hour? George Martin, leaning across his desk, stared resentfully at a patch of discoloured wallpaper in front of him. The question was pertinent, but was it really fair? Feiling, a man unknown to the police, had only obtruded himself at the very last moment. Now, of course, they knew a good deal more about him. Sir Oswald Feiling, his uncle, had supplied the information.

Martin looked again at the file in front of him. It contained a police report from Norwich of an interview with Sir Oswald, conducted by the local officer. Feiling had been living in France. He had gone to France in preference to the Colonies as the result of a private misunderstanding with his uncle – something to do with a cheque. Richard Feiling was evidently the black sheep of the family.

Martin got to his feet and began to walk up and down the office.

Come to think of it, the case against Feiling was pretty strong.

Feiling had probably been working in close touch with Throgmorton from the beginning. Almost certainly he had met Hermione Taylor in Paris and taken delivery of the French notes. There was no proof of the fact, but it explained one of the most exasperating features of the case, namely, why no trace of the notes had as yet been found.

Feiling, then, had been in charge of all the financial arrangements. The rest was pure conjecture, but one could see pretty clearly the course of events over the last week-end. Feiling had met Throgmorton by appointment with the car. They had driven away together. Throgmorton, perhaps, realising that he was in grave danger of arrest, had decided to fade away.

Or was there some as yet unknown purpose in their journey?

Why, if they had merely intended to abscond, had they left behind their female confederate? And why had Throgmorton bolted in his own car, as though he had almost invited attention and pursuit?

The car had been driven well away from traffic and observation, and there it had been deliberately destroyed. There could be no question of an accident. The preliminary report of the experts who had examined the car was quite definite. The whole machine and, more especially the body found at the wheel, had been soused with petrol and set alight. The murderer and incendiary had then departed.

Buttons identified as from Throgmorton's coat and the ruins of a gold watch with his monogram on the back of it had been found clinging to the charred remains of the clothes and body, the immediate inference being that Feiling had murdered his companion.

A general call for Feiling had accordingly been sent out. The ports were being watched. The BBC had been asked to co-operate and the Press had published a description of the man.

Martin sat down again at his desk. Chief Inspector McPherson had concluded his hortation upon a note of encouragement and appeal. He had pointed out that the tangled case before them was one in which inference and imagination were at a premium. They were dealing with a premeditated and ingenious series of crimes and the perpetrator had from the first set out to lead astray anyone who applied the ordinary methods and worked by rule of thumb.

To that view of the case Martin had instantly subscribed. Clearly, then, he must proceed on the assumption that such evidence as the police could collect easily, and such clues as in an ordinary criminal investigation would be accepted as positive and helpful, were more likely to be misleading than to be of any direct assistance in solving the mystery.

Inspector Martin, meditating upon the burnt-out car, found in the lonely lane near Little Missett, accordingly began to consider the evidence distrustfully, assuming, for the sake of argument, that the whole series of incidents had been deliberately staged to convey a false impression. The murderer had made no attempt to make the crime look like an accident. He had driven the car to a spot deliberately selected for the purpose. His main preoccupation was that the body of his victim should not be recognised and to that end he had sacrificed every other consideration. He could hardly have hoped to make it impossible for the police to identify the car. He had not even tried to do so. He had concentrated his attention upon the body. It was essential to his purpose that the charred remains of his victim should be physically nondescript.

Why was this of such importance to the criminal? Two men had started forth in the car. The police would inevitably assume, if a body which could not be identified were found in the vehicle, that one of them had murdered the other, and the murderer would not have been at the pains and risk to stand by the car and make sure that the body of his victim was unrecognisable unless *he had wanted to mislead the police into believing that it was the other man who had committed the murder and himself who had been killed and reduced to ashes.*

Inspector Martin rose from the table and walked to the window. He had recovered from his depression and his brain was alive again. The charred remains in the car had been identified as those of Throgmorton. Buttons from Throgmorton's coat and his gold watch had been found. If, however, as already inferred, it had been the purpose of the murderer to mislead the police as to the identity of his victim, he would have chosen just such a means of achieving his object. His aim, *ex hypothesi*, was to convey the impression that he had himself been murdered. He had arranged, according to this reading of the case, to disappear from this life completely. It would, accordingly, be part of his plan to discard his own clothes and effects and to foist them upon the murdered man.

The buttons and watch-case had thus become clues in the opposite sense. They were intended to identify the charred remains as those of Throgmorton. In reality, however, they pointed in the opposite direction. These obvious clues were in fact the product of the same intelligence as that which had planned the murder of Miss Haslett and successfully led the police into a blind alley upon a false trail deliberately laid for their undoing. The same brain was behind each of the two crimes, and the murder of Greening left a similar impression. There again, though less elaborately and presumably in greater haste, a false impression had at first been successfully conveyed.

Martin nodded in unconscious affirmation of his sudden, vivid conviction. It was not Feiling who had murdered Throgmorton, but Throgmorton who had murdered Feiling – the last brilliant stroke of a series. Throgmorton, wanted for the murder of Greening and Miss Haslett, had thereby intended to cover his traces for ever. Possibly, too, he had not been sorry thus to shake off his confederates. One he had killed and the other he had left to face the music, while he himself would presumably have made arrangements to cash the total profits.

Martin, in his mind's eye, swiftly reconstructed the events. Throgmorton, having shaken off the police in Piccadilly Circus tube station, had gone into hiding over the week-end. He had arranged for Feiling to meet him with the car. Martin imagined the two men driving through the night. Throgmorton would make some excuse to stop the car. In all probability he had killed Feiling as he had killed Miss Haslett and Joseph Greening, by applying the brutal pressure of his thumbs to the carotid arteries. He had then driven the car on with the body and hidden it well behind High Tree Wood. He had then changed clothes with the victim. Both were incidentally of the same height which made it all the easier. He had then set light to the car and vanished into the darkness, leaving behind him the ashes of his past.

Martin stared out of the window. Was it a true bill? He would at any rate act upon it in a moment. As a working hypothesis it was good enough.

Where and how was this man to be found? Surely that would not be difficult. Throgmorton had banked on the fact that the police would be looking for someone else. It was impossible in these days for a man to disappear from the world once the hue and cry was raised.

And this time it would be raised promptly and effectively.

First, however, there was an important and perhaps a serviceable factor to be considered. The woman, Hermione Taylor, was now in custody. What exactly was her part in the story? Was she, perhaps, privy to this design of Throgmorton? What exactly was her relationship to the master criminal? What would she make of the final puzzle of High Tree Wood?

Martin walked to his table and pressed a bell. He would see Miss Taylor at once and he would assume, in the questions put to her, that Throgmorton was still alive and somewhere to be found.

Inspector Martin smiled suddenly and reached for the telephone. There was time, before Miss Taylor arrived, for a word with Chief Inspector McPherson.

The Chief Inspector had rattled him pretty severely that morning. Now the tables were turned. He was going to rattle the Chief Inspector.

4   *Wednesday, December 16th, 2.30 p.m.*

'Busy, Elizabeth?'

Elizabeth raised her head as her uncle entered the room.

'Only these accounts,' she replied.

Hedlam was absent-mindedly stuffing a pipe. He looked at her kindly over the bowl.

'You are not looking very grand,' he said.

'I am not feeling very grand,' she responded. 'I slept badly last night.'

'Tooth still troublesome?'

Elizabeth nodded.

'Is it aching now?' continued Uncle Robert, as he struck a match.

'Just keeping on.'

'You had better go up to London to-morrow and see that dentist again.'

'I can't get an appointment with him till Saturday,' answered Elizabeth.

'Then we had better call up Dodson. He's the best man in Norwich. In the meantime I will find you something to soothe it.'

He unhooked the telephone receiver as he spoke, handed it to her and went in search of his remedy.

Elizabeth was touched. There were times when Uncle Robert could be quite considerate, and this was one of them.

She made an appointment with Dodson for the following after-noon and hung up the receiver just as Hedlam entered the room carrying a small bottle in his hand.

'This is what you need, my dear,' he said, shaking half a dozen pellets on to a sheet of notepaper.

Elizabeth eyed the pellets doubtfully.

'Sure they are all right, Uncle?'

'Perfectly all right,' he answered briskly. 'They call it sulphonal, or some such name.'

He exhibited the bottle

'It's stronger than aspirin. I had it from a doctor in the South of France.'

Elizabeth obediently swallowed the tablets and bent over her books.

Hedlam stood watching her for a moment.

'Are those accounts really urgent?' he asked.

'Not terribly,' answered Elizabeth.

'I was wondering whether we might run over in the car to Potter Heigham,' he continued. 'I promised to return a book to old Gregory and he sent me a rather snappy post card about it this morning. A breath of fresh air will do you good, and for once it is a fine day.'

Elizabeth looked towards the window. Pale sunshine streamed across the playing-fields, green and fresh after the rain. She rose to her feet.

'Very well, Uncle,' she said; 'but I must be back again by six.'

'Easily managed,' answered Robert. 'But we must be very firm on the subject of tea. We shall only just have time to call and leave the book.'

Elizabeth smiled. Old Gregory, retired business man, who lived on the broad near Potter Heigham was famed for his teas. He was a bit of a recluse and was interested in medieval church architecture. Uncle Robert, who took an interest in the same subject, had met him once in the County Club at Norwich. The two had struck up an acquaintanceship which had developed as the years went by. But old Gregory was what Uncle Robert described as 'tetchy,' and one had to avoid giving cause of offence. Hence this sudden expedition to return the second volume of Mâle's famous work on religious art.

Elizabeth rose and went to her bedroom. She examined her face in the glass with care. Was it imagination or was her cheek beginning to swell? The tooth at times had been very painful, but already Uncle Robert's drug was having a soothing effect.

The drive was pleasant enough. A pale sun struggled valiantly with the Norfolk haze and the big trees rested upon the flat fields like green clouds. The tooth, moreover, had ceased to trouble. Elizabeth was feeling pleasantly languid and relaxed as she turned into the gravelled drive of the Georgian red-brick house inhabited by Mr Gregory.

Their host himself opened the door, and on seeing the second volume of Mâle he smiled graciously.

'This,' he chirped, 'is delightful. How do you do, Miss Orme? Just in time for tea.'

Elizabeth, feeling increasingly languid, murmured a greeting and left the subsequent explanations to Uncle Robert. Mr Gregory, she noted, was inclined to take it ill that they would not stay to tea. Vaguely she heard her uncle refusing a bait of hot scones waiting before the fire and realised that Mr Gregory was grumbling reluctant farewells from the doorstep.

It was nearly five o'clock when she turned the car and drove it back towards the high-road. Her hands on the wheel seemed oddly uncertain, and, leaving the drive, she grazed one of the stone pillars of the gate. Straightening the car she pulled up beside the pavement.

'What is it, my dear?' asked Uncle Robert. 'Is the tooth still worrying?'

'No, but I am feeling most terribly sleepy. I think it must be that stuff you gave me.'

'Nonsense, my dear. It isn't a narcotic. But perhaps I had better take the wheel.'

They changed places and Elizabeth oddly at peace with the world, nestled back into a quiet lethargy.

She was roused by the stopping of the car in front of the garage at St Julian's. It was dark now. The promise of the afternoon had not been fulfilled and a thin rain was falling. The lights from the school a hundred yards away shone through the mist.

With a great effort she tried to rouse herself, but Uncle Robert laid a hand upon her arm.

'Keep quiet, my dear,' he said.

There came a roar as he raced the engine, and, with a jerk, the old Austin jumped forward into the dark recesses of the shed. Uncle Robert was proud of his garage. It was fitted with electric light and a door of the shutter variety which slid up and down in steel grooves.

Elizabeth waited in her seat. Waves of sleep were sweeping over her.

Uncle Robert had not yet stopped the engine. He seemed to be busy somewhere at the back of the car. From far away there came a rattle. It sounded like a big wave tearing at shingle on the beach. But that was a silly thought. She was not anywhere near the sea and here was Uncle Robert with a hand upon her elbow.

'Elizabeth,' he was saying in a voice incredibly soft and remote, 'You are only half-awake.'

He put one hand on her shoulders. Another was clasped about her knees. She made an effort to rise.

'It's all right, my dear,' he said soothingly. 'That stuff must be stronger than I thought. I shall have to carry you to the house.'

Elizabeth's eyes closed. She felt that she was being lifted from the car:

'Just like a bundle,' she thought.

5   *Wednesday, December 16th, 6 p.m.*

George Martin walked rapidly up the drive to the front door and rang the bell. He had come straight to St Julian's from the station with but one idea in his mind. He wanted to see Robert Hedlam. He wanted to see him at once. All other thoughts, wishes and intentions were for the moment suspended.

He rang the bell again and a minute later he was facing a regretful housemaid.

'I'm sorry, sir, but Mr Hedlam is not at home.'

'Miss Orme, perhaps,' suggested Martin.

'Miss Orme is with the master,' the maid informed him. 'But they were to be back by six, sir. And it's striking six at this very moment.'

George stood a while on the doorstep. Should he go to the police headquarters or wait at the school?

At that moment, however, came the sound of a car on the high road.

'That will be them, sir,' said the maid.

'The master is putting the car away,' she added.

'Then I will go and meet them.'

Martin turned about and walked rapidly down the curving drive towards the garage. Before coming within sight of it he heard a sound as of an angry sea tearing at pebbles on the beach.

'That,' he thought, 'will be the sliding door.'

He walked forward. The garage was shut and a thin line of light showed upon the floor. From inside came the sound of the engine, softly chugging.

For a moment he stood motionless. Then suddenly he dashed forward and grasped the handle at the foot of the door. With a jerk it sprang upwards and for a moment he was dazzled by the electric light which shone bright and steady from the roof.

Then he saw. The back of the car was immediately in front of him. The engine was still running. From the exhaust came a thin stream of blue vapour, and, beside it, a crouching figure held upon its knees the head of Elizabeth. Her eyes were closed and the blue vapour was streaming across her mouth and nostrils.

Martin sprang forward. The kneeling figure stirred and the light from the ceiling shone suddenly down upon its face, bringing all its features into sharp relief.

But Martin, at the sight of it, had no time for the revelation. The figure had jumped to its feet and was coming towards him. Without an instant's hesitation he smashed a straight left at the firm jaw in front of him. The man went down. Martin ran round the car, switched off the engine and pulled Elizabeth to her feet.

'What's the matter, George?' she asked drowsily.

'One minute,' said George.

The prostrate figure on the garage floor had risen. The pale blue eyes glared at him fixedly. The loose mouth was working.

Martin took a step forward.

'Robert Hedlam,' he said, 'alias John Throgmorton. I arrest you for the murders of Veronica Haslett, Joseph Greening and Richard Feiling. Anything that you may say may be taken down and used in evidence.'

6   *Monday, February 15th*

'Members of the jury, that completes the first part of the case for the Crown.'

The Attorney-General paused and threw back his gown. He had already spoken for two hours, and Inspector Martin's attention had wandered during the later portions of his statement. The court was packed to the limits of comfort or even of safety, and Martin felt a sudden longing for the open air. A sensation, almost of claustrophobia, had begun to afflict him and he had found it easy to understand the look upon the faces of the two calamitous figures in the dock – Hermione Taylor and Robert Hedlam, alias John Throgmorton – as the case for the prosecution advanced inevitably to its conclusion.

Inspector Martin was tired and inclined to nod – as well he might be. Two sleepless nights – the second spent in a mental survey or recapitulation of the case from end to end – had left him with little zest for the result.

The Attorney-General, wishing to conduct the prosecution in a way which would be least confusing to the jury, had decided to present it in the first instance as a case against Throgmorton of Shaftesbury Avenue, leaving aside for the moment the question of the identity of Throgmorton with Robert Hedlam of Norwich. The case against Throgmorton was now complete. The Attorney-General had traced in detail the whole series of events in which the prisoner had participated under that name and character from his meeting with Miss Haslett, as the mystery man with the black patch over his right eye, to the moment when he had arranged for his charred remains to be misidentified in the burnt-out car on the

London-Cambridge road. Martin had been over that story so many times himself that he found it difficult to follow it again with any real interest – except that he was now and then moved to admiration by the force and clarity with which the facts were presented. He had listened with half an ear to the long recital of events, his eyes going often to the prisoners in the dock or to the judge sitting on high in his oaken seat under the great sword. For this was Court No. 1 at the Old Bailey, the authorities having decided that Hedlam should be brought up for trial in London and not at the local assizes in Norwich.

Only once had Martin been stirred to a painful interest in the indictment. There was one chapter in his conduct of the case for which, despite the successful series of inferences he had subsequently drawn, he still blushed in shame and astonishment. The fact that he had allowed himself to be influenced for a moment by Throgmorton's alibi for the night of Greening's murder still rankled. The alibi had rested on the assertions of Hermione Taylor, a possible confederate, and the fact that Throgmorton's wireless had been heard by his neighbours until past midnight. The wireless had presumably been left to play in an empty flat. Throgmorton had, in fact, produced no real or convincing proof of his statement that he had spent the evening of Monday, December 7th, nursing a cold and soothing his savage breast with concord of sweet sound.

The Attorney-General, however, had used this episode, which Martin in retrospect felt to be a blot on the scutcheon, merely to emphasise the intelligence and resource of the prisoner.

The Attorney-General, having rearranged his papers, was preparing to resume.

'Members of the jury,' he continued, 'we have so far confined our attention to the individual known as John Throgmorton, registered moneylender and unofficial dealer in stocks and shares. That part of my task was materially simplified by the fact that one of the prisoners, Hermione Taylor, accused of complicity in the murder of Veronica Haslett, has made a statement to the police and has elected to give evidence for the Crown. I have described to you several remarkable features of the case, and you will already have formed your opinion of the ability and resource whereby Throgmorton successfully compassed the murder of his three victims and whereby he hoped to convince the police that he had himself been done to death by his male confederate. All these facts and circumstances, however, will seem to you relatively normal and straightforward as compared with the bewildering situation with which you are now to be confronted. I have submitted to you an indictment of John Throgmorton. I am now to show you that this indictment applies in every particular to the man whom you see before you in the dock this morning under the name of Robert Hedlam, proprietor of St Julian's Preparatory School in Norwich.

'Here I would, with the permission of the Court, allow myself a short parenthesis. It is not often that a public prosecutor, in presenting a case for the Crown, ventures upon observations regarding the police investigations on which that case must necessarily rest. In this instance, however, some such observations seem to me not only just but even necessary to a clear exposition of the facts. I have already described to you, in presenting the case against Throgmorton, how the officers in charge of the case, by a process of inference, came to the conclusion that the charred remains in the burnt-out car were those of Richard Feiling and not those of the prisoner at the bar. I have now to describe how, partly as a result of inference and partly as a result of prompt action taken by the officer directly responsible, Robert Hedlam, alias John Throgmorton, on the evening of Wednesday, December 16th, was caught red-handed in the act of committing yet another murder and thus silencing for ever the only witness who, unknown even to herself, had accidentally stumbled upon a clue which established a direct connection between the two men – or, as we now know, between the two distinct personalities created for himself by the prisoner. Before entering in detail upon this aspect of the case, I would like to congratulate the responsible officer upon this remarkable achievement.

'There is a preliminary feature of these extra-ordinary events to which I would draw your immediate attention. It will be easily understood that a man, electing to live a double life, would find no difficulty in doing so provided those who knew him in his two characters were an entirely different set of persons. The amazing feature of Robert Hedlam's impersonation is that, in the period under investigation, from November 27th to December 14th, he was seeing at least two people who knew him in both characters. The police officer who interviewed him on several occasions as Throgmorton knew him also as Hedlam. The unfortunate Mr Greening, who was Hedlam's employee at St Julian's School, also had dealings with him as Throgmorton, the moneylender. You will wonder how it was possible for anyone, let alone a trained officer of the police, to meet and carry on a long conversation with one and the same person masquerading as two different individuals without detecting the imposture, and you may be tempted to think meanly of the powers of observation thus displayed. It is the more fortunate that I should be able to submit as exhibits in the case photographs of the two men, or perhaps I should say two photographs of one and the same man. The first was taken of Robert

Hedlam in his study in Norwich. It is a snapshot and has not been faked or altered in any way. The second is a photograph of Throgmorton, taken by a professional photographer. I shall ask you to examine them carefully.

'It is said that the camera cannot lie. These two photographs are a faithful representation of the form and features of Robert Hedlam and of Throgmorton respectively. At first sight there is little resemblance between them. If, however, you look at them closely you will recognise them to be photographs of the same person. The superficial differences are due to four very simple devices. Robert Hedlam is bald, with dark eyebrows. He has pale blue eyes, which are clearly visible. He has lost most of his front teeth. John Throgmorton has light eyebrows and an abundant and striking head of hair. He wears spectacles that distort and partially conceal his eyes. He has excellent teeth which give a characteristic full-lipped appearance to the mouth. The Crown will produce in evidence the properties which were necessary to effect a lightning change from the one likeness to the other – a wig which cost no less than a hundred and fifty pounds, purchased from the famous M. Blanchard, of Paris, of such superb workmanship that not even those that lived with him in the greatest intimacy suspected that the hair was not his own; a pair of tortoise-shell spectacles, a set of false teeth which exactly correct the dental deficiencies of the prisoner; and a bottle of hair-dye of a kind whose effect is at once removed by the application of a well-known chemical preparation.

'I do not think that anyone examining the photographs which I am submitting to you as members of the jury could be fairly expected to recognise them offhand as portraits of one and the same individual. Careful inspection shows that the essential features are identical, but I am sure you will agree that the risk of Hedlam being casually seen and recognised as Throgmorton, or vice versa, was negligible.

'Hedlam's disguise, however, was put to a much severer test than that of a casual recognition. I have described to you the circumstances in which Throgmorton the moneylender murdered Miss Haslett. For him it was a troublesome coincidence that the Inspector in charge of the case who questioned him as Throgmorton should have known him also as Hedlam, and that the unfortunate Joseph Greening, assistant-master at St Julian's, who saw him daily as Hedlam, should have visited him as Throgmorton in his London office. I would point out, in passing, that these coincidences, seemingly accidental, were in fact an almost inevitable result of the crime. The prisoner, when he decided to make use of his knowledge and position as Hedlam to murder Miss Haslett in the character of Throgmorton, was necessarily establishing a connection between his twin existences in Norwich and in London. He had deliberately to face the risk of creating this perilous link between his separate entities. He knew, in planning the murder of Miss Haslett, that both as Hedlam and as Throgmorton he would henceforth be associated with his victim, and that he must be prepared to face inquiries into her death in both his characters.

'Robert Hedlam, alias Throgmorton, considered and met this difficulty. He did not further complicate his disguise, but as Hedlam he twisted his ankle, developing a fictitious limp while as Throgmorton he was attacked with a severe cold, developing a fictitious affection of the larynx, which rendered his voice and intonation extremely difficult to recognise.

'It is an admitted weakness of the case for the Crown – but a weakness which in view of the overwhelming evidence at our disposal it is well able to sustain – that no one ever caught or detected the prisoner in the act of changing from one character to the other. Robert Hedlam, finding his existence as a respectable citizen of Norwich to be tedious and inadequate, has, we allege, been leading a double life for the last six years. He went regularly up to London, as Hedlam, to stay with his mother. Mrs Hedlam was devoted to her only son, and it is one of the sad features of this terrible case that it is from her own personal statements to the police that we are driven to infer that only a small fraction of his time in London was actually spent at her flat in West Kensington. How and when he effected his transformation, in the absence of direct evidence can only be inferred, but we are fortunately assisted in our inference by a circumstance which I will recall to your memory. I have already described to you how Hermione Taylor, acting upon the advice of Throgmorton, changed her clothes and her appearance when impersonating Miss Haslett on November 28th. She made use for that purpose of public lavatories at the Gare du Nord in Paris and at Victoria in London. I think we may assume that Throgmorton was in this instance recommending to his confederate what was to him a familiar procedure.

'I admit that this is only a matter of inference. Our evidence goes to show conclusively that Hedlam regularly disappeared at certain definite times and that he as regularly reappeared in the character of Throgmorton, or vice versa. The place and method of transformation cannot, however, be ascertained. The prisoner took no living soul into his confidence. Not even his mother, not even his mistress, knew of his double life or can throw any light on this special point.'

Martin glanced at the clock. At this rate the court would rise for the luncheon interval long before the Attorney-General had finished. He felt a tap on his shoulder.

'Mr Felton wishes to see you, sir,' a police constable whispered.

Martin rose. Felton was the Crown Solicitor and must be humoured. The Inspector made his way with difficulty from the crowded court and it was half an hour before he could get back again, having settled a trivial point in the evidence which he would be shortly called upon to give.

The Attorney-General appeared to have made considerable progress.

'Members of the jury,' he was saying, 'I have described to you how Robert Hedlam, throughout the period under review, without exciting the least suspicion on the part of the police or of those with whom he came into personal contact, passed from London to Norwich and from Norwich to London, from his respectable life as the proprietor of St Julian's School for Boys to his criminal activities as John Throgmorton of Shaftesbury Avenue. I have submitted to you a schedule or time-table of his appearances and disappearances in these two distinct characters and indicated how, as Throgmorton, the prisoner, for his criminal purposes, turned effectively to account the knowledge he had acquired as Hedlam of the habits and circumstances of his victims.

'We come now to the last stage in this eventful history. The dramatic character of these final incidents, in the course of which a material witness for the Crown, Miss Elizabeth Orme, was nearly done to death, will need no emphasis from me. The facts speak for themselves. But I would point out, that behind this obvious drama of attempted murder and rescue at the eleventh hour, there was in progress a drama, less spectacular perhaps, but of greater signifi-cance to the general conduct of the case. I am alluding to a drama in which the resources of New Scotland Yard were silently at grips with a criminal intelligence of the highest order.

'Hedlam, alias Throgmorton, by a last brilliant stroke, had set the police an almost insoluble riddle. On Monday, December 14th, he visited Inspector Martin as Hedlam, and in that character he proffered evidence which, as he knew, would probably lead to the immediate detention of Throgmorton. He was, in effect, inviting the police to proceed to his own arrest, and he was thereby hopelessly confusing the issue. For how could anyone possibly imagine that the man who thus denounced Throgmorton was none other than Throgmorton himself?

'Nevertheless, members of the jury, it was precisely this master stroke which first aroused the suspicion of the authorities. Robert Hedlam, as I have said, on December 14th gave evidence, obviously vital to the case, which was almost bound to lead to the ultimate conviction of Throgmorton. But Robert Hedlam had been in possession of that evidence for over a week, and in a previous statement to Inspector Martin he had made no reference to it whatever. He was well aware that this striking circumstance needed apology and explanation. The prisoner, members of the jury, is a fine actor, and his performance on the morning of December 14th was undoubtedly superb. He represented himself to be just the worried, absent-minded old gentleman who would be capable of such an incredible lapse of memory, and, for the moment, he successfully imposed this view of the matter upon the police.

'But not for long. The police, when, as a result of Hedlam's evidence, they went to detain Throgmorton, found that he had vanished, and, following the discovery of his burnt-out car near the London-Cambridge road, it became evident that he was unlikely to be seen again. He intended them to assume that he was dead and it was part of his plan that they should also assume that he was guilty of the murder of Veronica Haslett and Joseph

Greening. Justice would then be satisfied. There would be no further hue and cry and he would thenceforth be safe from molestation or pursuit.

'The conduct of Robert Hedlam, reviewed in the light of these developments, took on quite a different aspect. He had withheld vital evidence from the police at a time when it would inevitably have led to the detention and probably to the successful conviction of Throgmorton, but he had come forward with this same vital evidence at the very moment when Throgmorton was arranging to disappear and when he wanted the police to believe that the murderer of Veronica Haslett and of Joseph Greening had himself been done to death. Robert Hedlam, in fact, when he made his statement to the police on December 14th, was not in effect acting against Throgmorton. He was playing into Throgmorton's hands. He had withheld his evidence so long as it was damaging and he produced it as soon as it had become useful to Throgmorton.

'On Wednesday, December 16th, there was a conference at New Scotland Yard of the officials in charge of the case. As a result of that conference Inspector George Martin went to Norwich on the afternoon train. He had as yet no inkling or suspicion that Hedlam and Throgmorton were one and the same person, but he was by this time firmly convinced that Hedlam was Throgmorton's confederate. He went to Norwich in order to discover to what extent the proprietor of St Julian's School for Boys was implicated in the murders and to ascertain whether he knew where Throgmorton was to be found.

'I come now to the last sensational phase of this remarkable case.'

At this point, however, there came a movement from the high seat in which the quiet figure had sat for so long motionless, following the case for the Crown.

'I think, Sir Giles,' came the slow voice of Mr Justice Halkett, 'this would be a convenient point at which to take the luncheon interval.'

'Certainly, Melud. As Your Ludship pleases.'

There was a stir and shamble of feet.

7   Monday, February 15th

It was half-past three in the afternoon before Inspector Martin was able to return to the Court. Felton had again required his advice as to the order in which the witnesses for the Crown should be taken and Martin had also contrived a hurried meeting with Elizabeth in the great hall, waiting her turn to be called and standing in need of encouragement.

He found, as he pushed his way into the crowded chamber, that the Attorney-General was nearing the end of his statement.

'My concluding observations, members of the jury, have special reference to two exhibits in the case on which the Crown relies to establish beyond any possible doubt that the prisoner, Robert Hedlam, in the character of John Throgmorton, committed the series of crimes with which he is charged.

'The first of these exhibits has a direct bearing on the attempt to murder Elizabeth Orme on the evening of December 16th.

'I have described to you how Inspector Martin arrived only just in time to prevent the commission of that final crime, but I have yet to supply the motive which drove the prisoner to this desperate and apparently unaccountable step. John Throgmorton, as a man of business, was accustomed to carry a brief-bag. The bag will be produced to you shortly, and you will observe that it is easily recognisable, one corner of the bag being burned and stained with acid. On the occasion of the last visit which he made to his mother's flat in the Addison Road he left that bag in his dressing-room while taking a bath. It so happened that on this very afternoon, the afternoon of Monday, December 14th, Miss Elizabeth Orme arrived at the flat and asked to see the prisoner. She required him to sign a cheque to settle the weekly accounts of the tradespeople supplying the school. The prisoner's mother brought her the brief-bag, which Robert Hedlam had left in his bedroom. Miss Orme had never seen the bag before, and she concluded quite naturally that it belonged to her uncle. Members of the jury, *that same brief-bag, stained and marked in the same place with acid, was found two or three yards from the burnt-out car in which what the prisoner hoped would be taken for the dead body of Throgmorton was discovered.* The prisoner, unaware that Miss Orme had seen the bag in his mother's flat, had deliberately left it beside the car as further evidence that its owner, John Throgmorton, had perished in the flames.

'Now mark carefully what followed.

'Robert Hedlam, alias John Throgmorton, having murdered his confederate, returned to Norwich on December 15th. He had successfully accomplished his purpose. His life as Throgmorton was now a thing of the past and nothing remained to connect him with his second self. On the same day, however, he had a conversation with his niece in his study at St Julian's School. They talked, among other things, of Christmas presents, and Miss Orme, remembering the brief-bag she had seen at the flat in the Addison Road, suggested that she should give her uncle a new one to replace it.

'Consider the awful significance of this allusion, a significance of which Miss Orme herself was wholly unaware. Hedlam realised that his niece had only to set eyes on that brief-bag, old and acid-stained, which he knew to be in possession of the police, to have it in her power to establish a clear connection between himself and Throgmorton. She had seen Throgmorton's bag in the flat of Robert Hedlam's mother. She remembered it well enough to be sure of its identity. You may object that the risk of her being informed that such a bag was in the possession of the police was relatively slight. But Robert Hedlam was not the man to allow such a risk to remain. He had murdered Joseph Greening because that unfortunate young man had stumbled upon evidence which, if properly used, would have brought him to the gallows, and he now decided to murder his niece for a precisely similar reason.

'I come now to my second exhibit. My first supplies the motive for the attempted murder of Elizabeth Orme. My second supplies the motive for the whole series of crimes for which the male prisoner is mainly responsible. It is a valuable exhibit, members of the jury. It is, in fact, worth not less than fifty thousand pounds.

'We have so far understood that Veronica Haslett was murdered owing to the fact that she was in possession of a lottery ticket which entitled her to receive the sum of seven hundred and fifty thousand French francs. That sum of money, however, was required by the male prisoner and his accomplices for a special purpose – namely, the purchase from Sir Oswald Feiling of Tenby Hall of a reliquary valued by himself at five thousand pounds, but which was known by his nephew Richard Feiling to be in reality worth many times that amount. Sir Oswald will inform you later how, on December 11th, he received the visit of a Mr Bannister to whom he sold the reliquary in question. Sir Oswald has since recognised in Mr Bannister John Throgmorton of Shaftesbury Avenue as portrayed in the photograph which we are submitting as evidence. It was

John Throgmorton who bought the reliquary on account of himself and his confederates and the reliquary was still in his possession when he left London with Richard Feiling on Monday, December 14th. It was his declared intention to accompany Richard Feiling to Hull, where an appointment had been made with a client who was prepared to purchase the reliquary for the sum of fifty thousand pounds.

'You already know what happened on that journey. Throgmorton killed his companion and returned to Norwich. For the moment he was unable to sell the reliquary. In order to dispose of it he must await a favourable moment and a suitable customer. That reliquary, members of the jury, purchased by John Throgmorton, was subsequently found at St Julian's, locked away in the drawer of a desk belonging to Robert Hedlam.

'I have nothing further to add to my opening statement of the case for the Crown. I have undertaken to prove that the male prisoner, Robert Hedlam, is guilty of the charges brought against him – namely, that on Friday, November 27th, he wilfully and of malice aforethought murdered Veronica Haslett in order to obtain possession of a lottery ticket entitling the bearer to the sum of seven hundred and fifty thousand French francs; that on Monday, December 7th, he murdered in the same way Joseph Greening, who was on the point of giving evidence to the police which might have led to Throgmorton's detention; that on Monday, December 14th, he murdered Richard Feiling, his confederate, with the double object of revenging himself upon a rival in the affections of his mistress and of providing for his own effective disappearance from the world; finally, that on December 16th he attempted to murder Elizabeth Orme, who had stumbled upon evidence which put it within her power to establish a connection between his separate and distinct activities as the financier of Shaftesbury Avenue and the proprietor of St Julian's Preparatory School for Boys.

'To each and all of these charges the prisoner pleads not guilty.

'The charge against the female prisoner, Hermione Taylor, is that she was an accessory to the first of this series of crimes. She pleads guilty to the charge, and I propose to call her as first witness for the Crown.'

Inspector Martin glanced at the two figures in the dock. The man had hardly moved during the long statement of the Attorney-General and neither of them had once given the least sign of being aware of the other. On hearing her name, however, the woman raised her head and looked at her companion. For a moment they gazed directly at one another. The man's expression was at first hard to read. Was it a last appeal that he made? Or was it merely a prelude to the malignant stare with which he finally met the settled hatred which he read in the eyes of the woman he had left to bear in desolation the consequences of their common crime?

'She cares nothing for herself,' said Martin to himself, as his eyes rested for a minute on that tragic face. 'She cares only that her confederate shall be taken from this place and be hanged by the neck till he be dead.'

EPILOGUE

Mr and Mrs George Martin sat at breakfast in the crowded veranda of a small hotel in the Austrian Tyrol. Outside the sun was shining and the gleaming snow, turned by the plough, lay in piles along the mountain road which passed just under the window.

Elizabeth, after the trial, had pleaded that a change was necessary, and Martin had successfully insisted that the change should include a swift transition from the status of Elizabeth Orme, spinster, of this parish, to the status of Elizabeth Martin, wife of George Martin, who had, in the opinion of his superior officers at the Yard, earned the right to a really satisfactory holiday in congenial company.

Between them lay an English newspaper. Elizabeth had opened it first and she had passed it without comment across the table.

Martin took up the paper. His eye fell upon the middle of a paragraph under thick headlines:

'Robert Hedlam, the Norwich murderer, was executed at nine o'clock this morning at Pentonville in accordance with the sentence passed upon him by Mr Justice Halkett at the Old Bailey on February 18th last. The prisoner, who maintained silence to the last and refused to make any statement or admission, met his end with the same indifference which he had assumed throughout his trial and at the moment of conviction.

'It will be recalled that Hermione Taylor was recently removed to Holloway, where she is now serving a sentence of twenty years' imprisonment as accessory to the first of the murders laid to his account.'

Martin rose from the table. He went round to Elizabeth and put his hand on her shoulder.

'Lizzie,' he said, 'all that happened ages ago. The sun is shining and there are forty centimetres of powder snow on the nursery slopes. I suggest we wax the skis and get down to it.'

THE END